THE LADY
VANISHED

A gripping detective mystery

GRETTA
MULROONEY

Published 2016 by Joffe Books, London.

www.joffebooks.com

ISBN- 978-1-911021-54-4

CHAPTER 1

In the dream, the knife slashed into Swift's thigh and he felt again the sharp, stinging pain. The blood ran instantly and strong. In reality, he had been surrounded by lights, the screams of women, men shouting in several languages and the swift thump of boots as his colleagues scoured the building. In the dream, he lay in a grey mist, alone, knowing that his blood would keep streaming away, that no one would be coming to help him. He thought that if he could just press on the wound and stop the blood, he might have a chance but he was too weak. He could only lie and feel his life flowing warmly away on to the hard floor. He was resigned and hopeless. He blinked and tried to tear at the cobwebs that were spinning over his eyes and then his head, forming his soft shroud.

He woke a moment before his alarm clock rang and lay dazed, hot and dry mouthed. He touched his thigh, felt the slight indentation where the stitches had been, traced the line and ran a hand over his eyes. He rose and made strong, almost bitter, coffee, then stood under a cool shower. For months now he'd had respite from that particular dream. He knew people who said they never remembered their dreams and he envied them.

He opened the kitchen window and let the chill morning air touch his skin. Birds were darting to and from the sycamore tree at the bottom of the small walled garden. He noted the blue tits were back at the nesting box and watched them for a few minutes as he ate a bowl of cereal and finished his coffee, clearing the last dream shadows from his mind. He filled his water bottle and moved through to the centre of the living room where he did ten minutes of muscle-warming exercises, then set off for his boat and his therapy.

* * *

The dark water streamed from his oars as Swift sculled steadily. The river was calm and quiet below a soft April sun on this Tuesday morning, with the wind and tide in the same direction. He had seen only three other rowers and a cormorant near Putney Bridge and he luxuriated in the warmth and solitude. When he was rowing he knew he was alive, part of the turning world. He loved the brackish scent of the Thames and the movement of the light on its surface. He often thought of the riverbed as he rowed and of the secrets that lay submerged in its mud; bones, jewels, timbers of ships and the more mundane bedsteads and prams. The Celts had believed that water was the route to the otherworld and had honoured rivers as bestowers of life, making offerings to gain favour with them. Although Swift didn't contribute any small tokens to appease the waters, he sometimes trailed his fingers through it thankfully. He closed his eyes behind his sunglasses for a moment and concentrated on his breathing, exhaling during each stroke, inhaling in between. A kind of contentment that he rarely felt, and usually only when he was on the water, crept over him.

Yet the thought of Ruth intruded. He had met her again recently for lunch, reawakening all the love and misery. He had held her slim hand as they sat side by side on a bench in St James's Park, not saying much. When they parted at Victoria he had cupped her face between his hands and pressed his forehead to hers. Then he had watched her slight figure disappear into the flow of passengers heading for the South Coast. Now he was back in the limbo of waiting. He would put himself through the same pain in a month's time. Seeing her was a delicious torment; he knew he should stop but couldn't find a way of doing it. He rowed faster, building speed and heat in his muscles, forcing the image of her out of his head. Sweat dripped down his face as the oars sliced the water. There was nothing but velocity and sun and the flow of his blood.

His phone rang, startling him. Usually, he turned it off when he got in the boat but he had forgotten, too keen to take the oars. *Unknown number*, it told him and he almost pressed ignore but then thought it could be work. He steadied the boat with one oar, manoeuvring into the river bank.

'Tyrone Swift.'

It was a woman, with an impatient tone and a slight lisp. 'Is that Swift Investigations?'

'That's right.'

'My name is Davenport, Florence Davenport. I'm ringing about a matter I'd like to discuss. Could I come and see you?'

'When were you thinking of?'

'As soon as possible, really. I think I've already left it too long. Later this morning?'

He calculated how long it would take him to row back to the club; conditions were kind, on a falling tide. 'I could meet you at eleven thirty. You have the address?'

'Yes, thank you. I'll see you then. I'll have to bring my little girl with me, is that all right?'

He was dubious. He had limited experience of children and parents were usually distracted in their company. But, business was business.

'No problem.'

He tucked his phone away and applied himself to the oars. He passed the old Harrods Depository and was back at Tamesas, his rowing club near Hammersmith Bridge, by ten thirty and stowed his boat away. He ran back to his house. It didn't overlook the river but was still within sniffing distance of it. He showered, towelling his thick curly hair, dressed in jeans, T-shirt and suit jacket and unlocked his office in the basement. His great-aunt Lily, who had left him the house, had kept two Labradors and he was convinced at times that he could smell wet dog on the stairs. Lily had been a chiropractor and had converted the basement room into her clinic; with its own outer front door, it had made an obvious choice for his office. There was still a washbasin in one corner which he meant to have removed some time. Clients seemed to find it odd; certainly their eyes often strayed to it. His answerphone told him that a man wanted him to help with a boundary dispute with a neighbour — he would call him back and advise a solicitor — and Mrs Brewer had rung to ask if he had any updates on whether her husband was cheating on her with her daughter-in-law. The answer was yes, but he would put off calling her until Florence Davenport had been, as he had a feeling the conversation would be lengthy and involve tears and recriminations.

The bell rang at just gone eleven thirty. He opened the outer door to a small, plump blonde woman, fortyish, with a small, plump child who was straining on a rein. He showed them in, asked her to sit down and seated himself at the other side of the desk. Florence Davenport unclipped the child and unbuttoned her cardigan.

'This is Helena,' she said. 'Say hello to Mr Swift, Helena.'

Swift nodded at the child, who looked at him, smiled coyly, then tottered against her mother, rubbing her chin into her arm.

'I've come to see you because I'm very worried about my stepmother,' the woman said, rummaging in her bag and producing a book for Helena. 'There you are, Helena, you can sit on the carpet and look at your book. My nanny is ill,' she added for Swift's benefit, 'that's why I had to bring her.'

'No problem. What's worrying you?'

Ms Davenport crossed her legs, which were encased in skintight jeans that strained at the calves. She looked for a moment at her ankle boots, rearranged her scarf and hooked her chunky yellow leather bag, of a type Swift suspected was very expensive, over her chair back.

'Carmen, my stepmother — she's a widow — went missing several months ago and there's been no trace of her since. My brother says that she's probably playing games but I don't think so. No, Helena, don't put the book in your mouth, darling.'

'Why would your brother think she's playing games?' Swift couldn't help looking at the child, who was chewing the book and beating it on the floor.

'Well, she has been difficult in the past, going away without telling us.'

'Holidays?'

'Yes; so she said, anyway.'

'And she's definitely not at home?'

'No and she hasn't gone to stay with friends — not that she has many. She's one of those women who likes attention and doesn't much like her own sex; a man's woman, I think they used to be called.'

Swift nodded. So presumably she doesn't like you either, he thought. He had experience of disliking a stepmother so he made some allowance for the cattiness of the remark. Part of the book, which had a colourful dragon on the front, had become detached from its cover and was dangling.

'Helena, Mummy will take the book away in a minute and you'll have to go on the naughty step. I'm sure Mr Swift has got one.'

Swift cleared his throat. 'Have you been to the police?'

'Oh, the police! They've been involved but they've found no trace of her. You may have seen a bit about her in the quality papers, because she's Daddy's widow.'

Swift looked at her, his memory nudging him. She was pretty but her face lacked animation and she wore too much foundation, probably to try and conceal the slight acne damage to her skin. She sighed and bent to wrestle the book from Helena, who started screaming.

'Your stepmother is Carmen Langborne?'

'That's right.'

Swift could barely hear her above the child's screams. She finally gave Helena the book back, apparently resigned to seeing it mauled. Swift recalled a report in one of the papers and a grainy photo of Lord Justice Langborne and his wife taken when they were younger and attending the opera.

'What have the police told you?'

'Not a great deal. They say there's no evidence that she has been harmed. On the other hand, there's been no activity in her bank accounts. She can hardly be living somewhere without any money. She's never gone away for this long before.'

'Passport and mobile phone?'

'Her passport is in her house and she doesn't believe in mobiles, always sticks to her landline. Helena, please stop pulling at my bag. I'm going to count to six and if you haven't stopped, Mummy will get cross.' She spoke in a thin, cajoling tone.

Swift had noticed this new technique for dealing with children's behaviour in various public places. It evidently didn't work, as the children merely carried on with whatever destruction they were engaged in.

'Why don't you just say no and get cross?' he asked as Helena, who seemed a strong youngster, tugged away; the bag looked ready to be ripped from the chair and Ms Davenport swayed with it.

'Pardon?' She looked at him as if he had uttered an obscenity.

'Doesn't matter. I haven't got a naughty step.'

He sat back and watched as Helena listened from one to six, continuing to pull the bag. The strap snapped and it fell on the floor, disgorging a mobile phone and a huge purse. Unbalanced, Helena fell on her bottom. Startled by her achievement, she opened her lungs and bawled. Swift rose, strode round the desk and stuffed the items back into the bag, handing it to Ms Davenport.

Then he said to Helena, 'Want to feel my muscles?'

Surprised, she stopped mid-bawl and watched as he took off his jacket and held his arm out.

'This always works with boys,' he told her mother, putting the child's hand on his right bicep and tensing it. She frowned, then laughed and looked at him, eyes glistening with tears. He thought it best to quit while he was ahead and spoke to the mother as he tensed the muscle as tight as possible, Helena squealing, but now with delight.

'Maybe it would be best to talk this through when you're on your own. I think I can help you but I need more details.'

'I just don't think the police have treated it seriously enough because she's an old woman.'

'Not that old, surely?'

'Sixty-eight. But she looks older.'

Ouch, Swift thought.

She smiled at him and jingled Helena's harness at her. 'I hope you will help us,' she said. 'I've heard good things about you.'

'Oh yes. From?'

'A friend of mine knows your cousin, Mary Adair.'

'I see. Are you free later today? I could come to your home. In the meantime, here's a list of my charges. You'll see that I always ask for a cash deposit once I agree to take a case.' He reached into the desk drawer. Helena had now trotted round to his side and was poking vigorously at his upper arm. 'By the way, does your brother know you're asking for my help?'

Ms Davenport rolled her eyes upwards. 'Oh, Rupert . . . I've told him and he says he thinks I'm wasting my money. Says Carmen will turn up like a bad penny. Come on, Helena, let's get home and if you're a good girl you can watch "Baby Jake."'

In answer to this, Helena ran to the other side of the room and angled herself beside the washbasin. There was more cajoling, tears, forcible harnessing and finally they disappeared out of the door, Ms Davenport calling out her address in Putney and saying that Helena had a play date later in the day; she would be in and could guarantee peace and quiet at four if he could call round then.

Swift shook his head as he pushed the door closed, then switched on his coffee machine, turned on his computer and googled Carmen Langborne. There were brief stories in The Guardian and The Times about her disappearance on January 31. She had last been seen in her home that morning by her GP. The paragraph in The Times was the most interesting:

Known as a rather eccentric character, Mrs Langborne has devoted her time since her husband's death five years ago to supporting animal charities. She was involved in a lengthy dispute last year with neighbours about their basement excavation and succeeded in persuading the council to review the planning permission, when part of the roadway caved in. Police say that there is no evidence in her home of a struggle or any kind of force being used. Mrs Langborne was expected to see friends to play bridge on the evening of the thirty-first and when she failed to arrive and they couldn't contact her, they phoned her stepson Rupert Langborne, who is a Permanent Secretary in the Civil Service.

The story had then dropped out of sight; eccentric old ladies weren't that interesting when there were items about dodgy politicians, film stars and young fashionistas to fill the pages. Further web pages contained details of Lord Justice Neville Langborne's career and photos of him and Carmen at society events; Chelsea Flower Show, theatre first nights, The Lord Mayor's banquet. They were a sleek-looking couple with that unmistakeable patina of wealth; Swift thought Carmen had a look of Wallis Simpson, with her thin, lined face and angular body. He was interested because nobody else seemed to be, apart from Florence Davenport and a half-hearted brother. He wondered why she was concerned; he hadn't got the impression that she was missing her stepmother. He guessed that money might be a motivation; unresolved disappearances caused all kinds of difficulties about property and inheritances.

He fetched his coffee and sipped it, emailing his cousin:

Hi M, I hear you've been saying nice things about me. You might have brought me some work. Buy you a drink in one of those wine bars you like?

He rubbed his shoulders and sat back, coffee cradled against his chest. He loved his cousin not only because she was a good woman and had been one of his closest friends in childhood but also because she resembled his much loved dead mother; the same brunette curls and smile, the same light and steady voice. Mary Adair was an Assistant Commissioner in the Metropolitan Police and had been enthusiastic about his decision to turn private detective when he left Interpol and was casting around for a role in life. His email pinged:

Hi, I'm always saying nice things about you. How's the trench coat and trilby? Ring me later in the week, M.

He made notes about Ms Davenport's information, while he finished his coffee, and then rang Mrs Brewer.

Given the details he could provide about her paunchy husband's hotel assignations with his lissom daughter-in-law, he suggested it would be better if she came to see him but she insisted on hearing it over the phone. He listened to her sobbing; he had advised her, when she had contacted him, that she should only pose the question if she wanted to know the answer. There was certainly going to be an interesting family scene. He let her cry, and then advised her to sit down and speak to her husband before she contacted her son. She said that he had been very helpful, very kind. He didn't think so and he wondered if she would in a month's time. He said that he would email her the details with his final bill and ended the call.

He closed his eyes for a moment, remembering the smooth river, and then looked up directions to Ms Davenport's address.

CHAPTER 2

With the house, Swift's great-aunt Lily had left him a
sitting tenant; Cedric Sheridan was in his late eighties and
lived on the top floor. Cedric and Lily had known each
other for years, meeting during the war, when they worked
in Intelligence. In his teens, Swift had visited Lily
frequently, escaping his stepmother in Muswell Hill; he
had once asked her if she and Cedric were involved with
each other. Lily had laughed and said no; adding that
Cedric was bisexual and she wouldn't be keen on a man
who couldn't make up his mind. Lily's husband Wilfred
had died aged only thirty-eight, the age Swift was now, and
Lily had never stopped missing him. She never referred to
him but on that occasion when he enquired about her and
Cedric, she told Swift that Wilfred had been the only man
for her and no one else had ever come near. He had
recalled that remark when he got engaged to Ruth, and Lily
had raised her glass to them at the party. He had thought
that Ruth felt that way about him but he had been proved
wrong.

   He met Cedric coming back from his afternoon walk,
as he set out for Putney. Cedric was with two friends,

partners in the dominoes tournament at the Silver Mermaid most lunch times and they were heading back for a game of cards. Cedric had an erect military bearing and, other than slight arthritis in his hands, was fit and energetic. He waved languid fingers at Swift, asked him how the river had been, said he should call by later for a G and T, then weaved up the steps between his companions who were swaying slightly after several hours in the pub. Swift sometimes thought that Cedric had a busier social life than he had himself; most evenings, his lights burned late and music and conversation drifted down through the house.

* * *

It was a fine afternoon and the exercise of the morning had left him with a taste for more, so he walked the five miles along the Thames path to Putney Bridge. Florence Davenport lived in a terraced house not unlike his, with steps to the front door, but no basement. She answered the door wearing jodhpurs and asked would he mind waiting while she changed, as she had just got back from a hack.

She showed him into the living room and vanished. It ran the length of the house and was full of light but the walls had been painted a pale, chilly blue that was unwelcoming. The room was decorated with abstract prints and the heads of a fox, giraffe and elephant constructed, he thought, from newspaper and cardboard. A large plasma TV covered the wall opposite the sofa and a huge plastic box containing toys stood on the polished floor boards. A group of photos in fussy, faux-Victorian style silver frames were clustered on a coffee table next to a pile of horsy magazines and he bent to look; they were of Florence and Helena and, he assumed, Mr Davenport, who was a thin man of medium height with wispy hair, a trim beard and lines under his eyes that made Swift less concerned about his own. No image of Stepmother, he noted. Given the nanny and the horse riding, the place wasn't as expensively furnished as he would have expected. The beige sofa and chairs seemed small and cheap; he sat in one of the armchairs and confirmed that it resisted his six feet two. He was accustomed to finding furniture uncomfortable but this chair seemed particularly rigid. He swapped to the sofa which was only marginally more accommodating. Florence appeared to be a lady of leisure; he wondered what the husband worked at. His interest was now piqued enough to inform him that he had decided to take the case. He heard her on the stairs and took out his notebook. She had dressed in the very tight jeans again and had put a kind of floral smock over them; with her hair scrunched back in a ponytail, he thought her top half looked like Pollyanna, her bottom half Lolita. She offered him tea or coffee and he refused.

'I think I'll be able to help you,' he said. 'Are my rates acceptable?'

'Yes, thank you.'

He flicked his pen open. 'How did you find out your stepmother was missing?'

She perched on one of the armchairs, her hands around her knees. 'Rupert, my brother, rang me that evening, January thirty-first. Paddy Sutherland — that's the woman who was expecting Carmen for bridge — had contacted him. He hadn't been able to get hold of Carmen so he phoned me to see if I knew where she was. Not that that would be likely.' She gave a little laugh.

'You didn't see your stepmother often?'

'About three or four times a year; Christmas, Easter, her birthday. Same with Rupe.'

About the same as he saw his stepmother. 'So, were you worried, did you call the police?'

'No, we assumed she'd got her dates wrong or mixed up and like I said, Carmen had taken off before without telling us, although her housekeeper was always in the know. But the next morning the housekeeper, Mrs Farley, rang Rupe to say that she wasn't there and the cats hadn't been fed. She had arranged to sit with Mrs Farley that morning to go through the menu for a supper she was giving at the end of the week. Mrs Farley did catering when needed. So Rupe rang the police; well, got his secretary to ring them. Rupe has staff, you know.' She made a little lemon sucking movement with her mouth.

'And the police spoke to you both, you and Rupert?'

'Oh yes. They were bustling around to start with but I'm not sure what's happening now.'

'Does your stepmother have a car?'

'No, she's never had a licence; Daddy used to drive them. Even for her age, she's old-fashioned in that way, likes a man to open doors, pull out a seat for her, all that stuff. When Daddy died she sold the car.'

'How many times has she gone away without telling you and where did she go?' Swift removed a cushion from behind his back and put it on the floor, trying to get less uncomfortable. It was chilly in the room and not just because of the blue décor.

'I think four or five times before and she never said where she'd gone but she looked tanned so it must have been abroad. Carmen wasn't one to holiday in the UK; too cold and rainy for her. She and Daddy used to travel loads so she knew lots of places. But with no passport . . .'

'She's Spanish, isn't she?'

'Hmm, from Barcelona; but she left there years ago, came to London at eighteen. She never had any contact with family there, as far as I know.' She giggled. 'I've always thought they were probably glad to see the back of her, bought her a one-way ticket.'

Swift looked levelly at her and she blushed, rubbing her cheek.

'How did you get on with your stepmother when you were younger, did you live with her and your father?'

'Well, goodness, that was years ago; what's that got to do with anything?'

'It's always useful to have as complete a picture of someone as possible, in this kind of circumstance,' he said mildly. 'She was younger than your father?'

She shrugged. 'We never really hit it off. Yes, she was almost twenty years younger than Daddy. He was seeing her before he and Mummy divorced so, you know, there was quite a bit of tension. I lived with Mummy in Sussex; she moved there after the split and stayed there until she died. I used to stay with Daddy in the school holidays. Carmen was really only interested in Daddy so I was a bit of an inconvenience. We didn't have much to do with each other. Rupe's ten years older than me so he never actually lived with her. She liked the status that being married to Daddy gave her. She was the general dogsbody at his dentist when they met so marriage gave her quite a leg up the social ladder.'

'When was the last time you saw Carmen or spoke to her?'

'Like I told the police, at Christmas. We went round there on Boxing Day for tea.'

'Was Rupert there?'

'No, he was at his wife's place in Berkshire. He called in to her at New Year; he always comes back to London for the sales to buy his shirts in Jermyn Street.'

Swift arched his back and flexed his legs, rubbing his cramped right thigh. 'So, Carmen didn't seem worried about anything, upset by anyone?'

Florence shrugged. 'No. She was her usual self, talking about her social activities, some gala she was attending to raise money for elephants in Thailand.'

'Did she have health problems? I read that her doctor had seen her the day she vanished.'

'Oh, I'm not sure. She always seemed well to me, although she liked having health checks; you know, BP, cholesterol. She has a private GP and they come running if you sneeze. Not like us ordinary mortals who have to beg for an appointment. I had tonsillitis a couple of weeks ago and I couldn't see a GP for days! I was offered a nurse instead, trying to fob me off.'

Swift smiled sympathetically. 'And your husband, did he see your stepmother with you?'

'Paul? Yes, he came when we visited. Actually, my DH gets on okay with Carmen, better than me probably. But then, as I said before, she's a man's woman.'

'What do you think has happened to her?'

There was a pause. 'I just don't know. I'm worried that she might have come to some harm, I suppose.'

'If she has, do you know who benefits from her will?'

Florence sat up straight. Her eyes were suddenly shrewd. Swift thought it was the most animated he had seen her.

'When she dies, Rupe and I share the house; that was all left in trust by Daddy. She's said she's also leaving us both money and some to animal charities. Cats and donkeys, probably. I ask you!'

'You don't approve?'

'I've nothing against animals but I happen to think humans should come first where inheritance is concerned.'

'You could do with the money, then?'

He wondered how she would react to the rudeness. Her colour rose but she forced a bright tone.

'Who couldn't do with money these days? But I work, you know, I do earn money myself.' Her head twitched.

'Oh? What do you do?'

'I'm a personal stylist.'

'Yes? Sorry, I'm sure I'm dense but I don't know what that means.'

She looked astonished. 'I help people to choose their wardrobes and make-up, accessorise jewellery. If they want, I go shopping with them to make sure their clothes match their lifestyle. I write a blog too.'

'Fascinating,' he lied.

She gave him a sideways glance. 'If you came to me, for example, I'd suggest a shorter hairstyle, maybe some gel to sculpt those curls and definitely softer colours.'

'Thanks, I'll think about that. What does your husband do?'

'He works in the city.'

'Right. Can you give me some contact details now? I need to speak to Rupert, Paddy Sutherland, Mrs Farley, your stepmother's GP. Also, it would help to have a look around her house, if that can be arranged. Where does she live?'

'Holland Park. You could ask Mrs Farley to let you in when she's there; she's still going in every day to keep the place ticking over and to feed the cats.'

She flicked through her phone and gave him the contact details he'd requested.

'What's a DH?' he asked. 'You said it about your husband.'

'It's shorthand for Darling Husband; women use it all the time on Mumsnet.'

'Ah; well, I don't have much reason to use that website.'

She giggled. 'I meant what I said, about giving you some style tips. With your raven hair and slate eyes, a sage green would really suit you.'

'Okay, I'll bear it in mind. I'll contact you in about a week and give you an update. I need that cash deposit, please.'

She rummaged in the yellow handbag and gave him the money. He handed her the receipt he had prepared and a contract for her to sign. The transaction seemed to relax her.

'Listen,' she said, cradling one hand inside the other, 'it's true that I've never been close to Carmen and we've had our differences. But in the end I always remember that Daddy loved her so I feel some family obligation towards her. I think I need to try and help because I'm sure she's in some trouble. Does that make sense?'

Her sincerity sounded forced to Swift. 'Yes, it makes sense.'

'Will you talk to the police?' she asked at the door.

'I'll let them know you've engaged me, yes.'

* * *

Swift waited for Mary Adair in a wine bar off Regent Street. It was tucked down one of the parallel side lanes that tourists rarely explored as they swarmed up and down the main drag. Swift always thought of London as two cities: one, the teeming beehive where you had to be careful not to get knocked off the pavement; the second, the backstage capital where, if you had the knowledge, you could walk, eat and talk in comparative tranquillity. At six thirty the bar was quiet, inhabiting the lull between offices closing and true night owls appearing. Miles Davis played plaintively in the background. It had started raining and it was snug to sit by the window, watching the misty droplets slide down the pane. Swift had already ordered a glass of Merlot; if it was going to be wine, it had to be red, as far as he was concerned. Mary went for white or red depending on her mood.

As children, he and Mary had enjoyed Cluedo, reading Sherlock Holmes, writing with invisible ink and sending each other messages in secret codes. As adults, they had continued their interest in concealment and exposure, joining the Met within a year of each other, as graduate entrants. After a couple of years, he had been seconded to, then taken a permanent post with Interpol, tracking illegal arms sales across Europe. Mary meanwhile had risen rapidly through the ranks, enjoying her fragmentation of glass ceilings. These days she seemed to spend most of her time in interminable meetings and committees, which he would never have been able to stomach. Mary had consoled him after Ruth, saying little, buying him a case of

Rhone Syrah with which to drown his sorrows. Close as they were, he hadn't told her that he had been seeing Ruth again. No one knew; his heart was too troubled to talk about it.

Mary dashed in, shaking her head, smiling, chucking an umbrella on the floor. He stood and hugged her; she was tall too, her head just below his shoulder.

'White or red?' he asked her, signalling to a waiter.

'Better make it a sauvignon, I have to read a report later and red beckons the sandman.'

When her drink arrived, they clinked glasses.

'You look well,' she said, 'been out on the river?'

'Twice so far this week. How are you?'

'Fine. I gave an inspirational talk at a girls' school this afternoon, about the Met as a career; at least I hope it inspired one or two of them. They asked good questions. I saw Mark Gill earlier in the week, he was asking after you.'

'That's a happy coincidence. I'm planning to ring him tomorrow to ask him if he knows about a case I've taken.'

'The one I may have unwittingly sent your way?'

'That's it; the disappearance of Carmen Langborne. Her stepdaughter, Florence Davenport, has a friend who knows you.'

Mary removed her dark-framed glasses and rubbed the lenses with the hem of her scarf. 'Who would that be?'

'No idea.'

'Oh well; Mark will point you in the right direction. She's still missing, isn't she?'

'That's right. Florence wants me to try and track her down. There's a brother, Rupert, who seems to think she'll turn up.'

'Rupert Langborne? I think I've met him at some committee or other at Westminster. He's a civil servant?'

'Yep. I'll be arranging to see him, although according to his sister, he thinks their stepmother is possibly game playing, gone away somewhere. Do you know much about him?'

'No; I recall a tall, stout chap but he was in another working group to me. You know, Ty; one of those ones where you have coloured post-it notes and you brainstorm and come up with ideas and then afterwards someone distributes them to be read and they disappear into the great ideas rubbish chute.'

Swift groaned. 'I miss that world so much, I really do.'

Mary ordered two more drinks and asked for some olives and bread. She was looking very chipper, he thought; her handsome, strong face and quick eyes gave her a commanding presence and she was wearing a beautifully tailored suit.

'Do you think I should wear sage green?' he asked her as the wine and food arrived.

She laughed. 'You what? When did you start caring about what you wear?'

'Florence Davenport is a personal stylist,' he said with affected dignity. 'She wants to give me a makeover.'

'Ha!' She popped an olive in her mouth and shoved them towards him. 'Maybe she wants your bod too. Do you fancy her?'

'There are so many things wrong with that question, Mary. One, she's married, two, she's a client and three, no, I don't.' He dipped bread into oil and vinegar; it was dark and delicious.

Mary tore a piece of bread. 'I've got some news on the romance front,' she said slyly.

'Go on.'

'I met someone at a conference. Her name's Simone. We've seen each other a couple of times. So far, so good. I like her a lot.'

He took a deep sip of wine. 'Good on you. She a cop?'

'No; she's in forensics, so we can talk ghoulish stuff in comfort. How about you? Seeing anyone?'

'Not at the moment.' *Only my married ex.*

'Looking?'

'Not really.'

Mary knew when to drop a subject and went on to talk about her plans for a summer break in Crete.

'Have you had a birthday invitation from Joyce?' she asked him.

Joyce was his stepmother. 'Mm, it came last week. I suppose I'd better go. Are you?'

'I'll show my face,' Mary said. 'How old will she be?'

'Sixty-five. I expect most of the neighbourhood will be there, so I should be able to get away with a fleeting appearance.'

Mary clutched his arm and imitated Joyce's fruity, breathy voice, 'Oh Tyrone, I never see enough of you, you dreadful man and you're so thin, I'm sure you're not eating properly!'

'Don't!' he said, shuddering.

She finished her drink and pushed his to him. 'Drink up, I have to get home and bury myself in this report.'

* * *

He left Mary at eight and set off for Seven Dials to follow up a case he had taken a few weeks back. The client was Ed Boyce, a slick, fast-talking man in his late twenties. He was convinced he was being stalked by his jealous ex-girlfriend and his jittery manner certainly indicated that he had anxieties. Boyce had asked to meet in a café near his office, explaining unnecessarily that his work schedule was mental. He had played with his phone throughout the consultation, taking only a few sips of his banana smoothie before abandoning it. He had jet black hair, tiny brilliant teeth and pale, almost translucent skin. He just wanted Rachel, his ex, to stop being ridiculous, he said, and let him move on with his life and his new partner. If Swift could get some photos and details of her behaviour collated for him he could challenge her and he was sure she would back off.

The rain had eased, so Swift walked. He avoided the tube when he could, hating its hot, crammed carriages. He wondered what he should get Joyce for her birthday. Probably, he would fall back on the usual scarf or theatre voucher. His father had remarried just eight months after Swift's mother died, when he was fifteen. Joyce taught history at the school where his father was deputy head. Swift remembered his tall shadow as he came into the garden on a summer evening and explained that he had proposed to Joyce; *it's just that I feel terribly lonely, you see*, he had said, almost apologetically. Joyce was a friendly, boisterous, bossy and well-meaning woman but she tried far too hard and flooded remorselessly around Swift's life, giving unwanted advice on studies, diet and exercise. She had no children of her own and appeared to regard her stepson as a project to embark on. Swift didn't want another mother; the one he had lost had meant everything to him and had left him a deep reservoir of all the maternal love he would ever need. He shrank away when Joyce approached him, questioning, prying, poking her nose in where it wasn't wanted, not comprehending that an adolescent boy needs privacy. He was a perceptive young man and didn't want to hurt Joyce's feelings, understanding that she was well intentioned if unbearable.

He started spending time at Lily's, where it was peaceful and he could make himself scrambled eggs at any hour instead of having to sit down at six on the dot to three-course meals with loaded questions about how school had been and what his plans were for the future. He employed the excuse that Lily's house was useful for rowing practice and he thought that his father was relieved that he had it as a bolt hole. He had applied to red-brick universities because Joyce kept telling everyone that he was *terribly bright, Oxbridge material and of course he can be in the Boat Race!* She failed even to understand that his enjoyment of rowing was as a solitary activity, an escape. His father died just before he graduated from Warwick, leaving him with an uncomfortable sense of having Joyce as an extra, unwanted family member. Florence Davenport's comment about feeling an obligation towards her stepmother had chimed with him.

He checked the time. Ed Boyce had indicated he would be leaving a private members' club called *Abode* around nine. He worked in TV production for a company called *Purple Spark*. He had told Swift that Rachel, the stalking ex, was 'like you know, a major head case,' and making his life unbearable. He said he'd had odd phone calls and constant emails from her, had seen her loitering regularly near his home and 'just felt he was being followed as he moved around.' Swift had a photo of her on his phone; a likeable, average face, dark hair swept up in a topknot, a pleasant smile. Boyce appeared an excitable type, full of himself and good-looking in a smoothly self-conscious way. He seemed used to hobnobbing with low-grade celebrities from TV reality shows. Swift thought he might have been listening to too many of their car-crash life stories and felt the need to inject some drama into his own. To date, he had tracked Boyce on half a dozen occasions, to and from business meetings, restaurants, nightclubs and his gym and had seen no evidence of anyone following him. Still, Boyce maintained that he felt uncomfortable, as if there was a shadow at his back and wanted Swift to continue a while longer. Swift wondered if the shadow was imaginary, the product of guilt or a vivid imagination but he was happy to take payment, so he wandered along a row of shops, looking for the club and finally saw a discreet sign with the name above a fanlight on a door tucked between a designer boutique and a delicatessen.

Swift crossed the road and stood at the window of an upmarket men's clothing shop. There was a shirt in the display in a shade that he thought might be sage green. The street was empty except for the odd passing car. He checked his phone and sent a text to Mark Gill, saying he would ring him. He heard the door to *Abode* opening and watched as a group of people spilled out on to the pavement, Ed Boyce among them. They all immediately checked their phones and started replying to messages or calls. Some air-kissing took place and Boyce set off towards Covent Garden tube, his man bag slung diagonally across his chest. Swift started after him, keeping to the other side of the street and caught the same Piccadilly Line train to Turnpike Lane. He thought Boyce looked self-important, being observed by his own private detective, and imagined him bragging about it at work. At Turnpike Lane he shadowed Boyce on the five-minute walk to the block of flats he lived in and watched him enter. He waited for a few minutes and saw no evidence of a stalking woman who looked like a major head case, only young professional types like Boyce heading for home. Hungry after his snack of bread and olives earlier, he bought fish and chips and ate them as he walked, enjoying the soft night air and the hit of vinegar on his palate.

CHAPTER 3

Carmen Langborne's house was in a mews just off Holland Park Avenue, a beautiful Georgian property with gleaming white paintwork, wide black front door and carefully tended window boxes full of white and purple pansies. The hushed, pristine street looked as if it was scrubbed and polished every day. Swift felt that if he dropped even a scrap of paper, he would be apprehended. He rang the bell and the door was opened almost immediately by a tall, rangy woman of around sixty with short brown hair and a warm smile. He introduced himself, holding out his ID, and she raised her glasses which were on a chain around her neck, held them before her eyes and examined it carefully. She nodded, satisfied, and pulled the door wider.

'Come in. Could you take your shoes off, please? Mrs L's rules. We'll go to the kitchen, I've the kettle on. You'll have a cuppa?'

'Coffee would be good, if that's okay.'

'Of course. There are some of those individual coffee filters here in the cupboard, Mrs L prefers those. I only ever drink tea; I was given it in my bottle as a baby, so I suppose you could say I'm an addict.'

He untied his laces and left his shoes by the umbrella stand. He could smell cigarette smoke from her clothes as he followed her along a wide hallway; she had the slightly worn-looking, dry skin that dedicated smokers developed. Her apron rustled as she walked. She was wearing slip-on paper covers over soft flat shoes, presumably so that she didn't mark the burnished parquet flooring. The spacious kitchen was at the back of the house, refurbished in minimalist style, all stainless steel, whites and greys but in an alcove there was an incongruous well-used pine table and chairs with cushions tied on and a small armchair. Two of the cushions were occupied by the longest, most lithe and handsome cats that Swift had ever seen. He wasn't a great cat lover, being allergic to their hair but he could acknowledge their beauty. Both were sleeping; one of them opened one eye, gave Swift a lazy look, then closed it again. The air held delicious scents of chocolate and vanilla.

'Sit yourself down,' Mrs Farley said. 'This is Perseus and this is Apollo. Paris is out and about for now.'

Swift drew out the chair furthest from them. 'They're incredible looking animals.'

'Bengals,' Mrs Farley said, lining up cups and pouring milk. 'Their price is something out of this world, with their pedigrees and whatnot and of course they only eat the best. I reckon they cost more to feed a day than I do.'

'Thanks for seeing me, Mrs Farley. Mrs Davenport said it would be all right to take a look around the house.'

'Call me Ronnie.'

'I'm Tyrone.'

'Aye, Mrs Davenport rang me. To be honest, I'm glad she contacted you. The police are very smart and efficient-looking but I don't think they have any idea what's happened.'

She turned down the radio, which was tuned to an easy-listening station, finished placing tea, coffee and biscuits on a tray, checked that everything needed was on it and brought it to the table.

'Are you from Aberdeen?' Swift asked, accepting coffee and a chocolate biscuit.

'I am, right enough. Well spotted.'

'I used to work with someone from there, it's a distinctive accent.'

'It's a bit watered down now, after forty years in London. Is there enough milk in that coffee?'

'It's fine, thanks. What do you think has happened to Mrs Langborne?'

Ronnie crossed her legs and tapped her chin with a forefinger. Swift reckoned she was a woman who enjoyed recounting a story and it was, after all, of dramatic interest when your employer vanished.

'Haven't a clue, is the truth of it. I was here the morning of the thirtieth of January. I usually come in three days a week in the morning for two hours to do general cleaning and any other jobs Mrs L wants. That day I hoovered the ground floor — the cats are short-haired but even so, you get some moulting — and emptied the dishwasher, did a bit of ironing although Mrs L has most of her stuff dry-cleaned.' Ronnie took a sip of tea but pushed the plate of biscuits towards him. 'I'd love one but I'm on a diet, so it'd be a kindness if you have another. I make them because it relaxes me, not to eat them.'

He took another. They were good, buttery and with chunks of chocolate. 'How was Mrs Langborne that day?'

'Same as always. Organised, looking smart; she always dresses well, even if she isn't going out. She wasn't upset or anything. I said to the policeman, if anything, she seemed chipper.'

'She hadn't seemed any different during the weeks before?'

'Nah. She's a very ordered person, everything done to schedule and in the proper way. I think that's why we get on okay, I'm the same. She had a bit of a clear-out at the end of December, just after Christmas; some of her husband's stuff that she still had, clothes and golf clubs and such, and some scarves and perfume she decided she didn't like any more. I copped some Chanel No. 5! She got me to take the bags of stuff to the charity shop.'

'How long have you worked for her?'

'About five years. I came soon after her husband died. Her previous help was a friend of mine, Kate, who went to live in Cyprus when her hubby retired, so that's how she knew about me.'

'You seem to get on with her okay; how would you describe her?'

Ronnie gave him a knowing look. 'Some folk find her difficult, including her family, but I get on fine with her. We never discuss personal matters. We're just straightforward with each other. She likes everything just so but then, as I say, I'm the same. I suppose she comes across to some as a wee bit chilly and rigid, maybe a tad snobbish. I think she was bereft after the husband died; Kate told me she depended on him, he was the centre of her life really and she was in a bad way for a while after he died. As far as I'm concerned, she pays well and this is a handy wee job. More coffee?'

'No, thanks. Who finds her difficult?'

Ronnie poured herself more tea. 'Well, now, I'd say that there's no love lost between her and the stepdaughter. I don't think Mrs L has much maternal instinct and I heard her once on the phone talking to Florence, being critical about her wee girl's manners. They'd been round here and the wee one had broken a tea pot. Mrs L could be sharp, you see. I believe too that Florence was very close to her daddy and of course the divorce meant she had to live away from him. That kind of scar never truly heals, does it? Mrs L likes Rupert better; I saw them together here once and he was complimenting her on her dress. He has a way with the ladies, that one, I can see how he'd attract a string of wives; I believe he's on his third marriage. He and the sister don't care much for each other, I'd say. I've heard them both drop snide comments about the other one.'

Ronnie was well into her stride now, pulling her chair in to the table, folding her capable freckled arms below her bosom. Swift nodded, not wanting to interrupt her flow.

'I can tell that Dr Forsyth finds her a bit of a nuisance,' Ronnie continued, 'even though she's paid well enough for her time. Mrs L worries a lot about her health; she had a cancer scare a couple of years back although it turned out just to be a kidney stone. She's always phoning Dr Forsyth and getting her round here; any little mole or cough or headache. She called her that last morning I saw her because she had a painful finger and the doctor said she'd be round the following day.'

'What about friends, does she have close ones?'

'I don't know about close; she likes Mrs Sutherland, who she plays bridge with. She's RC, quite devout in her own way I think but never discusses it. She goes to mass on Sunday but I've never had the impression she gets involved in the church otherwise. She seems to go out to lots of social events and she's held the odd coffee morning and supper party here in aid of her animal charities. I do the coffee and hand round the cakes and biscuits and I make or buy in quiches and puds for the evenings. The guests are mainly ladies, at the coffee mornings anyway. I don't think men go for that kind of thing much. There's been some fellas at the suppers. But to be honest, she isn't one to talk about anything to me except matters to do with the upkeep of the house.'

'You keep your staff at arm's length?' Swift suggested.

Ronnie laughed. 'Aye, right enough. She likes me to call her "madam" and she calls me "Farley." Mind you, that's fine with me. I go to do for another lady near here who's always telling me about her family troubles and it gets a bit much. I'm a housekeeper, not a therapist. If I earned the kind of money they earn, I could have a villa in

Cyprus too! Ah!' she held a hand up as a song came on; 'The Wichita Lineman. I adore Glen Campbell. D'you like him?'

'Not too keen, but I agree the song tells a good story. If I listened to country music, it would be Kris Kristofferson. Mrs Davenport said that her stepmother had gone away without telling her family a couple of times. Did you know about those trips?'

One of the cats stood, circled his cushion and settled down again with a yawn. Swift sneezed rapidly, three times. It was always three times when it was an allergic reaction.

Ronnie reached to a worktop and passed him a box of tissues. 'Bless you. When my ma sneezed three times she'd say, "God bless me, Christ bless me, all the saints in heaven bless me." Mrs L told me she'd be away but she didn't say where. I had to come in every day, you see, to feed the cats. But three weeks was the most time she was gone for. I know she didn't tell Florence and Rupert that she was going. I think she liked to cause a bit of a stir sometimes. I've met other women who live on their own who get like that; maybe it's a way of making sure people take notice of them. Would you mind if we step into the garden? I'm dying for a ciggie and there's no smoking allowed inside.'

She unlocked a side door and they stepped out into a small garden, mainly paved, with steps leading to slim terraces that held urns and pots of flowers and shrubs. There was an iron table and chairs, so they sat in the sun. Ronnie reached into her apron and took out a tin with ready-made roll-ups inside.

Swift stretched out his legs, enjoying the warmth of the sun on his head. He shifted his chair to make sure he was out of drifting distance of Ronnie's smoke.

'Mrs Langborne doesn't have a gardener?'

'Nah; she likes doing her own tubs and this is small enough not to need any other help.'

Swift clasped his arms behind his head. 'One of the papers said that Mrs Langborne is eccentric. Why would they say that?'

'Oh, the papers!' Ronnie snorted. 'Maybe that was to do with the argument she had with the neighbours. They're young and oozing money. They started having a basement dug and the noise was awful, with the constant drilling and dust everywhere. I mean, why not just buy a bigger house? She'd already had words with them and started a local petition. She was constantly badgering the council about it. Then the pavement and some of the road caved in which really made her feel justified. They were allowed to carry on with the basement eventually but there was a big to-do about it all and she was knocking on their door most days about the noise. I think the neighbours referred to her as a 'mad old bat' to a journalist who was hanging about; at one point they threatened to get an injunction against her for harassment. When Mrs L felt she was in the right, she was like a dog with a bone.'

'Which house was this?'

'Number Eleven, two doors up. They're called Stafford.'

Swift added to his notes and read them over. Ronnie looked on, interested.

'Must be a fascinating job you do. Do you get to know lots of secrets?'

'A few. People usually have things they want to hide.'

'I can imagine. Folk tell me I'm an open book but I don't think that's true of anyone. We all like to draw the odd veil, don't we?'

Swift smiled at her. 'Ronnie, I know that you've said you and Mrs Langborne have a fairly formal relationship but I can tell that you're a keen-eyed woman, who doesn't miss much. I would imagine that if you're in someone's home three times a week there must be stuff you pick up on. Are you sure there's nothing else you can tell me? In a case like this, even the most apparently insignificant things can be helpful.'

He could see that she knew she was being flattered and why; no flies on Ronnie. But she liked it nonetheless. He thought it must be odd for her in this house, coming to its emptiness every day, with just the cats to talk to, not knowing where her employer was. He wondered if she was alone too much; there was an intensity to her warmth, as if she lavished it when she could and she obviously loved a good chat. She was clearly also making her stewardship comfortable, judging by the TV and celebrity magazines he had seen stacked by her bag with its long straps hanging over the kitchen worktop and the foot stool pulled up to the arm chair. He had detected a faint smell of alcohol coming from her and wondered if she was helping herself to some of her employer's stock.

'You've a clever tongue,' she said, taking a deep pull on her cigarette and blowing a smoke ring. 'I ought to give these up but I started when I was fourteen and you've got to die of something.'

There was a pause. Swift looked intently at the garden.

'Well, I don't know, Tyrone; when I said to the police that Mrs L seemed chipper on the thirtieth, it did cross my mind later that maybe she sniffed a romance or at least had met some fella she liked. She didn't like being on her own, I could see that right enough. My friend Kate told me that the husband had put her on a pedestal and cosseted her, treated her like some kind of princess. Whatever she wanted, she got. Must be hard to suddenly not have that kind of attention and be on your own. I've never had it, so I've never missed it. The way she acted around men, you could see she was a bit desperate; you know, coming on a bit too gushing. Men aren't keen on that, are they?'

He held his hands up. 'I don't know, not sure it's ever happened to me. But I can imagine it might be off-putting.'

Ronnie gave him a look. 'I'd say you're being modest, a good-looking, fit man like you would get plenty of offers. Are you married?'

'I'm not, no. So, was Mrs Langborne acting like that around some of these supper-party men?'

'Aye, but not to one in particular, as I recall. But, you know, she'd do that Princess Di kind of thing, holding her head to one side, fluttering her eyelashes and being girlish. It was funny to me, seeing it, because I only know this rather formidable woman. A wee bit sad, too, because she's not in the first flush anymore and she isn't that much of a looker, although because she's slim and beautifully dressed, she can make some other women feel a bit frumpy. I heard one of the wives muttering to another one in the hallway about it. She said, "Carmen looks grotesque when she's flirting, it's awful at her age, I do wish she'd stop it."'

Ronnie had adopted a posh accent for her quotation and Swift laughed.

'So she isn't popular with wives?'

'Aye, you could definitely say that.' She leaned forward. 'Do you think one of them has bumped her off for poaching?'

'Seems unlikely; I think that's Agatha Christie territory. Does Mrs Langborne keep an appointment diary?' He was hoping she had relied on pen and paper rather than an electronic record.

'Aye; the police took it away but they brought it back a couple of weeks ago. I'll show it you.'

'How about a computer? Did she have one or use email?'

'No, she disliked technology, said she had no time for it. Oh, here comes Paris, the third bundle of trouble.'

A lissom, grey-and-brown striped cat, like a mini tiger, was picking his way among the terraces. He ignored them and vanished through the cat flap into the kitchen.

'He's the troublemaker,' Ronnie said. 'There'll be madness in there in a minute.' She stubbed her cigarette out carefully in an ashtray and swept up all evidence of her pastime with a duster she took from her pocket. She turned to him as she was leading the way back into the house, frowning. 'I can tell you that something's happened to Mrs L; she'd never have left her cats unfed or gone away from them for this long, she was devoted to them.'

She gave Swift the diary, a thick, hardback book with the RSPCA logo and a cover featuring kittens and told him to look around the house; she could stay for another half hour and had things to get on with. He sat on a Queen Anne chair in the hallway, reading through the pages from the beginning of January. Most days had one entry and all looked like the moderately interesting social activities of a wealthy woman; *Animals in Need supper; bridge, PS; hair 230; National Trust talk 6pm; Wigmore Hall @ 7; CPL coffee morning.* No suggestion of assignations with a 'fella.' Carmen's writing was elaborate, with curlicues and loops. On January 31 she had written *Dr F 930*, then *Re WP* and *Haven.* February held a similar series of entries, never fulfilled. March was almost empty. There was no repeat of *WP* or *Haven.* He took a photo of the January 31 page with his phone.

He looked around the house, knowing that the police would already have searched and fingerprinted. Every room was shining and orderly. There was a great deal of chintz and numerous knick-knacks in the form of china shepherdesses and ladies in crinoline. Mrs Langborne's bedside table held a small plaster statue of the Virgin Mary, a bottle of sleeping tablets and a copy of *The Lady.* He picked up the magazine and flicked through. There was a page with two apparently identical prints of a seated woman in twenties fashion, asking the reader to spot ten differences between the pictures. Swift found them all within seconds, thinking it wasn't exactly taxing on the brain. Just along the upstairs landing was a box room which was clearly used for sewing and knitting. Downstairs in the sitting room there were more copies of *The Lady* and *Country Life*. Swift looked at an array of photos on the mantelpiece, over a coal effect gas fire. There were several of Carmen and her husband, one outside a hotel and one on what looked like a cruise ship. In each one he was looking at her, an arm around her slim waist. Her hair was very dark and looked dyed and Swift could see how expensive and elegant her dresses were. She wore gold earrings, necklaces and bracelets. Her face was a little hard and quite lined but she had a confident smile that lifted her expression. Her well-preserved figure would certainly annoy many other older women. There was another photo of Carmen with a tall man and a petite woman dressed in cream and holding flowers; he thought he recognised the steps of Chelsea register office. He took the photo through to the kitchen. He could hear a cat squealing, some thuds and Ronnie admonishing them. He put his head through the kitchen door and saw that two of the cats were squaring up to each other, Paris clearly being the originator of the ruckus. Ronnie shooed him out of the door and locked the cat flap.

'He can stay out there and cool his heels for ten minutes,' Ronnie told Swift, who was pleased that she wasn't going to count to six. He noted that she had put on lipstick while he was looking around and there was a floral fragrance that he didn't care for in the air; like cat hair, perfume often made him sneeze.

'Just a couple more questions,' Swift said. 'What's CPL?'

'That's the Cats Protection League.'

'And these entries on the day she disappeared, *WP* and *Haven?*'

'Aye, the police asked me about those. I haven't a clue. The photo is her with Rupert and Daphne at their wedding three years back.'

'Thanks. Could I keep it for now? It's a very clear close up of her.'

'Aye that's fine. Are you done? I have to be at my next lady at two.' She took a cream mac from the back of a chair and gave it a shake.

'Thanks for your time.' He gave her a card. 'If you think of anything else, do ring me. Or, of course, if Mrs Langborne turns up.'

Ronnie slipped the card in her pocket. 'I don't reckon that'll happen. I hope you find her. It's odd to be coming here and she's not around. I worry that some harm has come to her; it must have, surely, or there'd be some trace of her. I've no idea how long I'll be wanted here if she's not found.'

'Who's paying you in the meantime?'

'Rupert's taking care of it.'

She saw him to the door, one of the cats following her and brushing around her legs.

'You've got my number too, Tyrone, if you want to give me a wee call,' she said softly, waving.

He waved back and walked away, a little startled, suspecting that he had just been propositioned. After a minute he stopped, retraced his steps and rang the bell of number eleven. No one answered. He looked at the new steps leading from the side of the front door down to a basement window. He went down them and looked through the window but the obscured glass revealed nothing. The area around the window was newly planted with dark green shrubs and smoothed with gravel. The chaos that had so annoyed Carmen had been made harmonious.

* * *

Back at his office, Swift wrote up his notes and looked at the photo of Carmen Langborne's diary. A haven for what or whom? He felt that he had learned a fair amount about Carmen, who seemed a tricky kind of woman and possibly tiresome, but nothing that suggested any reason why she should have vanished.

He headed upstairs to his flat to forage for some late lunch. The place was still pretty much as Lily had left it; a well-proportioned square sitting room at the front, behind that a bedroom, and at the back a long galley kitchen and bathroom. Now and again, Swift considered redecorating, but the truth was that he loved the place as it was, albeit it was growing shabby. Lily had favoured the Arts and Crafts style; the sitting room was decorated with William Morris Strawberry Thief wallpaper, a console table with shield and cross motifs, a Victorian chaise longue and deep armchairs in a thistle-patterned fabric. The buttery-yellow woodwork and glazed ochre tiles in the kitchen over the butler sink, and the open shelves with copper pans and spice rack; all these things were a pleasant reminder of Lily and the sanctuary that the house had always offered him. He had friends who lived in homes that were minimalist, with plain walls and stark, modern furniture that made him feel edgy. Mary said that shabby chic summed him up, with his fraying shirt collars, unkempt curling hair and random pairings of suit jackets and jeans, so in her opinion, the décor suited him perfectly.

He made a cheese and tomato sandwich, adding a dollop of damson chutney made by Cedric, who regularly cooked up batches of jams, marmalades and relishes. While he ate he rang Mark Gill who suggested he come round for an Indian takeaway that evening. There was an added enticement that Mark had some new additions to his collection of vintage detective magazines. He and Mark had met soon after he joined the police and had worked together on several cases. Mark was now an inspector operating in digital investigations but said he could take a look at what was happening regarding Carmen Langborne.

Swift then emailed Rupert Langborne, asking for a meeting and giving his contact details. He made coffee, went back to his office and tidied up some accounts, checked the tides and decided that he could get an hour's rowing in if he was quick. He donned a blue all-in-one Lycra suit and picked up a woollen hat to ward off the breeze. After he had changed, he ran up to Cedric's flat with half a dozen empty glass jars. Cedric was back from the pub and when he opened his door there was a mouthwatering smell of fruit.

'Ah, terrific timing, my boy!' he said, waving Swift in. 'You look like an elongated super hero in that outfit, about to save the world. I'm just making lime marmalade with Milo. You remember him, don't you?'

Swift certainly did remember Milo, who had fallen down the stairs at midnight due to inebriation, several months back, and fractured his wrist. Swift had been woken and had to call an ambulance and accompany Milo to hospital. He was older than sprightly Cedric, slightly bent and slow-moving; they called themselves the hare and the tortoise. They were both wearing aprons and there was an amazing mess in the kitchen. On the cooker a deep pot was making noises like a rumbling volcano.

'Tyrone, my dear one, my rescuer,' Milo called, waving a wooden spoon. 'Come and taste this.'

He held out the spoon and Swift licked it.

'Lovely. Has it set?'

'Almost,' Cedric said, prodding a glob of the mixture that was chilling on a plate. 'We must keep close watch now; we're reaching a critical point.'

Milo was ogling Swift. 'Dear one, that outfit leaves very little to the imagination. If I was younger I might pounce on you!'

Swift waved a warning finger. 'You concentrate on your marmalade, Milo.'

'Yes, Milo,' Cedric said. 'Tyrone isn't of your persuasion so behave nicely.'

'Ah,' sighed Milo, 'there was a time when I was young and fleet and I might have turned him. Now I get my thrills boiling fruit and sugar.'

Swift left them to it and set off. So far that day he had been propositioned by a sexagenarian and an octogenarian; perhaps by night time a nonagenarian would eye him up.

CHAPTER 4

Mark Gill's flat in a small modern block in Ravenscourt Park wasn't so much minimalist as almost empty. Swift had been there a couple of times in the eight years Mark had lived in it and apart from a few expensive pieces of furniture and state-of-the-art TV there was little evidence of his personality. He rarely ate in, so his kitchen gleamed in the same pristine condition the builders had left it when he bought it off-plan. Mark was a medium-height, intense man who spoke, moved and acted rapidly. Even when sitting, he was restlessly tapping his fingers on the chair edge or drawing imaginary diagrams on surfaces. He talked constantly, in a stream of thoughts that were often hard to follow. It was hard to imagine that he ever slept and when he did he kept the TV in his bedroom flickering all night with the sound muted. He loathed being on his own and if not working, which he often did until late in the evening, he sought the company of others. His nickname at work was *twitcher*. Swift, who could be seen as solitary and taciturn, watched his friend jittering around the room. He found Mark's volubility oddly restful; his friend never noticed if his companion was unforthcoming. He had often wondered what Mark's childhood had been like, to cause such inability to be peaceful, but it wasn't the kind of friendship that allowed such questions. And ultimately, Swift believed that everyone was a survivor in some way and to some degree of childhood experiences.

They met now and again and always discussed their joint interest, detective magazines and particularly pulp fiction. On wet days when he wasn't busy Swift sometimes called in to a shop in Soho that stocked an extensive selection of the magazines, and which for some reason played sixties music. He would spend an entertaining hour or two in the musty atmosphere, listening to The Troggs and Dusty Springfield; and he occasionally bought a couple of magazines if they particularly interested him. Mark was a dedicated collector and after phoning the food order and pouring beers for them both, he brought a box file to the S-shaped glass coffee table.

'Here,' he said gleefully, 'look at my latest acquisitions. I picked up an early 1930s *Casebook of Cardigan* on eBay.'

Swift looked through a copy of *Dime Detective* which featured the usual garish cover with private eye Jack Cardigan in *The Dead Don't Die*. After it there was a story with Patricia Seaward, the female detective who gave Cardigan a run for his money. Mark also had a *True Detective* from 1952 featuring *Jail for the Jezebel* and Swift was taken with a magazine he had not come across before called *Uncensored Detective* with a cover of a horrified woman and the title, *Murder Stalks the Bobby-Sox Bride*.

'Terrific,' he said. '*Jezebel* is not a word you hear much nowadays. Did Cardigan ever fail to solve a mystery?'

'Not in any I've read.'

'Unlike the Met, so far, with Carmen Langborne.'

'True. I'll tell you more about that in a minute. I'm trying to find some copies of *Black Mask* with Tough Dick Donahue; tip me the wink if you come across any.'

The door buzzer rang and Mark leapt out of his chair to receive the takeaway. They sat at the table, helping themselves to various curries, rice and pakoras. Mark fetched more cold beer. He ate as quickly as he spoke, stabbing his food.

'I had a look at the Langborne case. No fingerprints in the house other than hers, the GP's and the housekeeper's. No signs of a struggle. No blood. Nothing known about her movements after the doctor visited. She doesn't own a car. No activity in her bank accounts or on credit cards. Passport in her bedroom. A load of nothing.' He shrugged and took a swig of beer.

'What about those neighbours she argued with over the basement?'

'They were checked out; away on holiday in South Africa, where they always go in January.'

'Family?'

'There's a stepson and stepdaughter, right? Both could account for where they were that day. It wasn't one of the housekeeper's days for cleaning and she was at another client in South Ken.' He clicked his fingers. 'The lady vanishes, all right.'

'It's the stepdaughter, Florence Davenport, who's asked me to look into it. I haven't spoken to Rupert, the stepson yet. Doesn't look good, does it?' Swift helped himself to more rice. The food was spicy but not too hot, and he was hungry after his time on the river.

'You know the score as well as me; she should have turned up by now if she was okay.'

'The housekeeper said she'd never leave the cats unfed or stay away for so long.'

'Hmm. Maybe a random attack; I know they're actually rare, but it is possible. Maybe she was carrying cash, wearing good jewellery and it was a mugging that went wrong.'

'In London though, unseen by anyone?'

Mark swept his fork efficiently across his plate. 'You can find empty places in London. Given that the city is constantly being dug up, there are always opportunities to hide a body. I don't know. It's a DI Morrow who's in charge of the case. I don't know her but I can have a word with her about you and ask her to give you a ring.'

They cleared away and sat talking and drinking beer, Mark expounding on the latest changes in the Met, the ever-growing bureaucracy and targets to be met. Swift let most of it wash over him. Mark frequently leapt up as he talked to straighten a curtain, glance out the window or check his emails.

'How are you finding life after Interpol?' he asked. 'Not as exciting?'

'I had enough excitement, thanks. I like what I'm doing.'

'Did you leave because of that stabbing — in the leg, wasn't it?'

'Partly. It was a flesh wound in the thigh muscle but it took some time to heal. We were investigating a suspect's house and I didn't see the knife coming. They'd transferred me from arms-tracking to sex-traffic investigations. A year of that was enough for me; I could handle gun trading but those abused women, some just kids . . . my aunt had died and left me her house and money, so I did the sums and decided to bail out.'

'You're still missed in the Met, I can tell you that much. Some of the old team talk about you, hanker after your clear thinking.'

'That's good to know. But we all have to move on; life changes.'

Mark's phone rang and he took the call, mouthing it was important. Swift was relieved to move away from the subject of Interpol. That year of investigating the brutality of the sex trade, speaking to hollow eyed, abused and terrified women and children, seeing the squalid conditions they lived in, had left him revolted and jaded. He had seen much in the Met and at Interpol that exposed the layers of human degradation but for him sex trafficking was in a place apart. Even thinking of it now, sickened him.

He fetched another beer from Mark's state-of-the-art, almost empty fridge and looked through the magazines again. He selected and started reading a Jack Cardigan story, where at least the crime was straightforward, if vicious; a murder, a nightclub owner, a beautiful blonde, a tough-talking gambler and plenty of shooting with hard boiled Cardigan sorting them out.

* * *

Dr Forsyth surprised Swift with her American accent. Boston, he decided, as he sat opposite her in her consulting room in Notting Hill. It wasn't opulent but certainly better appointed than any GP surgery he had ever been in, with padded chairs, gleaming paintwork and vases of flowers. Also, doctors in his experience didn't wear silk shirts and pearls. He explained why he had come and Dr Forsyth nodded, sitting back in her chair, legs crossed, regarding him through heavy-lidded eyes.

'Seems a total mystery,' she said. 'I talked to the police weeks back. I think they were disappointed that I couldn't tell them anything important.'

'Mrs Farley, Mrs Langborne's housekeeper, said she was often concerned about her health.'

'Sure, she was a worrier but there was nothing wrong with her the day I saw her, except some arthritis in her finger that caused a tiny swelling. It was a bit painful so I told her to take aspirin. I offered a referral for an X-ray, even though I didn't really think she needed it, and she accepted. That was it. I was there about fifteen minutes max. And, no, I didn't notice anything unusual, she didn't seem odd, looked about the same as always.'

'So there was no health problem that might have caused a sudden incident?'

Dr Forsyth folded her arms and raised an eyebrow. 'Well, Mr Swift, I'm a doctor, not a psychic. Any older person could have a stroke or an unexpected fall. All I can say is that on that morning there was nothing I found to cause concern. Mrs Langborne was what we call in the trade "the worried well." Polite terminology for hypochondria.'

'Had you known her long?'

'Couple of years. She fell out with her previous GP so came knocking on my door.'

'And how did you get on with her?'

Dr Forsyth gave a deep, dry laugh. 'Well, after her first shock at finding out I was black and a subsequent frank exchange of views about her response, we got on fine.'

Swift was interested. 'She was openly racist?'

'Sure. Nothing new to me, I pretty much expect it in older patients and I see it as their problem, not mine. This is a woman who calls her housekeeper by her surname; she thinks she's living in some kind of old-fashioned *Downton Abbey* world. When I first met her she got tight-lipped and said she'd prefer "a doctor with blue eyes." I said fine, she could look elsewhere but I pointed out to her that she had dark eyes herself.' Dr Forsyth gestured. 'Same colour as yours, I'd say. She did a recalculation when I squared up to her. I think she kind of liked it. She said she'd see how we got on. We did okay; she's a bit wearing with her trivial complaints but she pays her bills on time and that's all I require. I don't need my patients to like me; there are plenty of them I don't like.'

Swift found this approach refreshing. She was one of the most attractive women he'd met in a long time, with her candour and dry tone; she was a woman you could have a laugh with. His eyes had started itching. He sneezed suddenly, then twice more and pulled out a tissue.

'It'll be the flowers, they're highly scented.' He blew his nose and rubbed his eyes.

Dr Forsyth took the vase of freesias from her desk, opened the window and placed it on the ledge.

'I don't actually like cut flowers,' she told him, 'but my receptionist insists on putting them around the place. She used to work in a florist in another life. Want an antihistamine? I've got some freebies here somewhere, from a pharmaceutical rep. They're non-drowsy, just in case you're driving.'

'Thanks.' He took one from the box she produced from a drawer and passed it back, but she shook her head.

'Keep them; there are ten more boxes in there.'

He swallowed the tiny tablet. 'That last time you saw Mrs Langborne, did she mention that she was going anywhere that day? Was she dressed up?'

'Nope. She didn't mention going anywhere. Apart from her niggling finger, she seemed in good spirits. She was always dressed beautifully at any time of day; I remember what she had on that morning because it was my favourite colour, turquoise. It was a wool suit, Jackie O style with a waisted jacket. She had a round necked white blouse under it and she was wearing her usual excess of gold jewellery. I told Detective Morrow, the Met officer who came here, that one of those cats was circling as I left and she called to him that she'd make sure he had food for later. You know how cat lovers talk to their pets. It was the warmest tone of voice I ever heard from her.'

'So it seems she was planning to go out.'

'I guess. It was an unusually sunny day for January, good for going out, and I think she had a pretty busy social life from some of the names she dropped; Lady this and Earl that.'

'Does the word *Haven* or the initials *WP* mean anything to you?'

Dr Forsyth shook her head. 'In connection with Mrs Langborne? No.' She glanced at her watch. 'I do have a patient in ten minutes, so if that's everything . . .'

'Yes, thanks.' Swift gave her a card. 'If you do think of anything else . . .'

'Sure,' she gave a generous smile and stood, smoothing her skirt. 'Hope you find her; I don't like, literally, losing any of my patients. And you know, I kind of like her. I think she's lonely and like a lot of needy people, she covers her vulnerability with an attitude. That's my two cents' worth of added psychology. Maybe I should have majored in what goes on in the mind rather than the body. Stay away from flowers, now, honey.'

* * *

Ed Boyce sent Swift an electronic copy of his weekly calendar to assist monitoring. It was crammed with meetings, pitches, presentations and lunches. Swift had noted that many of the lunches went on for hours and as it was just after three o'clock decided to take a look around a restaurant on Queensway which was a short bus ride from Dr Forsyth's surgery. He saw Boyce through the window, leaning forward in his seat, shirtsleeves rolled up in the way politicians used when showing they meant business. Boyce was holding his laptop, demonstrating something to the two women sitting opposite him. Swift glanced at the calendar and saw that the meeting was named *lunch @ Savour with NY cable*. One of the women was fiddling with her hair and pushing a salad around her plate, the other leaning back in a way that didn't look promising for whatever Boyce was trying to impress them with. Swift bought a coffee and walked up and down the street, which was busy with taxis and tourists with cameras, but no stalkers. A French couple holding a map between them and looking perplexed stopped him, asking the way to the Diana memorial in Kensington gardens. He turned the map the right way up and he told them it was very near, pointing across the road. They thanked him profusely, the man giving a little bow. The woman told him that they loved Diana; she was a lost angel who had had a beautiful heart. Swift smiled, unable to think of a reply and waved them on, adding that they should also take a look at the statue of Queen Victoria. It always entertained him that she sat, po-faced, looking in the direction of an expression of public sentiment that would not have amused her. He scrutinised the street again and glanced back through the restaurant window. One of the women was paying the bill, the other was on her phone, and Boyce was typing. Swift considered following him back to his office but decided against it. He was convinced that the man had an overactive imagination or persecution complex and he wanted to sit and take some thinking time.

Within an hour he was sitting in his garden on the canopied swing seat. It was ancient and rusting slightly but wide and comfortable. He had taken his notes, iPad and a coffee out there in the late afternoon. It was west-facing and bathed in sun. As he added to his notes and read them through, he could hear the clatter of saucepans from Cedric's kitchen above and smell delicious aromas of garlic and herbs. Cedric often gave him leftovers, so he hoped there would be some later. He finished his notes and googled Rupert Langborne, finding that he was forty-nine, had been to Oxford and Sandhurst, then joined the Civil Service where he had risen quickly to permanent secretary. He was married to his third wife, Daphne, who was heiress to a biscuit fortune.

Swift lay full-length on the padded, striped seat and set the swing rocking gently back and forth. Gazing at the dappled patterns made by the sun and overhanging sycamore tree on the canopy, he let his thoughts roam over the missing Carmen; a needy, snobbish woman who wanted attention, responded well to straight talking, wasn't close to her stepchildren, loved her cats and socialising. He kept coming back to *Haven*; as her main interest seemed to be animal charities he had wondered if there might be a connection to such an organisation but when he googled the word he found nothing except holiday parks and private hospitals. He didn't think Carmen was the type to book a stay on a caravan site packed with families and she wasn't suffering with a health problem.

His phone rang and he heard a rushed female voice.

'Hi, this is Nora Morrow. Mark Gill gave me your number. You want to know about Carmen Langborne?'

He sat up. Nora Morrow's voice was light and attractive, a Dublin accent. 'Yes, thanks for ringing.' He summarised what he had already established. 'So, anything else you can tell me?'

There was the noise of a busy office in the background. He guessed open-plan.

'Let's see. We interviewed GP, housekeeper, stepdaughter and stepson, a Mrs Sutherland, parish priest. Stepson's a smooth character, still saying she might have popped off somewhere as an attention seeking device, despite the obvious problem of what she'd be doing for money. Nothing dodgy in her phone records. We doorknocked locally but nothing, no one saw her go out that day. That kind of hushed wealthy area, most people are either at work or on holiday or at second homes in the country.'

'I don't buy the going-away story. She wouldn't leave the cats unattended, even for a night, without making some arrangement. The housekeeper was very firm on that.'

'Quite. We have no leads currently.'

'What did the parish priest say?'

'Not much. She attended regularly but didn't mix with other parishioners. He reckoned quietly devout. She hadn't approached him with any problems.'

He heard Nora Morrow talking to someone else and waited until she spoke again.

'So, dead ends so far. We'll have a chat with some of her charity buddies but presumably they would have come forward if they thought they knew anything useful.'

'The one thing the housekeeper said had occurred to her was that she wondered if Mrs Langborne might have had a sniff of romance. She'd been quite upbeat the day before she vanished.'

'Cherchez l'homme? We've found nothing to indicate that.'

'What about her diary?'

'Yeah, *WP* and *Haven*. No idea. No one we've spoken to has a clue.'

'Must be relevant in some way, surely, they must have been appointments?'

'Maybe, maybe not. If you work it out, let me know.'

'Okay. Will you ring me if you find out anything you can share?'

'Sure. I'm not hopeful, though.'

Swift stared at the grass, which Cedric had just mowed to within an inch of its life. He wasn't feeling hopeful either. He checked his emails. There was one from Ruth, confirming that she could meet for lunch on Monday and another from Rupert Langborne, suggesting a lunch time meeting at a restaurant near Waterloo called Abelie. He replied to both and sent one to Ed Boyce, advising that he had not seen any stalking activity and suggesting that they call it a day. He attached a final account. He then sat for a while, swinging back and forth, lines from Thomas Hardy haunting him:

Woman much missed, how you call to me, call to me,
Saying that now you are not as you were
When you had changed from the one that was all to me,
But as at first, when our day was fair.

His reverie was broken by Cedric, who was leaning out of his window.

'I have far too much food for my friends, Tyrone. I've put some by for you. Do come and get it. I fed the lawn after I cut it, by the way.'

* * *

Swift was up at six the following morning and out on the river by half past. He had made a thermos of coffee and tucked a croissant into his pocket. The muted light beneath Putney Bridge was restful; the water gave off a rich, fishy odour, sluicing softly against his oars. Bird cries echoed from upriver, calling him on. He slowed near Barn Elms boathouse for a quick refreshment and despite a strong tide was back home by nine. As he neared the house he saw Cedric, on his way back from buying his morning paper, talking to a young woman. She was standing holding the handlebars of a bicycle, her blue helmet with green flashes still strapped on her head.

'Ah', Cedric said, turning and pulling a face at Swift and mouthing *excitable*. 'You have a visitor seeking you out, Tyrone. I'll say goodbye, then, my dear.'

'Can I help you?' Swift asked, fishing for his keys.

She had a small, oval-shaped face which was wearing an angry frown and she seemed familiar.

'You're Tyrone Swift, are you?' she asked nastily.

'That's right.'

'I thought you're supposed to be a detective of some kind, not a leftover from the Boat Race.'

'I'm a private detective for business; rowing is for pleasure.' He spoke mildly, aware of sparks emanating in his direction.

She propped the bike against his front wall rather more forcefully than was needed and came up close to him. The helmet added a menacing aspect to her grim look.

'How dare you!' she said. 'How dare you get involved in implying that I'm some kind of nutter!'

He was aware that the sweat inside his bodysuit was cooling and that he had spray on his face. He was also aware that Cedric was lurking inside the front door and that several passers-by were glancing at them.

'I don't know what you mean. Would you like to come into my office . . . ?'

'No, I bloody wouldn't! What I would like is for you to mind your own business and find someone to pay you who isn't . . . perverse and twisted!'

'I don't know what you're talking about. Who are you?'

'You're not much of a detective if you don't know that, are you?'

Oh God, he thought, we might be standing here all morning at this rate. 'Okay; I'm not much of a detective. So tell me who you are.'

She gave a twisted smile. 'I'm Rachel Breen. Got it now?'

Ah! He looked at her again, ignoring the helmet and recalling the photo on his phone. 'You're Ed Boyce's ex.'

'Exactly, thank goodness. And he's mine, the nasty little runt. He's been spreading lies, saying I'm stalking him, making his life a misery and he's got you running around backing him up.'

'I don't think you have been stalking him and I've told him so, but why has he lied about it?'

'Because, dimwit, I want half my share of the stuff in the flat we own and my quarter of the flat's value, but he doesn't want to give it to me. We split up six months ago after I found him in bed with someone else and I'm no further on. I'm living in a crummy rented room without my favourite saucepans. I've phoned and emailed him but he keeps avoiding me and he's dreamed up this idea that he'll persuade people I'm a crank. He's hoping that if he can embarrass me enough that I'll settle for less than my share. Also, he's a grandiose prat with more money than sense and a jumped-up view of his own importance. Will that do?'

Swift dabbed his face with the towel round his neck. 'You could wait until he's out and get what you want.'

'He's changed the locks, of course. Bastard.'

'Sounds as if you need a solicitor.'

'Oh, thank you; I'd never have thought of that. I was attempting to do things the civilised way and save myself money but I do have a solicitor now. Ed will be sorry he started this, believe me. My solicitor says you need to back off and stop believing his lies.'

'Well, I wish you luck if what you tell me is true. I've sent Ed my final bill so unless he gets himself another detective, you shouldn't be bothered anymore.'

She took a step back and sneered, reaching for her bike. 'You should be ashamed of yourself, getting involved in persecuting an innocent woman.'

'I've hardly been persecuting you; this is the first time we've met.'

She sat on her bike and adjusted her helmet. 'Private detective; isn't that a job for washed-up blokes who can't find a better way of making a living?'

Swift watched her cycle away. Ouch. Ed Boyce had better settle his bill promptly or Swift would engage in some persecution of his own. In the shower, he scrubbed himself vigorously, reflecting on errant husbands and self-aggrandising cranks.

CHAPTER 5

As always, Swift slept badly the night before he met Ruth. He lay awake in the small hours, alternately wishing he could stumble across someone who would inspire and overwhelm him the way she had and not wanting ever to replace her, because in the end there was only Ruth, there had only ever been Ruth. He no longer knew if his renewed involvement with her was love, obsession or addiction. It was now almost four years since she had suddenly ended their engagement and taken off with a barrister she met at a party, marrying him within a couple of months. When he first told Mary what had happened, she had misheard him on the phone and thought he'd said *barista*, which was the only humour to be found in a dismal story. He had blamed himself; he had been commuting between London and the HQ of Interpol in Lyons for too long and he believed he hadn't given Ruth enough of himself, of his attention. That was possibly true, Mary had said, but such temporary distances could be bridged if both parties were committed and determined. She had liked Ruth but had once commented to Swift that her perfect beauty was almost disquieting because she was clearly used to being adored. The rapidity of the marriage impacted on Swift as much as the end of the relationship, a second savage blow. He had been jettisoned swiftly and efficiently, and there was clearly no road back. He had been a pale, shadowy figure for a long time after Ruth left him, rarely communicating and as far as his friends could tell, doing nothing but working and rowing on the Rhone or the Thames. Sometimes he worried that he would turn into a male version of Aunt Lily, convincing himself that he'd had his true love and becoming resigned to a solitary life.

Three years after Ruth left him, married Emlyn Taylor and moved to Brighton, they had met again at the engagement party of one of their oldest mutual friends, Saul. Both had been advised of their invitations and Saul had stressed to Swift that he would understand if he didn't want to attend. Swift had decided he needed to face the test and rowed all afternoon before the party, pumping up his courage.

When he saw Ruth standing by a window, perusing the congratulations cards, he knew that he loved her as much as ever and thought he could see the same emotion reflected in her eyes when he said her name. The meeting had mirrored their first; a locking of gazes, a sudden recognition. They had stood talking for half an hour that seemed like only five minutes, while he felt a ridiculous, light-headed joy. He didn't need the wine in his hand to feel dizzily inebriated. Her long tawny hair still had the same scent, her clear hazel eyes glinted with that humour and intelligence he missed so much. Yet she seemed subdued and distracted. Emlyn was not with her, she had said eventually, looking away; he had developed MS. The onset had been rapid and he was unable to work full-time. There was a carer with him while she attended the party. When Swift said he was sorry, she shook her head, saying that was just the way things were and they were making the best of it.

Ruth continued to work as a psychologist, mainly in Brighton but one Monday morning a month taught a class in cognitive therapy at Holborn. Before she left the party she said goodbye to him and they stood, paralysed in the hall of the house, looking at each other, oblivious to the music and laughter around them. She asked, so quietly that he had to strain to hear, if he would like to have lunch sometime? He had replied that yes — yes, he would.

Afterwards, Saul had put a drunken arm across his shoulder, saying that he'd heard about Ruth's husband being ill. *Sorry for them, but makes you feel she got her comeuppance, bet she wishes she never ran out on you,* he'd commented with some relish. Swift had felt no glimmer of satisfaction at Ruth's predicament, only shock and sadness, but he was aware that others thought he might, perhaps expected him to.

And so they had started meeting once a month. It was almost a year now since that first lunch. They always met near Victoria so that Ruth could make her late afternoon train home. They were careful with each other, talking about everything except their true feelings, which were spoken of only rarely. Sometimes they held hands or touched fingers and, if there was time, walked in St James's Park. His irrepressible, buoyant Ruth had been replaced by a sober woman; she spoke more slowly, as if puzzled by the turn life had taken. She told him at that first lunch that she would never leave Emlyn and would understand if he didn't want to continue meeting.

He woke early, after just a couple of hours of light, unrefreshing sleep. He made coffee and stood drinking it at the kitchen window. The day was promising with a gentle light. Next door, the neighbour was watering her plants before she left for work and he watched as she removed dead leaves and picked a sprig of herbs, holding it to her nose. He knew he needed to stop seeing Ruth, end this madness, but the thought of losing her again made his eyes mist.

* * *

He went to see Paddy Sutherland. He had expected that, like Carmen, she would live in a large house, but her address indicated a flat. He turned up a side street near Holland Park tube and found her on the ground floor of a two-storey thirties block, set on the corner of a square replete with cherry blossom.

She showed him through a small hallway bulging with coats, shopping bags and shoes, into a cluttered living room, filled with bookshelves, two sofas and an oval dining table. The floor was covered in an expensive but frayed carpet and the walls were a faded and in places slightly grubby cream. The sofas had loose threads but were deep and spacious. Swift folded himself into one with pleasure. The four large oil paintings looked like originals but were somewhat forbidding portraits of gloomy, densely bunched trees in shaded woodland. Paddy was a large-bosomed, tall woman with a fresh complexion and thinning greyish hair, wearing a pleated tweedy skirt and an open-necked shirt with plain court shoes. Her pudgy nose was redeemed by wide, candid grey eyes. He accepted her offer of coffee and looked around, thinking how much more comfortable this lived-in room was, compared to Carmen's highly polished, trinket-strewn home. He could spy a small kitchen through an alcove, where Paddy was bustling, and guessed there was just one bedroom.

The coffee was served in delicate china. It was instant but hot and there were no biscuits. He wondered if Paddy was a woman who was asset-rich, cash-poor, and was making the best of it. On the other hand, she might just be exhibiting the natural stinginess and disregard for appearances of old money. She had a clipped voice, the kind that he thought of as 1950s BBC.

'Now,' she said, sitting opposite him and tucking her skirt under, 'this business of Carmen. Completely baffling! If you've come thinking I can tell you anything useful, you'll be disappointed.'

He added milk to his coffee, suspecting it was UHT, and he would regret it.

'I understand but you never know. The smallest things can be part of a bigger jigsaw.'

'I adore jigsaws,' Paddy said. 'They're terrific, especially on winter evenings. I have one on the go at present, a view of Hampton Court; tricky but satisfying.'

He smiled. 'How do you know Mrs Langborne?'

'Elephants. We met . . . oh let me see, about eight years ago at a charity event at the Festival Hall and discovered we lived near each other. Got chatting a bit, established we both like bridge, so Carmen joined the little club I have here.'

'You meet how often?'

'Fortnightly. That's how I knew something was wrong when she didn't turn up. Carmen never missed it, and if she was going to be away she told me so I could make up the numbers. That idiot stepson of hers, saying she'd probably made a mistake in her dates . . . complete rubbish.'

'Would you say you know her well?'

Paddy sipped her drink; he was amused to see that she held her little finger in the air as she grasped the cup.

'Not well, no. Carmen likes to chat about charities, news items, TV programmes, just light talk. I don't know much about her except she was widowed. I met Rupert, the stepson, once when I was dropping something off to her. Struck me as a bit bombastic, self-opinionated. I tried once to get her interested in becoming a magistrate, after Neville, her husband, died. I sit on the bench and I thought it might be a new interest for her but she didn't respond.'

She paused. Swift swallowed his disgusting coffee, which became more tasteless as it cooled.

'I don't know if I should say this, in case something dreadful has happened to her but I never thought that Carmen really liked me. I felt that she was interested in me because my cousin is a viscount and vaguely related to the royal family. She's very keen on people's station in life, you see.'

Ah, thought Swift, I was right about old money. 'A social climber?'

'Well . . . that's a crude way of putting it but yes, perhaps.'

'Did you attend her suppers?'

'Yes, a few. Again, I felt they were held more for show than because Carmen really liked the company. Oh dear, I hope I don't sound bitchy.'

'Well, what you tell me tallies with some other views. Did you ever form the impression that she might have a gentleman friend?'

Paddy picked up a cushion and smoothed the fabric, giving the question careful consideration.

'No, I don't think so. But you see, as I've said, she's quite a closed person, gives very little away. Always polite and a bit formal, perhaps even guarded at times.'

Swift thought he knew why: if, like Carmen, you were an emigrant who had risen from the lowly status of dental receptionist and managed to break through the class barrier via marriage, you would always harbour a lingering anxiety about your origins and the possibility of committing social solecisms. You would watch your step and especially so after your passport into your new world had left you on your own. Paddy was a pleasant woman but she was clearly secure in her class and station in life; her frayed furnishings spoke volumes about her confidence in her social position. He could imagine Carmen visiting here from her immaculately kept home, never quite being able to put her finger on how this effortlessness was achieved.

'I really have no idea what can have happened to Carmen,' Paddy continued. 'Have the police got nowhere?'

'Not so far. Do you know why Mrs Langborne might have written *WP* and *Haven* in her diary?'

'As in appointments?'

'Probably. She wrote them on the day she went missing.'

Paddy shook her head. 'No idea. Sorry I can't be of more help.'

As he left, Paddy coaxed him to buy a raffle ticket for Spiny Friends, the hedgehog sanctuary she supported. He parted with a pound and saw as he walked to the bus stop that the first prize was a visit to the sanctuary; he couldn't wait. His phone rang as the bus trundled past The Albert Memorial and he heard Dr Forsyth.

'Hi, Mr Swift, how are you doing?'

'Fine, thanks. You?'

'I'm fine too. You said to call if I remembered anything. Well, I was soaking in the tub last night and I thought of something. You know, the way you get a random memory?'

Swift had a sudden image of Dr Forsyth's elegant limbs stretched out in her bath and blinked. 'Go ahead.'

'Last autumn, September, I believe, Mrs Langborne took herself off to stay in a residential facility for a couple of weeks. She was convinced she needed to convalesce after a virus. A few long walks would have done her more good, but there you go.'

'You mean like a home for old people?'

'Sure. An upmarket one, I should think. A hotel in the sun would have been just as good but I guess a home for elders with uniformed staff at the call of a buzzer played more to her idea that she was feeling frail and needed looking after.'

'Do you know where she went?'

'Afraid not. She asked me if I could recommend anywhere and when I couldn't she made her own arrangements. That's all I know.'

'Okay, thanks. I'll look into it. You didn't tell the police this?'

'Like I said, I only just remembered. Should I have?'

'Oh yes, they need to know.'

He rang off and called Ronnie Farley.

'Oh, hello,' she said, 'I'm just at Mrs L's now, feeding the hungry horde.'

He explained about Dr Forsyth's information. 'Presumably you know about this, as you'll have been in to look after the house and cats?'

'Aye, I recall that now. She'd had a bad cold and chest infection and she reckoned she needed to recuperate. Would it be of any significance? That was months ago.'

'Probably not but I might as well look into it. Do you know where she went?'

'Hang on a minute. I put it in my phone calendar. It was a fortnight, as I recall.'

Ronnie whistled softly. The bus driver was arguing with a woman who wanted to board with a buggy. There were already two by the crowded stairwell and he said he couldn't allow any more. The woman raised her voice and her baby started bawling. They were nearly at Victoria and Swift was early so he hopped off the bus, leaving the argument in full swing.

'Are you working part-time in a nursery?' Ronnie asked.

'Not likely. Found anything?'

'Aye. She went to a place called Lilac Grange in Kingston upon Thames on September fifth for two weeks. Shall I text you the number?'

'Please. How was she when she came back?'

'Fine. Said it was very nice, lovely food and service. It seemed to have done her good.'

'Ok, thanks a lot. Give my best to the cats.'

'They miss her. I can see they're disappointed when they realise it's only me again.' Her voice lowered. 'Don't forget to call by for a coffee some time, Tyrone.'

Swift walked along Buckingham Palace Road, zipping up his leather jacket against the breeze, thinking that it was only the cats who truly needed and missed Carmen; for the people in her life, her disappearance was a worry or an inconvenience but they didn't miss her. He had begun to feel a tug of sympathy for her and an understanding of how isolated her husband's death must have left her.

* * *

He and Ruth always met in the Evergreen, a small pub tucked away off Ebury Street. It was quiet on Mondays, and by now they were on first name terms with Krystyna, the waitress. Ruth was there when he arrived, sitting at their usual table by a side window decorated with stained glass. She was reading and twisting a strand of hair around a forefinger, just as she had been the first time he ever glimpsed her in the British Museum café. He had sat opposite her with his coffee, she had moved her bag to make room and smiled at him and that had been that; six years together and then the day she had been waiting for him when he came back from Lyons. He had run up the stairs to their flat in Dulwich, anticipating the sight of her. She had kissed his cheek, made him a coffee, offered him his favourite almond pastry and told him in a tight voice that she had met someone else. Since Ruth, there had been no one significant, no one he could imagine wanting to go home to.

She looked up and saw him, smiled, tucking her hair back. He sat, sliding his jacket off.

'Hi. How are you?'

'Okay. The class this morning was a bit oversubscribed but went well anyway. You?'

'Fine. You look a bit tired.'

'Emlyn had a broken night, that's all. But he's managing to do some work today, so that's good.'

They ordered drinks and food; Ruth had become a vegetarian, as Emlyn was, and opted for a mushroom ravioli. While they ate, Swift told her about his new case and how he'd made little progress.

'Don't you find it frustrating sometimes, after the Met and Interpol,' she asked, 'working on your own with no backup?'

'Rarely and I can always contact old colleagues.' He laughed and told her about Rachel Breen's insults.

'Sounds like you got involved in a domestic there.'

'The unwitting fate of the private detective.'

'But what can have happened to this woman? Surely if she'd been murdered, a body would have been found?'

'You'd have thought so. Maybe it's well hidden.'

'You do hear about skeletons being found behind walls and fireplaces. Her family must be so worried.'

'Hardly. I've yet to meet the stepson but there seems to be no love lost.'

They had coffee. She knew far more of his world than he did of hers, being familiar with his extended family. He updated her on Cedric and told her about Mary having a new partner. She spoke of her work and her plan to study for an MSc. Then they were silent for a while. There were only two other customers, men in suits with laptops, discussing sales margins. Krystyna polished glasses and bottles at the bar, making busywork for herself on a slow day. There was usually a point like this, when it became too painful to talk.

'We're like secret agents,' Ruth said at last. 'Regular clandestine meetings, walks in the park, lives compartmentalised.'

He nodded, touching her hand. 'I've missed you.'

'Yes. I never stopped loving you, Ty; I temporarily misplaced the love, lost my way. And I am so fond of Emlyn and I married him. We both go through so much pain and I'm the cause of it. If it's of any comfort, I feel it too, every day. But regrets are pointless. I keep hoping that one day you'll email me to say you've found someone special and you need to say goodbye. Then I could stop tormenting you and myself. I could stop feeling guilty, selfish.' She rubbed the back of his hand gently.

'We both know that I would need to say goodbye for myself, for my own reasons alone, and that I probably won't be able to focus on anyone else until I do.'

She nodded. 'Then you should, you should.'

They had time for a short walk under the trees in the park before turning back for the station. He walked her to the ticket barrier and kissed her forehead. He could feel her trembling and backed away, holding up a hand in farewell. He walked through back streets as far as World's End, hardly noticing his route, where he caught a bus to Hammersmith. Closing his eyes, he dwelled for some moments on Ruth's face, bathed in the lemony light from the stained-glass window, thought of the roughened skin on her fingers, from where she had been sanding a door. Then, annoyed with himself, he rubbed his head vigorously and raised and lowered his shoulders three times, causing a woman sitting opposite to give him a strange look. He took out his phone and rang Lilac Grange. He asked for the name of the manager and was told it was Maria Berardi. He asked to speak to her and after a brief wait he was put through and explained his reason for calling.

'I don't see how we can help you,' Ms Berardi said, her voice rising and falling with Italian inflections. 'Mrs Langborne only came here once.'

'I don't know if you can. I just need to follow up anything that might contribute to understanding her disappearance.'

She sounded hesitant. 'Why have the police not been in touch?'

'They don't know about this. Her GP just remembered today and informed me. I advised her to tell them but I don't know if they'll think it significant enough to follow up on.'

'Well, we are very busy here . . .'

He softened his voice. 'I do appreciate that but Mrs Langborne's family are very distressed about this and so far there has been no trace at all of her. I will be as brief as possible when I come. If I could just speak to you and any staff who worked with her. It would mean a lot.'

She capitulated and agreed to see him on Wednesday afternoon. Back at the office, he wrote up a synopsis of the information he had gleaned that morning, then polished off the casserole Cedric had given him for supper. He sat watching a game show on TV, aware that he was in danger of drifting into the kind of fugue that often crept over him after a meeting with Ruth. He was checking conditions on the river when there was a knock on his door.

'Hello, my dear one,' Cedric said.' I was wondering if you could come and take a look at my boiler. I can't get any hot water.' He was wearing a gold-and-blue Hawaiian print shirt and yellow Bermuda shorts, and lit up the shadowy hallway.

Swift followed him upstairs and managed to relight the pilot in the boiler. By way of thanks, Cedric insisted on taking him to the Silver Mermaid, where worse for wear after too much red wine and several card games, they staggered back around midnight, holding each other up, Cedric singing *it ain't what you do, it's the way that you do it.*

* * *

The Abelie was a two-storey restaurant overlooking the river, all snowy white tablecloths and stark décor. Swift had assumed that a permanent secretary wouldn't be slumming it and had put on one of his classier suit jackets, an ironed white shirt and his least frayed jeans. Langborne was there when he arrived, sitting at a table overlooking the river and drinking bottled water. He looked up as the waiter escorted Swift across the room and stood, holding out a hand.

'Mr Swift, good to meet you.'
'Hi. And you.'

'A drink? I stick to water during the day. The minister is teetotal and doesn't appreciate alcohol on the breath.' His voice was deep and smoothly confident.

Swift's head was still slightly cloudy from the night out with Cedric. 'Water's fine for me, thanks.'

Langborne poured him water as the waiter brought two menus. He was tall, almost Swift's own height, fleshy and big boned and nearly bald with dark freckles on his scalp. There was little resemblance to his sister except around the mouth, with a full lower lip. His eyes were slightly bloodshot but his look was penetrating. He had the sleek, assured appearance of a man who ate well and had a wardrobe of tailored clothes. His suit on this occasion was dark blue, his tie grey; a gesture of idiosyncratic colour was added by the buttonhole he was sporting, a small spray of thistles and heather on a blue ribbon.

'Shall we choose our food before we discuss my stepmother? Everything in here is good. I always have the steak and kidney pie. My wife only allows red meat occasionally, so I cheat when I lunch out.'

Swift ordered a cod bake, Langborne his pie with seasonal vegetables. He smoothed his tie and spread his broad hands on the table. His fingers were thick, the nails square and short.

'So, any idea where Carmen might be?' he asked.

'Not as yet. I understand that your view is that she's gone away and will be back.'

'It would follow previous form, that's why I thought it originally. Obviously, as time goes by, it does seem less likely.'

Swift sipped his water. It was warm by the window. The river rippled enticingly in the sun.

'I don't believe it was ever likely. Mrs Langborne left her cats unfed overnight and that is something she just wouldn't do.'

'Hmm. Carmen can be capricious, you see. She does like to create an air of mystery at times.'

No, Swift thought, it doesn't add up but he changed tack.

'How do you get on with your stepmother?'

'We manage fine. I find her a little rigid and opinionated at times and we don't see each other that often but when we do, we get along okay.'

'I've had the impression that she gets on better with men.'

'That's true, she likes male company, especially since my father died. I expect my sister has told you that she and Carmen don't rub along too well. Flo has never really forgiven Carmen for breaking up our parents' marriage.'

'And you?'

Langborne held his hands up. 'Live and let live, say I. And it would be a case of pots and kettles for me; I left my second wife for my current one, you see. Although no children were involved.'

Something about his affability struck Swift as surface deep; he sensed a more complex and difficult personality below. 'I think I read that your mother died?'

'That's correct. A couple of years ago.'

'When did you last see Carmen?'

Langborne tapped his fingers on the table. 'New Year's day. I called in about four thirty and we had a glass of wine. I was with her for about an hour. Duty done, I went off to my flat in Knightsbridge.'

'You live in London?'

'I have a flat here where I stay several nights a week. My other home is in Berkshire. I rang Carmen once during January, can't recall exactly when, just to check in. She seemed fine.'

The food arrived and they were silent while the waiter fussed around. Langborne attacked his pie with relish, cutting it open so that it released a heavy scent in a steamy vapour. Swift disliked the smell of offal and felt his appetite vanish as Langborne speared a glistening hunk of kidney. He bet Langborne was the kind of man who liked steamed puddings with custard.

'Do you think it's possible that Mrs Langborne was seeing someone?'

Langborne chewed, dabbed gravy from his mouth with his napkin and looked interested.

'Seeing someone as in a romantic attachment? Well, always possible I suppose. She socialises a good deal, you know, often out and about. Perhaps she had met someone. She's not one for confiding, you see, that's not the kind of thing she would have told me or Flo. Come to think of it, she was getting rid of some of my late father's things a couple of months back. Clearing the decks? What makes you ask that?'

'Her housekeeper said she seemed in a good mood the day before she vanished. It was just a thought.'

'Well . . . I hoped she might meet someone, give her something to focus on other than charities. One doesn't want anyone to be on their own in older age. I wasn't sure she would, though; she could be rather black-and-white in her views, lacking flexibility. A man doesn't always appreciate that.'

Swift suppressed an urge to laugh. Rupert's pomposity and physical heft made him seem older than his years. 'Your father didn't mind her rigidity?'

Rupert took the thrust in his stride. 'He was infatuated with her, thought she could do no wrong. Love is blind, as they say.'

Swift could detect annoyance behind the bland response. There was a practised smoothness about Langborne, which he found unsurprising given his profession, and also an air of authority; polished in the Sandhurst days, no doubt.

Swift declined pudding and asked for coffee. Langborne chose sticky toffee pudding and ice cream. He winked conspiratorially.

'Puddings; another item forbidden by the memsahib apart from weekends. Why are women so obsessed by their husbands' diets?'

'An expression of love?'

Langborne inclined his head. 'A thoughtful response. How long have you been a private detective?'

'A while.'

'Is it lucrative?'

'I do okay. I got the impression you weren't all that keen on your sister engaging me.'

Langborne tucked into the gooey mess of his pudding, his eyes glazing with pleasure.

'The police are presumably doing their job; I couldn't see why you were needed. Of course Flo is concerned about Carmen being found, because of the money, as well as worrying about her.' He looked at Swift, clearly making a calculation about his next statement. 'You're an intelligent man with a police background, you know about the seven-year rule regarding death in absentia. If there is a worst case scenario and Carmen is never found Flo has to wait seven years before a death can be assumed and property dealt with by the family.'

'The same applies to you.'

'Yes, but I have no immediate need of money. Flo's husband was made redundant last year and has only recently found another job at a lower salary. They're used to a certain lifestyle; I would hazard a guess that a lot of debt has been built up on credit cards. Seven years would be a long wait for Flo and I don't think she makes much out of whatever she does pampering to people's vanity.'

'Personal styling.'

'That's it; what a waste of a good education. She's not that bright but she went to Roedean, you know.'

Swift thought that personal stylist was exactly the kind of occupation that women who had been to Roedean might end up in.

'Your stepmother had down *WP* and *Haven* in her diary, for the day she disappeared. Any idea what she meant?'

Rupert scratched his forehead. 'Not at all, means nothing to me.' He glanced at his watch. 'Well, *tempus fugit* and all that.'

Swift had no more questions and had had enough of Langborne's heavy presence. He offered to pay his half of the bill but Langborne waved his hand and insisted on settling it. Swift allowed him, wondering if the lunch had been on the taxpayer.

* * *

Swift browsed the shops on the Waterloo station concourse after lunch and found an apricot-patterned silk stole that he thought Joyce would like. The assistant gift-wrapped it for him and he took it to a coffee shop where he bought an espresso and rang DI Morrow. It was always worth keeping a line open to the Met once you had a useful contact and he wanted to emphasise that he had done her a favour with Dr Forsyth's information. A man answered, said he thought she was about, and then yelled her name. She came on the line with the same hurried tone.

'Hi, it's Tyrone Swift here. Did Dr Forsyth contact you?'

'Yep, thanks for telling her to ring us. I've a bit of news for you; we've brought Paul Davenport in for questioning about Carmen.'

'Oh? What's happened?'

'I can't tell you now; I'll try to catch you later.'

'I've talked to Rupert Langborne today. Have you time for a drink after work?'

'Ahm . . . okay, just a quick one. Say at seven. Do you know the Parterre off Portobello Road?'

'No, but I'll find it. See you there. I'll be parked just inside the door with a copy of the *Evening Standard*.'

Swift thought for a moment, then rang Florence Davenport's number. It went to voicemail and he left a message, asking her to call him. At last, there was a development and if Paul Davenport did have something to do with Carmen's disappearance, it would conform to the statistics that the perpetrator of harm was usually to be found within the family.

CHAPTER 6

Florence Davenport still hadn't returned Swift's call when he arrived at the Parterre just before seven. He wondered if she was at a police station or busy with a solicitor. He looked around but couldn't see any women on their own. The place was low-lit and furnished with distressed leather chairs and benches, oriental style, multicoloured scatter cushions, rag rugs that snagged underfoot and wall tapestries covered in abstract designs. Swift ordered a beer and sat in a chair by a scarred table just inside the window. He browsed his *Evening Standard* and when Nora Morrow still hadn't arrived by seven fifteen, started on the crossword.

Five minutes later the door banged open and a woman erupted through it, clutching a briefcase, laptop and bulging rucksack. She looked around and Swift rose.

'Nora? Can I help you with your luggage?'

'Please. Here, take the rucksack. Ta.'

Swift put it under the table, noting the trainers and sweatshirt sticking out through the top. Nora Morrow yanked a chair out with her foot and slumped into it, placing her laptop and briefcase on the bench beside her.

She blew her hair back, shucked her shoes off and waved a finger at a waiter.

'Want another of those?' she asked Swift.

'No thanks, I'm taking it slow.'

'Small whisky please,' she told the waiter, 'and some of those pretzels you have stashed.'

She was medium height, wiry and dark-haired, with a short Audrey Hepburn style; Swift knew that this was called a pixie cut because a girlfriend at university had once had it done. There was nothing gamine about her though; she had a good-looking, square-shaped face, straight nose and grey-green eyes like a cat. She stretched her arms above her and rolled her head clockwise, then anti-clockwise. *Limber* was the word that occurred to Swift.

He held out a hand. 'Good to meet you.'

'Oh, yes.' She held hers out. She had a cool, firm handshake. 'Hope you don't mind this place with its Afghan market/ethnic look; I find it an antidote to soulless offices. So you're Mary Adair's cousin?'

'That's right. I didn't think you knew her?'

She looked at him appraisingly. 'I've heard her speak. I worship her from afar. She's my kind of woman — no-nonsense, pragmatic.'

He smiled. 'She's one of my favourite people.'

Her whisky arrived and she took a mouthful, murmuring with pleasure. 'Tyrone's an Irish name. Are you one of my tribe?'

'My mother was from Connemara.'

'Oh, you're a wild sea-blown man.' She took a couple of pretzels and flipped one into her mouth. 'No time for lunch, just the distant memory of half a sandwich,' she said.

'I lunched with Rupert Langborne and watched him juggling kidneys. He wasn't much help although he did acknowledge that his stepmother is unlikely to be voluntarily missing at this stage. He did tell me that his sister is strapped for money and I wondered why he chose to divulge that piece of information.'

'The perm sec, Mr Smoothie? I suppose they're trained to be as bland as that in the Civil Service. He kept calling me "my dear lady." Interesting what he told you about Florence, given what her husband has been squawking to us this afternoon. Want a pretzel?'

Swift took a couple. 'What can you tell me?'

Nora massaged her neck and shoulders. She was wearing a grey two-piece suit, a navy shirt and a small grey string bow tie which Swift found particularly fetching and quirky.

'Yesterday we had a call from a neighbour of Carmen Langborne who lives just up the street, other side. Name's Bruno Dacre. He'd been away in Florida for three months since January. I loved the way he said, "one can't tolerate the winter in Blighty." So once he'd unpacked and caught up with his *Financial Times* he noticed that his neighbour had gone missing. He knows her because he signed her petition about the basement showdown; diggers at dawn etc. He told me that he saw Paul Davenport walking away from Carmen's door the morning she vanished, at about eleven a.m.' She took another draught of whisky.

'How does he know Paul?'

'Saw him at Carmen's once when he dropped off a UKIP leaflet.'

'And according to Florence, the last time they saw Carmen was on Boxing Day.'

'Correct. And of course, Paul is arguing Jesuitically that it wasn't a lie; he says he didn't see Carmen that morning because she wasn't in. Says he called on the off-chance.'

'Did you interview him at the station?'

'I certainly did. Gave him a nice fright. He says he spoke to Carmen on Boxing Day about a loan of twenty thousand. He was out of work for a while and they've got significant debts. Carmen said she'd think about it and he hadn't heard from her so he called round because he had a business meeting in Kensington and it was on his way.'

'Why was he asking her and not Florence?'

'Good question and I asked it. Because, he said, he and Florence thought Carmen would respond better to him because she prefers chaps.'

Swift nodded. 'Chimes with what I've picked up.'

'Hmm. Anyway, he sticks to his story that he rang the bell, there was no reply so he left.'

'Did Florence know he was going round that morning?'

'He said yes, so then we got her in and she gave the same story. Of course, they've had plenty of time to patch it together. They both said, surprise, surprise, that they hadn't given us this information before because it might throw suspicion on them and detract from the search for her, blah blah.'

'Did you believe them?'

Nora shrugged. 'Probably. He seems an ineffectual kind of man; can't see him harming anyone myself but . . . money is a powerful driver.'

Nora finished her whisky and dusted pretzel crumbs from her lap. Swift rolled his glass in his hands, feeling annoyed with the Davenports.

'Explains why Florence hasn't returned my call from earlier,' he said. 'I suppose, if they have done away with Carmen, they could have decided to employ me to cover them and maybe also come up with the body.'

'Maybe; you would then handily resolve the seven-year problem of having to wait for the dosh.'

'None of their fingerprints were in the house, though.'

'No. I can't see them in the frame, they're too gormless. We'll be checking on this business meeting he was supposed to be at that day and we'll double-check Florence's whereabouts. I have a feeling you'll be taking to them.'

'Yeah, as soon as I can. From what I've learned about Carmen Langborne, I'm not sure she'd approve the request for a loan. Given that the Davenports are clearly living beyond their means, with a nanny and horse riding for Florence, I have a feeling she'd be the kind to suggest they cut their expenditure.'

'She does seem to be a bit high-handed; not exactly a wicked stepmother but not a cherisher of her family.'

Swift nodded. 'By the way, I've arranged to see the manager at the home in Kingston upon Thames where Carmen stayed in September.'

'Okay; I'm not pursuing that at present, haven't got the staff. Don't forget to share. Makes me bloody annoyed; those Davenports have been banging on about us not finding her and they've been withholding information. She contacted their MP, you know. I was called in to talk about a letter from the Right Hon.' Nora smiled. 'I did enjoy pulling them both in, because of that. Anyways, much as it's a pleasure to take a drink with a handsome private eye and cousin of my idol, I have to be on my way. Where do you get the muscles?' She tapped Swift's upper arm but impersonally, as a doctor might.

'I row as often as I can.'

'Really? Terrific; I used to row a bit back in Dublin but haven't for a while. Maybe we could go out some time, as long as it's a rowette; I'm a bit rusty.'

She was collecting together her various bags and slipping her shoes back on.

'Sure,' Swift replied, thinking it was just one of those things people said. 'I'll walk you out. Are you driving?'

'No way in this city. I'll catch a cab. See you, then.'

Swift watched her stride away, hitching up her rucksack, her tie flapping in the breeze.

He made his way home, leaving another message for Florence Davenport, stating sternly that he would be visiting them the following evening at seven thirty to discuss information he had received from the police.

Cedric had been married briefly and, Swift had gathered, disastrously in his forties. The unhappy union had produced one son, Oliver, who lived in Greenwich and visited his father now and again; usually, it seemed, to have a row with him. Swift was fascinated by the random genetic soup that could result in a benign, cheerful man like Cedric producing such an ill-tempered offspring who looked nothing like him. Oliver was a square-shaped, densely boned man with a heavy tread as he clumped up and down the stairs. He wore a permanent look of resentment. If there was slight to be taken, Oliver was the man to take it. Cedric appeared to accept his visitations as a kind of penance because he felt guilty at not having been much of a father when Oliver was a child. This would have been difficult as Oliver's mother had taken him to live in France after the divorce, marrying three more times before dying in a road accident. Oliver made sure that he explored the rich seams in the deep mine of Cedric's parental guilt. Lily had described Oliver as a conniving, self-absorbed, unpleasant piece of work who visited his father in order to abuse him and extract money.

Swift had heard Oliver banging up the stairs that morning, after he returned from an early row. The river had been choppy and exhilarating in a downpour. As he towelled himself dry, he felt the sense of wellbeing it always brought him. He spent some time checking his bank accounts while he ate breakfast. His savings were healthy, due partly to Lily's legacy and his low overheads and lack of mortgage. His current account could be better padded but he wasn't worried; he lived cheaply, had a reasonable work stream and Cedric's rent added a regular monthly income. He became aware of Oliver's voice from the floor above, becoming louder and angrier and Cedric's mild answers. The ceiling shivered as he stomped up and down his father's living room. Cedric never revealed what Oliver was angry about; the only comment he had ever passed about him to Swift was that 'he had his funny ways.'

He was opening the door to go down to his office when Cedric's door slammed and Oliver came down the stairs, mouth twisted.

'Hello,' Swift said. 'Been to see your dad?'

Oliver shot him a look of pure poison. He was supposed to be a sculptor of some kind and used this as a reason to wash infrequently. He was wearing a khaki smock daubed in streaks of clay over denim shorts. Swift was unsure if this was a fabric design or a public promotion of his craft. His muscular legs were also clay-streaked in places. His hair flopped greasily on his shoulders and a scent of mildew hung about him. His fury crackled, igniting the air.

'Him? That excuse for a father?' he said and pushed past Swift, leaving the door swinging.

There was a lovely silence in the hallway. Swift breathed it in and then, concerned, ran up to Cedric's flat. He knocked and after a few moments Cedric opened the door, a small glass of brandy in his hand. He looked weary and pale, as he usually did when Oliver had visited.

'Come in, dear boy.'

'I just wondered if you're okay. Oliver seemed upset so I thought you might be.'

Swift followed him into his living room which was always neat and orderly, everything in its place, pens lined up with military precision besides the morning paper, ready for Sudoku.

'Oh, you know, he gets worked up. Brandy?'

'No thanks, bit early for me. It's not too good, having someone shouting at you.'

'No, no.' Cedric sank into a chair and swirled his drink, looked into it as if it might reveal something. He laughed nervously. 'Apparently I'm a fascist because I suggested that if he's broke, he could try getting a job that pays a wage. It was just a thought. Didn't go down well.'

It was the most he had ever said about his son. Swift saw that his hand around the glass was trembling.

'You know,' he said gently, 'you don't have to see Oliver if he's offensive to you. No one has to put up with that.' Cedric's wallet was on the coffee table and Swift guessed that he had parted with money.

'No. It's just not that simple, dear boy, when it's family . . . Oliver's had his troubles and struggles . . .'

Swift didn't buy into that model of thinking; everyone had troubles and struggles, it didn't excuse treating other people like dirt. But he knew that family webs were intricate and layered. 'Can I make you a coffee?'

Cedric shook his head and downed his brandy, rallying. 'Not at all, I'm fine. Just a tiff, you know. These things happen in families. I have to get myself shipshape; I'm off to the quiz at the library.'

'Ok, if you're sure. Boiler okay?'

'Fine now. You escaped from the young cyclist who seemed out for your blood?'

Swift told him about his meeting with Rachel Breen and Cedric laughed, his face relaxing, the colour returning to his cheeks.

* * *

Swift caught the train to Kingston upon Thames, then took a cab to Lilac Grange which was situated a couple of miles to the south of the town. It was raining heavily and the streets looked dank and bleak.

He had expected a large old house adapted to a care home but Lilac Grange was a purpose-built home, opened in 2005 and operated by a national chain. It was set back from the road behind low brick walls and laurel hedges and was a bland, two-storey building with a wide central doorway with glass panels that hissed open automatically. The reception area was light and airy with numerous plants and vases of flowers. Swift introduced himself, showed his ID and signed the visitors' book. The tiny, doll-like woman at the desk who was wearing more make-up than he had seen on any face for a long time, said she would fetch Ms Berardi and invited him to take a seat. Instead, he stood and scrutinised the noticeboard. He read about activities of the friends of Lilac Grange, the weekly lunchtime concert — a pianist was expected today — availability of visiting hairdresser and chiropodist and the day's menu. He noted that fire evacuation procedures featured and the names of first aiders.

He detected a musky scent and turned to see a small rounded woman in a smart light blue jacket and skirt. She held out her hand. Her smile was a little tight in her jowly face so Swift switched on full-beam charm.

'Good morning,' she said in a nasal voice, her Italian accent more pronounced in person. 'Welcome to Lilac Grange, Mr Swift. I am Maria Berardi.'

'Hello, I'm very pleased to meet you.'

She nodded. 'Perhaps you would like to come to my office.'

It was a command rather than a request. Swift followed her, watching her purposeful, pigeon-toed walk and thick ankles. She was wearing flat ballet pumps which seemed too insubstantial to support her broad feet and ample frame. They walked along a wide corridor, passing several care assistants in pale green uniforms, shepherding old people with sticks and Zimmer frames. One elderly man smiled and Swift smiled back, adding a good morning, glad that Cedric wasn't likely to end up in such a place. A radio was playing classical music and there were the muted sounds of running water and cisterns flushing. Ms Berardi's office was small and bright, with photos of residents and staff engaged in various activities. Rotas and holiday charts were pinned to a notice board. She indicated a chair for him and sat, clasping her hands before her on her plump abdomen. She was in her late thirties, he guessed. He wondered what had brought her from Italy to spend her days with the ailing population of Lilac Grange.

'I'm here to find out if anything happened while Mrs Langborne was staying that might throw some light on her disappearance. I have told the police I'm visiting. They're not planning to contact you at present.'

Ms Berardi nodded, turned to the computer behind her and unlocked the screen, bringing up a chart. She was wearing what looked like false nails so Swift guessed she didn't do any hands-on work with the residents.

'Mrs Langborne was here for two weeks last September, from the fifth. She'd had a virus, said she felt under the weather and required rest. She stayed in Acorn wing, which is for private guests. Her record shows that she ate and slept fairly well, rarely mixed with other residents and did not wish to participate in activities. She read a good deal, knitted and walked in the gardens.'

'Sounds as if she was a little aloof.'

She looked at Swift. 'I believe so. I did not see a great deal of Mrs Langborne until she came to my office two days before her leaving date.'

'There was a problem?'

Ms Berardi took a breath. 'I have contacted our personnel department about this and they say I can tell you some details.' She turned back to the screen and scrolled down the page, checking something. 'Mrs Langborne informed me that she had discovered that one of our night carers had another job during the day. She had overheard this carer on the phone, discussing her other employment. Mrs Langborne had already commented to my deputy that she had seen this carer asleep in the staff area when she should have been awake and checking vulnerable residents; Mrs Langborne had gone to the kitchen for a drink in the early hours. We do not allow our full-time staff to work at other jobs that might compromise their caring abilities and especially those who work a night shift as they need to be alert. I had to look into it and I confirmed that this carer had another job in a bakery in the day. I'm afraid we had to dismiss her.'

'Did Mrs Langborne know this would lead to the carer being sacked?'

Ms Berardi picked at a button on her jacket sleeve. 'I did not discuss this with her. I told her the matter would be investigated and left it there. She was, I found, a determined kind of person and told me that she had to do her duty. The carer's dismissal took place about four weeks after Mrs Langborne left so I doubt she knew.'

'And the carer? Did she know that Mrs Langborne had reported her?'

'I did not inform the carer and my deputy was the only other person who knew; she would not have passed this information on. However, I can't say that the carer might not have found out somehow. There is a large staff group here and one cannot always prevent rumours and gossip.' She had an asthmatic wheeze when she spoke and she patted her chest. 'It was correct that Mrs Langborne reported this to me but the carer was one of our best and I was sorry to see her go. But there we are; she had breached her contract.'

'Can I have this carer's name?'

'I can give you that but I have been advised that I cannot give you her address. Her name is Charisse Lomar.'

'And she left here the end of October?'

'That's correct.'

Swift noted the information. 'Was this carer, Charisse, friendly with any of the other staff here, someone who might know her whereabouts?'

Ms Berardi's look was not amiable. 'I'm not sure that it would be correct for you to talk to any carers.'

Swift nodded. 'I know it's a further imposition but there is an elderly lady missing, which is very worrying.'

She made a snuffling noise and cleared her throat. She stood and looked at a rota on the wall. 'Beata Jesowski is here this morning and I believe she and Charisse were friendly. She's due a break so I'll ask her if she will speak to you. It will be up to her; after all, you're not the police. I must ask you not to speak to her of Mrs Langborne's complaint about Charisse.'

'Yes, I understand.'

'Wait here, please, and she only has fifteen minutes for her break.'

She locked her computer, took an inhaler from a desk drawer and exited. Swift stood and opened a window; the air in the place was stifling, like a hospital. He stood in the office doorway, observing carers coming and going. A thin old lady wearing pink curlers of the type that Lily used to employ wandered up to him.

'Have you seen my Pete?' she asked Swift. 'He was supposed to be in for his dinner but he hasn't shown up.' She looked about, distractedly.

'I'm afraid not,' he said. 'Maybe one of the staff can help?'

She looked around him into the office, rubbing her hands anxiously. 'He's not in there, is he? He's a devil for forgetting the time.'

'There's no one else in here.'

She clutched Swift's arm. 'What if he's had an accident? I'm always warning him about those machines. The kids will be worrying. And I've done sausage casserole, his favourite.'

Swift took her papery, chilly hand, seeing the distress in her faraway eyes. 'Let's find someone who can help.'

'He cut his hand on one of those machines last year; there was a terrible lot of blood.'

A carer was coming towards them. She took the woman's other hand and rubbed it.

'What are you doing down here, Kitty? The hairdresser's looking for you.'

The three of them were standing holding hands, Swift thought, as if they were about to execute a dance.

'Pete's not been in for his dinner, I'm worried about him,' Kitty said.

'Well, let's go and get your hair finished and then we'll see if he's turned up. You want to look nice for him, don't you?' The carer took her other hand from Swift's and started to lead her away.

'Pete's her husband, died years ago,' she murmured to Swift over her shoulder.

He watched them progress slowly away, Kitty still wondering where Pete was, repeating all she had said to him seconds before. Swift felt a leaden bleakness. He couldn't imagine how anyone could work here day in and day out, dealing with the remorseless onset of second childhood. He turned back into the office and helped himself to stale-tasting water from a jug.

There was a tap on the door and a woman in a carer's green uniform came in. She was painfully thin with fair hair scraped back into a ponytail from a high, bony forehead.

'You want to talk to me?' she asked in a flat, pronounced accent that Swift thought was Polish.

He stood. 'Yes that would be helpful, Ms Jesowski. My name is Swift.'

She sat in an upright chair near the open window. Her eyes were almost colourless, and wary. Her whole appearance was of someone who had been pared back to the bone.

'I not done anything wrong,' she said dully.

'No, I'm sure you haven't. I don't know what Ms Berardi has told you, so I'll explain. I've come because a Mrs Carmen Langborne stayed here last September. She went missing in January and her family have asked me to try and find her. I understand that you were friendly with a carer called Charisse Lomar who has now left here.'

There was a pause. 'I knew Charisse a bit,' she said.

'Yes. Are you still in touch with her?'

Another pause, as if she was translating his words, or perhaps playing for time.

'She calls me sometimes, see how I am.'

'On the phone?'

A longer pause. 'Yes.'

'Did you know Charisse was sacked?'

'Yes. Everyone know.'

'Do you know where she lives?'

She folded her arms, blinked, and lied. 'No. I never been her house.'

Swift sat forward slightly and sighed. 'You're not in any trouble and Charisse probably isn't either. Are you sure you don't know where she lives?'

There was a long silence. A small red flush had appeared on her neck. 'You not police?'

'No.' He could almost hear her brain whirring.

'I told you, I don't know. I do good job here, is important to me.'

'Okay. Did you know Mrs Langborne?'

She relaxed a little at that question, away from the topic of Charisse. 'I help her a couple times.'

'What was she like?'

'Okay. Liked to give orders; do it this way, that way, be careful. But okay.'

'Did she get on with Charisse?'

The shutters came down again. 'I don't know, I just do my job, keep my head down. I got to go now.'

She got up and abruptly left the room. Swift scratched his head with frustration, adding an extra wild touch to his rain blown curls. Maria Berardi appeared but before she could speak her phone rang; she held a conversation about catering supplies while checking lists on her computer screen. As she replaced the phone, a carer hurried to the door, asking her to come quickly as Mr Blantyre had fallen heavily. She rushed away, forgetting to lock her computer. Swift closed the door quietly, then navigated to the desktop and scrutinised the icons. One was titled STAFF. He clicked it and mouthed *bingo* as he accessed a list with personal details. He scribbled down Charisse Lomar's address in New Malden and her mobile phone number, exited the screen and wrote on a post-it pad on the desk; *thank you for your time and help*. He made his way back to reception. A piano was playing from somewhere in the depths of the building and warbling voices sang along to 'Smoke Gets in Your Eyes.'

Outside, it was still raining; a warm, drifting drizzle. He called a cab and decided to visit Charisse Lomar while he might still have the surprise factor; he was sure that Beata would be ringing her at some point that day. As he waited his phone rang. He turned his face away from the rain to answer it.

'Is that Mr Tyrone Swift?' a deep, tired sounding voice said.

'That's right.'

'I'm calling from Paddington Green police, sir. Do you know a Ms Rachel Breen and a Mr Edward Boyce?'

'Yes.'

'Good. They're here at the station. We had to deal with an altercation in a restaurant and now they're both wanting to press charges against the other. Ms Breen has been saying that Mr Boyce got you to harass her.'

'No, that's not the case. I'm a private detective and Mr Boyce engaged me because he said Ms Breen was stalking him. I found no evidence of that and I'm no longer working for him.'

'I see. Frankly, we'd prefer it if they'd both shut up, go home and deal with their problems through solicitors.'

'What are these charges?'

'He has a minor cut on his lip, caused he says by a flying wine glass thrown by Ms Breen, she has a small bruise on her right arm where she says he grabbed her during their argument. Other diners at the restaurant say there was a fracas but can't verify who did what to who. There was quite a lot of lasagne on the floor.'

'Sounds like an interesting lunch. They're arguing over property and possessions after a split, is what I understand.'

'Like I say, best left to solicitors or mediation. I think Ms Breen's solicitor might be getting in touch with you about the harassment.'

'I wasn't . . . oh, whatever.' His cab was approaching. 'I have to go now; I wish you luck with them.'

He gave the driver Charisse Lomar's address and sank back. He was beginning to think that Ed and Rachel deserved each other. He emailed Nora Morrow, asking if there were any further developments regarding Paul Davenport. He didn't mention the information Ms Berardi had given him for now, deciding he would see if it seemed to lead anywhere. The rain was tumbling from a steely sky and when the taxi pulled up in front of a block of flats in a grimy, rubbish-strewn road Swift paid the driver and asked him to wait for five minutes. It was a six-storey block called Nelson House and Swift followed arrows telling him that number twenty-five was on the third floor. There was a lift with a sign saying it was out of order. He climbed concrete steps that smelled of oil and urine and were decorated with graffiti. He turned onto the third floor walkway. Twenty-five was halfway along, with a scuffed red metal door. There was no bell so Swift rattled the letterbox and knocked. When there was no reply he repeated his actions, then bent and looked through the letterbox. All he could see was a small square hall with shoes and a child's scooter.

'You looking for the Lomars?' He turned and saw a woman exiting her door a little further along the walkway, leaning on a walking stick and dragging out a shopping trolley patterned with daisies.

'Yes. I know a friend of hers and I said I'd drop by, see how she is.'

'You won't catch her in this time of day. They're out at work, aren't they?'

'Of course. What time does she get back?'

'About five usually.'

'Thanks. I'll call again.'

'Here,' the woman said, 'you couldn't carry this down stairs for me, could you? Bloody lift's broken again. It's not heavy but you look fitter than me.' She was small and rotund, wearing a woolly hat with bobbles, like a child's. Her salt-and-pepper hair straggled below it onto her shoulders.

'Certainly.'

Swift walked towards the stairs while she tapped her stick beside him. He carried the empty trolley down, going in front of her. She moved slowly, gripping the rail.

'Charisse works at a bakery, doesn't she?' he asked.

'That's right. She brings me leftover loaves and buns sometimes. Nice girl. Can't say as much for her old man.'

'What does he do?'

'Works in a fish and chip shop called Yummy Tummy.' She laughed. 'Yummy Tummy, I ask you!'

'You don't care for him?'

'You can say that again. Got a temper on him and handy with his fists. I don't mix with them as such. You from the welfare?'

'No. I know someone she used to work with, that's all.'

'Oh. I thought you might be round there about the kids. I reckon he wallops them sometimes. Someone might have reported him. Wallops her too, of course. Seen her with a split lip more than once and it wasn't from walking into a door.' She said this matter-of-factly, as if it was to be expected.

Swift was glad to see the taxi was still waiting when they reached the bottom of the stairs. He would have to return tomorrow as the Davenports were in his sights for that evening.

'There you go,' he said, handing over the trolley.

'Ta. Nice to know there's some gents left in the world. You stick out like a sore thumb round here, love.'

She tapped and rolled away, her trolley squeaking as it hit the uneven pavement. In the taxi, Swift checked his watch and saw it was three p.m., which explained why his stomach was groaning. He decided to head home, check on Cedric and have something to eat before calling on the Davenports.

* * *

The rain had stopped by the time he got back to Hammersmith and the sky was shrugging away the clouds, allowing a feeble sun through. He stopped to buy eggs, bread and milk on the way home, pausing to have a peek at the river, which was reflecting the watery grey of the sky. Rachel Breen was sitting on the front steps of the house, her bike propped below her, helmet in her lap. She looked glum. Swift approached cautiously.

'Don't you ever just phone someone rather than turning up? Haven't you got a job to go to?' he asked.

'I needed a ride to clear my head so I thought I'd try calling round.' She sounded suspiciously meek.

'Really? Aren't you worried I'll start harassing you?'

She sighed. 'I talked to my solicitor. She checked you out and said you have a good reputation and as Ed employed you, harassment wasn't applicable.'

'Great. So, why are you wearing a groove in my steps?'

She stood, tucking her helmet under her arm. 'I had an idea I wanted to talk to you about. I might want to hire you.'

Swift took his keys out, glaring at her. 'I thought I was a "dimwit" and "washed-up", or did I mishear?'

'Sorry about that. I was angry.' She looked genuinely remorseful.

'I'm hungry and I have an appointment soon. If you want to talk while I eat, that's fine by me. You can bring your bike into the hallway.'

He opened the door and waited while she parked the bike, then took her through into the living room. He chucked his jacket onto a chair and rolled up his shirtsleeves. She looked rather worn and down.

'I'm making scrambled eggs. Do you want some? I heard most of your lunch went on the floor.'

'How do you know about that?'

'The police rang me. Fighting in public; tut-tut, Ms Breen.'

She sank into a chair. 'What a lousy day. I am starving, since you mention it.'

'Well, stay there and don't get into any trouble while I cook.'

They sat with plates of scrambled eggs on toast and coffee, which they both wolfed down. Rachel had a scattering of light freckles across her forehead. When she wasn't cross she had a kindly expression and mischievous smile.

'These are good, lovely and creamy.'

'The secret is plenty of butter and no milk. Who started the fracas in the restaurant?' Swift asked.

'We met up to try and talk stuff through, at my suggestion. I pointed out to Ed that solicitors were going to cost us both a fortune. Then he started going on about how much he'd done for me when we were together, helping me with my career etc. etc. and he deserved to get more out of the property. My memory is that we supported each other, it was pretty mutual. So the temperature rose. I did throw the glass first, then he grabbed me.' She pulled up her right sleeve and showed him a bruise the size of a pound coin.

'Was it a combustible relationship when you were together?'

'No. Just the odd argument, like most people. Ed was always very money conscious though, a bit of a skinflint.'

'You didn't tell me what you work at.'

'I'm a radiographer. I work some weekends, that's how I have time off during the week.'

They finished eating. Her plate looked as if she'd licked it clean. She placed her cutlery neatly together and looked at him.

'I don't know what I ever saw in Ed now, I can't stand him, and in fact I'd cross the street to avoid him. He was lovely when we were in our own separate places; funny, attentive, charming. Once we moved in together he became more and more fussy and nitpicking about everything. Then he replaced me with some woman who works in advertising. But you don't want to hear about that. I want to make him sort out our property and belongings fairly and to stop being a prick. I have an idea as to how.'

'I'm all ears.'

'I'm pretty sure that Ed is illegally subletting a council flat in Tooting. We were together two years and he was renting a private studio in Camden when we met but I heard him a couple of times on the phone, talking about keys and bin collections and once I saw a letter headed Wandsworth council that he folded away sharpish. When I asked him about it, he looked shifty and said it was misdirected post. Ed's the kind of man who likes to buck the system, feel that he's getting one over on other people. I always thought he had more money available than I'd have expected, even though he only spent it on himself; you know, expensive clothes and electronic gear. He calls himself a post-production executive but he's got an average-paying job with a film company. I mentioned this to my solicitor and she suggested I try and get proof. It will be a long and expensive process taking him to court and this might be a good bargaining chip to make him come to an agreement without legal hassle.'

'If it's true.'

'That's where you come in; I thought you'd know how to do it. My solicitor is also a friend but even at mate's rates, she's more expensive than you; I checked on your website.'

'So you'd like me to find out if Ed is defrauding Wandsworth council.' It had a certain appeal, turning the tables on him. Swift wouldn't usually accept the previous subject of an enquiry as a client, but Boyce had irritated him so much, he decided to waive the principle. Rachel was certainly a pleasanter and more engaging person than her ex. As was often the case with couples, Swift couldn't work out what the attraction had been for her. He finished his coffee and offered her a top-up but she refused.

'Okay, I'll take a look. If you've checked my website, you know that there's an upfront deposit.'

'Yes, that's fine. Thank you so much.'

'I have just one request; stay away from Ed in the meantime. What happened in the end at the police station?'

'They persuaded us both not to press charges when we'd calmed down. The sergeant who dealt with us told us to go away and play nicely instead of taking up police time.'

'Sound advice. So, keep under the radar until I contact you.'

She smiled and wriggled in her chair; if she was a cat, she would have purred. 'Sorry again for being so nasty to you before. Actually, you seem pretty decent and dependable.'

'Always nice to know when someone has altered their opinion.'

When she had given him a deposit and her contact details and signed an agreement, he watched her cycle away. Cedric was approaching, a biscuit-coloured Labrador eagerly pulling him along on the end of a long lead. He had signed up to a local dog share scheme and walked the animal three days a week for his owner who was a time-challenged head hunter for an oil company.

'Hi, Cedric, being taken for a walk?'

'I'll say! Whoa, Bertie!' He pulled a couple of treats from his pocket and Bertie turned back and sat at his feet, looking up expectantly.

'Did that cross young woman come back to offer you more aggravation?'

'Far from it; she apologised and hired me. I'll tell you more later; I have to get to Putney. You okay?'

'Yes, dear boy, thank you. Bertie is making sure I enjoy this relict of the day and the morsel of sunshine it's affording; "it is a beauteous evening, calm and free."'

'Keats?'

'Wordsworth.'

Back indoors, Swift stacked the dishwasher and changed his shirt. In the mirror, he checked himself for dependability and attempted to smooth his hair down with a damp flannel. He read an email from Nora Morrow saying that for now, since their whereabouts in January checked out, nothing further was being done about the Davenports.

CHAPTER 7

Swift walked to Putney again; the clouds had cleared to wisps and the evening, as described by Cedric, was now the best part of the day. There was a feeling of promise to the year. A dozen or so boats were out on the river. He watched a rowing crew sculling past and felt a sympathetic pull in his own arms.

Florence Davenport opened the door and told him to come in, not looking him in the eye. There was a smell of spices from the evening meal and he could see through to a messy kitchen. He was relieved that there was no sign of Helena, apart from a scattering of toys. In the living room, Paul Davenport was sitting watching the television and turned it down as he nodded to Swift without getting up. Swift sat once more on the uncomfortable sofa.

'Do you mind turning that off?' he asked, nodding at the TV. No need to stand on ceremony with people who had lied to him.

Paul Davenport looked surprised but switched it off with the remote. He was wearing a striped shirt that looked too small even for his skinny frame, close fitting linen trousers and a gold stud earring in his right ear lobe.

He had a ferrety look, with his closely shaven beard, thin mouth and tiny eyes.

'You didn't return my call,' Swift said to Florence.

'No. We've been busy.' Her hair looked dingy, as if she hadn't had time to wash it, and there was a crumb of mascara in the corner of her eye.

'So I understand; with the police.'

She looked at her husband. 'Oh, for goodness sake, what a waste of everyone's time! Anyone would think Paul was a mass murderer, the way they went on at us.'

Davenport straightened a tassel on one of his suede loafers. 'It's clear the police haven't got anywhere so they decided to make the most of a nosy neighbour's gossip.'

Swift stared at him. 'Nosy neighbours are often very helpful in police enquiries, and mine. Do you want to tell me why they called you in?'

'Well,' Florence said, rolling her eyes, 'if you've already spoken to them you must know.'

Swift ignored her and kept eye contact with her husband. 'I'd like you to tell me. It does help if I'm fully in the picture.'

Davenport shrugged and crossed one leg over the other, holding his ankle. His socks were bright orange, matching the stripe in his shirt; Florence obviously managed his wardrobe.

'When we visited Carmen on Boxing Day, I asked her for a loan. We've had some financial problems and Carmen's loaded. She said she'd consider it, in that high-handed manner of hers. She hadn't responded, so on January thirty-first I decided to call in as I had a meeting in Kensington late morning. The personal touch always went down well with Carmen. It was about half eleven when I got there. I rang the bell a couple of times but there was no reply. I left again. That's it.' He laughed and said sarcastically, 'I didn't go in and bump her off and raid her purse or steal the silver.'

'How much did you ask to borrow?

'Twenty grand.'

Swift looked at Florence. 'You knew about this?'

'Of course I did; Paul and I discussed it and I was hopeful that Carmen would agree. It would be peanuts to her, she's a rich woman.'

'Even so, twenty thousand might seem a lot to someone of her generation,' Swift observed.

Florence tossed her head. 'It's all Daddy's money when you come down to it, she hadn't a bean when she met him so I didn't see why we shouldn't ask.'

Swift left a silence.

'Anyone with any decency would have made a decision and not kept us hanging,' she added.

'I'm wondering why you lied to me,' Swift said coldly. 'What's the point in paying me to look for Mrs Langborne if you start off misleading me?'

'You haven't found her, so what *are* we paying you for?' Davenport asked cockily.

'That's not an answer.' Swift smiled at him.

Florence rushed in. 'Look, I should have told you, I know but . . . well . . . it's pretty personal stuff and it really didn't seem relevant. Carmen wasn't there that morning, so it just seemed as if it would cloud things.'

'You didn't notice anything at all while you were at the door?' Swift asked Davenport.

'Nothing. I rang the bell twice, there was no answer, I walked away. End of.'

'What's your profession?'

'What's that got to do with the price of eggs? None of your business.'

'I see everything as my business when I'm asked to do a job.'

'Just tell him, Paul; he's not asking for blood,' Florence said wearily.

'I manage international accounts for an insurance company. Happy with that? I tell you what; I wish someone would find Carmen so we could get back to our privacy and not have people poking their noses in. Can I relax and watch my own TV now? I've had a hell of a day.'

'Just one more question: you do have the money to pay me?'

'Yes,' Florence said tightly. 'I'm paying you from what I earn, if it's any of your business.'

'I think it has to be my business as I'm doing the work.'

Davenport stood, looking belligerent, his reedy voice raised. He sounded like an annoying fly. 'So, have you found out anything at all to earn what my wife's paying you?'

Swift looked at Florence, ignoring him. 'I have some information that might prove useful. Mrs Langborne stayed at a home in Kingston upon Thames last September and something that happened there might be relevant. I can't say anything further as yet. I'll let you know when I can.'

'Right, okay. We do worry about her,' she added, as if remembering to be concerned.

She showed him out, asking him to step softly as Helena was a light sleeper. He walked away, feeling distaste. A tutor on domestic violence, in Swift's early days in the Met, had said that family disputes were always based on one of three things or any combination of the three; love, sex, money. (Love, he had explained reassuringly, covered hate, longing and jealousy.) The same was almost always true of murder but he agreed with Nora Morrow that the Davenports, although grasping and venal, were unlikely murderers.

* * *

Swift rang Charisse Lomar's bell at five thirty the next evening. The door was opened almost immediately by a small boy with an eyepatch and a chip in his hand.

'Is your mum in?' Swift asked.

'She's making tea,' he said. He sucked on the chip, satisfied with his answer.

'Could you tell her she has a visitor?'

'I'm a pirate,' the boy said solemnly by way of reply.

'So I see. Could you climb the rigging and ask your mum to step this way?'

He was one of those children who are impervious to humour. He licked his fingers and stared at Swift.

'Robert, I told you about answering the door!' A woman appeared, wiping her forehead with her arm, propelling the child back inside with her other hand.

'Ms Lomar?' Swift asked, holding out his ID and handing her his card.

'Yes. What you want?'

'I wondered if I could have a word. I'm Tyrone Swift, a private investigator and I'm looking for a Mrs Carmen Langborne, who has disappeared. I visited Lilac Grange and I understand you knew her when she was staying there.'

She immediately looked distressed and pushed the door forwards. 'I not want to talk about her. She not a nice person, cause me trouble.'

'I understand. I don't want to cause you any. I just need to find her.'

She shook her head. Her hair was black and shiny, pulled back into a ponytail. She wore a white overall and trainers. He saw that she had a small crucifix on a chain around her neck and behind her in the hallway was a print of a beautiful, pious young man gazing upwards, hand over his heart.

'Is that Saint Pedro Calungsod?' Swift knew his Filipino saints from his days working with Interpol; there had been a group of women from Manila, lured to Europe with the promise of work, then bought and sold by traffickers. They were finally released and taken to a safe house in Lyon. Swift had interviewed them there and many of them had pictures of their favourite saints tucked in among their pitifully small possessions. He had eased his way into conversations with them by asking about their beliefs and getting them to talk about the saints and their homes.

'Yes,' Charisse said, startled. 'You know him?'

Before Swift could reply, there were shouts and cries from within the flat and sounds of siblings engaged in desperate fisticuffs. Charisse turned and ran inside. Swift followed her, closing the door, grateful for once for the presence of children. There were two boys and a girl in the small living room. The girl was sitting at a table, eating sausages, dispassionately watching her brothers rolling on the carpet.

'Stop!' their mother shouted. 'Robert, take your plate, go eat in your room. Joseph, sit down now.' As the boys started to apportion blame she snapped her fingers. 'I not interested, do as I say now!' For a small woman, she had a powerful voice when cross.

The girl gave her brothers a sly look and squirted more ketchup onto her plate but she didn't escape her mother's attention.

'Marcia, you the oldest, you should keep your brothers in line!'

Marcia frowned. 'Who's he?' she asked, pointing her fork at Swift.

Charisse turned and sighed. Standing under the light, she looked weary. 'You finish your tea nice and quiet, then start your homework' she ordered. 'I talk to this gentleman in kitchen.'

The kitchen was compact and as cluttered as the living room but the place had been painted white throughout and there were numerous well-tended house plants covering the cheap cabinets and shelves. A large bag of bread, pastries and iced buns lay on a kitchen counter and Swift saw the logo; *Sally's Bakes*.

'You best be quick,' Charisse said, scattering more oven chips in a tray and shoving it into the oven. 'My husband be back soon. He won't want you here.'

Swift recalled what the neighbour had said about Mr Lomar and his fists. He stood against the fridge-freezer, which was covered in children's drawings.

'I know that Mrs Langborne found out that you had two jobs,' he said.

Charisse nodded. 'I was working nights at the home and afternoons at bakery. Now I work bakery full-time. A woman like that, what she know about having to work hard to put food on table?'

Swift thought that Carmen might know more about that than Charisse guessed. 'You must have been very upset when you got sacked.'

'Yes. Bad for me.' She glanced at the clock and rinsed a few cups.

'Did you know Mrs Langborne was the cause of your sacking?'

Her answer was guileless. 'She nasty woman. She said to me, before she went home, that she told the manager and I probably be got rid of.'

Righteous Carmen again, Swift thought. 'So, it must have been hard for your family.'

'Hard, yes.' Charisse turned around and folded her arms. 'Was good pay at the home, bakery not so good. Is hard to get another care job now because of sacking.'

'What did your husband say?'

She blinked rapidly. 'He very cross. He have to do extra evening shift now.' At the mention of him, Charisse looked at the clock again and made a pushing motion at Swift. 'You go now, that's all I know.'

'Did your husband know that Mrs Langborne was the cause of your sacking?'

'I tell him, yes, so he know it not my fault.' She bit at her bottom lip. Swift guessed that if anything was deemed to be her fault, she suffered.

The front door slammed and Charisse jumped, knocking over an empty saucepan. A man called sharply to Marcia to hang her coat up properly and pulled open the kitchen door.

'Who's this?' he asked Charisse, dumping a carrier bag full of tins on the floor. He was compact and beefy, running a little to fat around the middle, wearing a worn grey tracksuit. A pungent smell of frying fish hung around him. His stance was aggressive, legs wide apart.

'Vincent, this man just looking for someone,' Charisse said, casting an imploring glance at Swift.

Swift nodded. 'Yes, I was just looking someone up for an old friend but I had the wrong address. Sorry to have disturbed you. I was just going.'

Vincent Lomar frowned, folding his arms. 'So why are you in my kitchen? Front door not good enough?'

Charisse gestured at the cooker. 'I was in middle of making food. No problem, no problem.'

'Yes, I am sorry to have intruded, a bit pushy of me but the food smelled good. Well, I'll be on my way.'

Swift stepped forward. For a moment, Lomar didn't budge. Then he moved aside a fraction so that Swift had to squeeze past him so close he could feel the man's body heat. He followed Swift through to the front. Swift saw Marcia and Joseph sitting still at the table, watching their father carefully, their faces blank. Lomar slammed the front door behind him as he left, so hard that the walkway seemed to shudder.

Swift descended the stairs slowly, worrying about what might now happen in the flat and that he would be the cause of it. He knew that for men like Vincent Lomar, any small transgression could provide an excuse. The signs of domestic abuse were all too clear. He walked to the station, thinking that Lomar might well have been furious with Carmen Langborne. On the train, he rang Nora Morrow and updated her, stressing the delicacy of the situation and his concerns for the Lomar family.

'Well, you have been busy,' she said. 'I'll check if they're known to social services and see if he's got a record. Sounds like we'd better take a look. Did you see the Davenports?'

'Yes. She was a bit subdued. I checked they've got enough money to pay me; that didn't go down well.'

Nora laughed. He saw he had a call waiting so rang off and found Cedric on the line.

'Dear boy, I'm calling from the hospital. I'm afraid Bertie and I got entangled on our walk and I came off worst. Met the pavement unexpectedly, banged my arm. They want to keep me in tonight, make sure I'm not going to pop off.'

'I'll come and see you.'

'No, no; Milo's with me. He got Bertie home safe and then followed me here. I just wanted to ask if you'll check the flat; you know, everything turned off etc.'

'Of course. You sure you're okay?'

'Yes, no fuss needed. I have a few scrapes and bruises, that's all. Bertie was more alarmed than me.'

'Ok. Let me know when you'll be home tomorrow, I'll try to be around.'

* * *

Swift stopped off at a supermarket and bought a selection of vegetables. Once a week, he made a huge pot of soup and dipped into it as needed. He would make one tonight and leave some for Cedric's homecoming. In his kitchen, he chopped vegetables while listening to a radio play about espionage during the Korean War. Once he had the soup simmering, he switched off the radio and moved into the living room with a glass of wine. Dusk was falling so he turned on some lamps and drew the curtains. He had just picked up Cedric's spare key when he heard a faint shuffling sound from upstairs. He waited, listening, and detected the soft tread of someone trying to move about quietly.

He picked up a heavy torch that he kept on a bookshelf and climbed the stairs to Cedric's flat. The door was closed and he could see no sign that the lock had been forced. He eased the key in and turned, holding the handle and pushing the door slowly open. He could see from the small hallway that the living room was empty and stood, listening. Someone was in Cedric's bedroom at the rear of the house, opening drawers and cupboards. He moved quietly towards the open bedroom door and looked through. Oliver was in there, busy fingers walking through his father's wardrobe. Swift pointed the powerful torch at him.

'You're hard at it,' he said. 'I've never known you move so lightly.'

Oliver shielded his eyes, stumbling against the wardrobe door. 'What are you doing up here?' he asked.

'That's my question.' He knew that Oliver didn't have a key to his father's flat; Cedric was careful about his security and Swift had the only spare one. 'How did you get in?'

'Take that bloody torch out of my face.'

'If you tell me how you got in.'

'Dad gave me a key. Not that it's any of your business.'

Swift kept the torch on him. 'I don't think that's true. I'll ring him now to check.' He took his phone from his pocket.

Oliver moved sideways and Swift followed him with the torch beam. He was pinned in a corner by the window.

'I borrowed a key one time, just happened to still have it. Dad rang to say he's in hospital so I thought I'd get him some stuff.'

'In the dark?'

'Oh, shut up! It's none of your business anyway.'

Swift turned the light on and switched the torch off. 'You haven't rushed to the hospital to see your dad, then? That would be the usual response of a fond son.'

Oliver snatched up a rucksack lying on the bed. 'Don't bother trying your Hercule Poirot rubbish on me. I've every right to be here. Now get out of my way.'

Swift continued to block the door. 'You don't have a right to be here if Cedric hasn't invited you. I think I can take a Poirot-inspired guess at why you're rummaging around in the twilight. Looking for a will?' He could see that he had hit home. 'I can tell you you're wasting your time, it's not here.' It was in the safe in his office and he was the executor, not Oliver.

Oliver came towards him, swinging the rucksack at him. Swift put an arm out and blocked it, then held a hand in front of his face. This close, Oliver smelled of stale sweat and something acidic.

'You're a right bastard,' he spat. 'Stay out of my business.'

'Glad to. Now I'll just see you off the premises but give me the key first.'

'Sod off. You've no right.'

He tried to push past but Swift continued to block the door, placing his arms against the frame, staring at Oliver impassively. 'I could call the police, you know,' he said.

Oliver took the key from his pocket and threw it at him. It caught his chin as it fell. He thought of taking a look in the rucksack but decided that would be pushing it.

'Out,' he said, moving well aside in case Oliver took a swipe at him as he left.

He ran into the hallway and clattered down the stairs with a parting shout of 'fuck off, bastard.' He gave the front door its usual thunderous slam on his way out.

Swift picked up the key, assuming that Oliver had at some point had a copy made without his father's knowledge. He checked through the flat. Oliver hadn't bothered to close drawers and cupboards properly. He tidied, made sure appliances were turned off and locked the door. Downstairs, he bolted the front door and checked his soup. It was ready but his appetite had gone.

He sat and drank his wine, mulling over Florence and Oliver hiding their greed and self-interest behind masks of solicitude. He would have to tell Cedric about Oliver's visit and the key he had taken from him but he wouldn't mention his motive; it would embarrass them both and hurt Cedric. He felt bleak and chilled. He put a jumper on, poured another drink and thought of King Lear:

> *How sharper than a serpent's tooth it is*
> *To have a thankless child.*

* * *

Swift woke at seven a.m. in a sweat. He had been dreaming about a dimly lit roomful of women who were crying, but he didn't know the reason. One of them had looked up, stretching her hands out to him and he had seen that it was Ruth. As he went towards her, he woke. He sat up and breathed deeply, recovering. He saw through the open curtain that it was a fine day and was relieved; later on was Joyce's party and he would be able to meander in the garden and not get trapped at her side in the house. He made coffee, donned his rowing clothes and spent two hours on the river, still a little haunted by the crying women.

When he returned he had a text from Cedric, saying that he was on his way home with Milo. He showered and dressed in his one suit, a fine grey wool one that he had last worn for his Interpol interview. Under it he put an open-necked pale blue cotton shirt. He ladled some soup into a large bowl and took it upstairs to Cedric's kitchen, placing it in the microwave. As he opened a living room window he saw Cedric and Milo getting out of a taxi. He waved and waited while they came up the stairs, Cedric leading the way, sporting a plaster on his right cheek. He seemed undaunted by his adventure with the pavement and clasped Swift on the shoulder.

'Thank you, dear boy. Good of you to keep an eye on things.'

'You've recovered okay?'

'Absolutely. A good night's shut-eye and this morning they gave me porridge that was amazingly good for the NHS. Apparently they've had a celebrity chef in there recently who shook them up.'

'Love the suit, Ty,' Milo said, peering at his jacket and fingering the front. 'Got a hot date? If not, I'm available.'

'No, just my stepmother's birthday party. I've left some soup in the microwave, plenty for both of you. Do you want me to call in this evening?' He thought he would leave it until later to mention Oliver.

'That would be kind of you. I'm going to send Milo packing once I'm sorted, then I'll take it easy. Good luck with Joyce.'

* * *

Someone — Joyce probably, it was very much her kind of gesture — had tied bunches of multicoloured balloons to the porch of her house. Swift knew that it was inevitable and right that Joyce would make her mark on her own home, but he had never adjusted to his mother's quietly individual taste in décor being replaced by Joyce's flamboyant preferences. Joyce favoured bold colours, brassware and heavily patterned fabrics. He chided himself for his feelings, believing that a man in his late thirties should have overcome such pettiness; after all, he hardly wanted Joyce to live in a museum dedicated to his mother's memory. Still, as he was greeted by Joyce and went in, he winced at the wallpaper in the hall. It was green, patterned with gaudy red poppies.

'Tyrone!' Joyce said, hugging him close to her stout bosom, her chin just above his elbow, then standing back and examining him, hands on his arms. 'It's been far too long, you know. You look very well.'

'So do you. Happy Birthday.' He presented his gift and Joyce swept him to her again, standing on tiptoe to kiss his cheek.

She was wearing a highly floral scent and he pinched his upper lip, hoping to avoid sneezing.

'Come on through,' she said. 'There are loads of people here. Mary's around somewhere too.'

He followed her through the house to the sitting room at the back. Joyce had gone for a nautical look for her birthday; a white flouncy skirt topped by a navy-and-white striped shirt and a blue and white striped bandana in her hair. Although she grew ever plumper, she was light and graceful on her feet and fast moving. The house was heaving with guests and the noise level was high. Tyrone didn't recognise anyone so he just smiled vaguely and generally at anyone who made eye contact with him. To his horror, Joyce clapped her hands, as if bringing a class to order and called loudly.

'This is Tyrone, everyone; my handsome stepson and detective extraordinaire! Anybody want a crime solved, this is your man!'

There was laughter and some people raised glasses to him. He nodded and accepted a glass of wine from a man who was wearing an apron saying *I'm Only Here for the Beer*.

Joyce drew him away to a corner while she opened her present. 'Oh, how lovely!' she said, 'a beautiful colour!' She draped the stole across her chest and twirled around, as if modelling it.

'I'm glad you like it. How have you been keeping?' he asked quickly, worried that she might call the company to order again to display her gift.

'Very well indeed. I've taken up golf recently and it's wonderful, literally keeps me on my toes although, sadly, I don't seem to lose any inches here.' She patted her midriff. But Tyrone . . .' She drew close to him, a hand on his arm. 'How are you keeping really? I do worry about this private agency thing; it can't be as rewarding as a professional career, surely?'

'I find it rewarding enough, thanks. I like being my own boss.'

'Yes, but you're still young and at Interpol you had a career progression. I always thought you'd become an international head of something there. I worry that you're wasting your huge talents.'

'As I said, I like heading up my own business. I have what most people envy these days; a work-life balance.'

Joyce moved even closer so that he was backed against a corner cabinet, the edge poking him in the hip. He could feel her warm breath on his face and see the join between her foundation and skin along the line of her cheek.

'And have you met anyone nice? I worry about you being lonely after that bad business with Ruth. I do hope you're not still pining after her.' Her intensity was too much, her head to one side, her gaze soulful.

'Joyce, I'm fine. My life is fine. Now, you're neglecting your other guests. Can I get you a drink?'

He started to move forward, guiding Joyce by the elbow towards the man in the apron. As soon as she was involved in getting a Bacardi and coke, he escaped through the open doors to the garden and stood in the sun, watching several children dangling their feet in the pond. He drank his wine; unlike the house, the garden had changed little since his mother's time and if he squeezed his eyes, he could see her sitting in her chair by the plum tree, reading Muriel Spark and giggling. One morning, his mother had complained of pains in her finger joints; an initial diagnosis of rheumatism was quickly replaced by bone cancer and within six months she was dead. Even now, so many years later, he still thought he might pick up the phone and hear her voice.

An arm sneaked under his jacket and circled his waist. He turned to see Mary smiling at him, sunglasses perched in her hair.

'You've escaped to the outdoors, then,' she said.

'I have, but only after close questioning about my lack of career prospects and love life.'

'I'm not sure about Joyce's sailor look but she's certainly got a good crowd. Now, let me introduce you to Simone.' Mary beckoned to a woman in a cream linen dress, her hair curling below her shoulders. 'This is Ty; Ty, Simone.'

They shook hands; Simone's was cool and slender. She looked at him from huge, intelligent eyes and ran a hand through her curls, pushing them back as they glinted with reddish tints in the sun.

'Good to meet you,' Swift said.

'And you. I've never met a private detective before.'

Despite her French sounding name and café au lait skin, her accent was Geordie.

'Well, glad to be your first. Hope you're surviving Joyce. She means well.'

'Your stepmother is certainly a formidable woman. She insisted on me eating vol-au-vents that I didn't want.' Her voice was musical and droll.

'Ty pretty much had to run away from her in his teens. Do you remember she redecorated your bedroom without consulting you?' Mary giggled, nudging him.

'I do. I came home and found magenta ruched curtains and the waxed floorboards covered in a carpet with green foliage. It's exhausting, tiptoeing around someone who barges into your life with good intentions. That's why I'm a bad stepson and don't come here often.'

'Don't beat yourself up,' Simone advised. 'Isn't there a saying that friends are God's apology for families?'

'I haven't heard that before; I like it.' Swift raised his glass to the notion.

They stood and chatted for a while about their work. Swift saw the way that Mary and Simone exchanged fond glances, touching each other lightly now and again. His phone buzzed in his pocket and he moved away to take the call from an unknown number.

It was Charisse Lomar, sounding hysterical; 'That you, Mr Swift? You gone and told police about me.'

He could barely hear her through her gulps for air. 'I had to tell the police about what I'd found out because they've been looking for Mrs Langborne. Where are you?'

'Home. You done bad thing. Police have been here, they took Vincent away.' She started crying louder.

'Listen, try and breathe, please. What happened?' He heard one of the children shouting in the background and a door slamming. 'Charisse?'

She blew her nose and gulped. 'Police came and asked questions about where we were end of January and Vincent got mad. He punched policeman so they took him. That bad woman, we don't do nothing to her! She cause lots of trouble. Vincent don't do nothing!' She started weeping again.

'I'll come round', he said. 'Can you hear me?'

The line was dead. He looked up at the clear sky. He had better go there; he didn't like to think what might happen when Vincent got home, if the police released him.

'Trouble?' Mary asked.

'Yes, I haven't got time to tell you now, I need to go. Can you say goodbye to Joyce for me if I don't catch her? It's been great to meet you,' he said to Simone, heading back for the house.

The sitting room crowd had thinned out and he could hear why; Joyce was at her piano in the front room, singing from Gilbert and Sullivan. He was thankful that he would escape without fond farewells and false promises to visit soon. He slipped through the hallway to the strains of 'Three Little Maids from School' and closed the door quietly behind him. One of the balloons had come adrift and was lolling by the gate. He nudged it aside, calling a taxi, calculating how long it would take to get from Muswell Hill to New Malden.

CHAPTER 8

Swift asked the taxi driver to step on it, not liking to contemplate what the ride was going to cost him but knowing he owed it to Charisse. On the way, he rang Nora Morrow to find out the situation with Vincent Lomar but her phone went straight to answerphone. He left a message, asking for an update and adding that he was worried about the family. He sat back and watched the streets reel by. He knew that there was little he could do for Charisse about her abusive husband, except tell her where she could go for help. When he reached the flats, he rang Charisse's number, ready to put the phone down if Lomar answered or was there. She picked up after six rings, her voice dull and nasal.

'It's Tyrone Swift. I'm downstairs and I'd like to come up and see you. Is your husband around?'

'No. He rang from police. They keeping him overnight.'

'What about the children?' They might tell their father of his visit; abusers used their power to make everyone an informer.

'They at a friend.'

'Can I come up, then?'

'Okay.'

She was waiting at the open door for him, arms crossed, staring out at the cement pastures below. Her eyes were red and puffy. She led him in wordlessly, leaving him to close the door.

'I am sorry,' he said. 'I had to tell the police.'

She sank into a chair and stared at him. 'You bring trouble to my door,' she said simply.

He nodded in acknowledgement. 'Was your husband arrested?'

'Yes. After he punch policeman.'

'That was a bad move.'

'He has a temper.'

'Has he been in trouble with the police before?'

She looked down. 'Once, years ago before I knew him. He robbed a shop, got caught.'

'He's been in prison?'

'Six month. He not bad man.' She leaked tears again and dabbed at her eyes. The room was in a mess compared to his last visit, cups and glasses on the table and clothes hanging on chairs.

'Do you want me to make you a cup of tea?' Swift asked.

'No. What you want?'

'I wanted to see how you are. Did the police ask your husband where he was on January thirty-first?'

She nodded. 'He was off work sick. He say he was here on his own. I was at work. They ask him if he saw Mrs Langborne that day and he got angry.'

'What do you think; do you think he saw her?'

She put her hands to her face. 'Why should he see that woman? She nothing to do with us.'

'Perhaps because he was angry with her? He might have wanted to tell her what he thought of her reporting you, making you lose your job.'

She rubbed at her eyes. 'I know what you trying to say. Vincent wouldn't harm old lady. He had bad cough and cold, he stay in bed that day.'

Swift left a brief silence. 'There are people you can talk to if you sometimes feel frightened of your husband, or if your children do. People who can try to help.'

She stood. 'So that policewoman tell me. What she know? I want people leave us alone. You go now. You leave my family alone. My husband good man, good provider. What we do if he put in jail?'

'If he's innocent, he won't be going to jail. Okay, I'll go. But please ring me if you ever need help.'

She turned her back on him and straightened cushions, started to pick up toys and books. He thought it was good that she was busying herself, making order from the chaos. He let himself out and decided to walk to the station. Vincent Lomar was going to have a difficult time with the police, having indulged in assault and not being able to back up his story about January thirty-first. Swift was interested in his previous record, sure that there would be more history than one robbery and that the history would involve violence. He thought of his offer to Charisse, if she ever needed help, what could he do? His words had been those of the concerned, powerless bystander. He had seen the familiar look of cowed defeat in her eyes. They lived in different worlds and hers was a daily struggle with providing for her children and navigating her husband's aggression towards the family.

* * *

On the train, he reflected on Joyce's party and her questioning. Sometimes he thought maybe he should engage a female 'walker' to attend such events with him so that he wouldn't be asked about his love life, or lack of it. He had a friend in Interpol who did just that after his divorce; he became so fed up with sympathetic hostesses trying to pair him off with suitable women, he paid

Vanessa from an agency to accompany him to social gatherings. He sent Joyce a guilt text:

Sorry I had to rush away on business. It was a lovely party and you looked as if you were enjoying every minute. All the best, Ty.

Back home, he went straight upstairs to see Cedric, who was sitting with his feet on a stool, drinking claret and watching snooker.

'Hello, dear boy,' he said. 'As you can see, I'm almost mended and indulging in slothfulness. Glass of wine?'

'I won't thanks, I need to write up some notes. Can I get you anything?'

'No, no, all is well. Bertie's owner rang me, very apologetic, saying he'll understand if I want to give up the outings but I said not at all, I'll be back on form in a couple of days. Have to get back in the saddle. Do sit down for a minute, you're making my neck ache.'

Swift sat opposite him, looking at his amazingly youthful skin and fine bones and his kindly eyes, a little glazed with age. He remembered what Simone had said about friends being God's apology. He selected his words carefully.

'Oliver was here last night,' he said. 'I came up when I heard a noise. He didn't stay long.'

Cedric took a sip of his drink. 'Ah, I see. Well, I expect he forgot something last time he was here. Thank you for keeping an eye open, dear boy.' He touched the plaster on his cheek, checking the edges.

'He got in with a key, said he'd had it for a while. I thought it best if he left it with me. Shall I hang on to it?'

'Yes, that would be helpful.'

'That's okay. Well, I'll leave you in peace.'

'Good night. Oh, how was Joyce?'

'On fine form, dressed for a yachting trip. When I left she was at the piano, singing Gilbert and Sullivan.'

'Dear Joyce; so enthusiastic always. Well, I won't keep you.'

In his office, Swift checked his emails, hoping to see one from Nora Morrow, but she hadn't responded. There was one from Carmen's doctor, Poppy Forsyth:

Hi, I just wondered if your enquiries at the care facility were fruitful at all or if you've heard anything further about Carmen Langborne. She was annoying but I kind of miss her.

He thought for a moment and replied:

Hi, yes, I did discover something of interest. I could tell you about it over a drink if you'd like.

He wrote up his notes, looking back over the chronology. If Vincent Lomar hadn't harmed Carmen Langborne, he was no further forward. Lomar was hardly likely to confess and without a body, the police wouldn't be able to prove anything. He tapped the desk, frustrated at his ignorance of how the questioning was going but knowing better than to bother Nora Morrow again that day. He sat back in his chair, hands behind his head, gazing at the ceiling. He knew what to do in the meantime; return to the beginning and look again, check if he had missed anything. He texted Ronnie Farley, saying that if it was ok, he would like to call round to the house again the following morning. Then he thought he had better make a start on the work Rachel Breen had asked him to do, glad to cause annoyance for the irksome, time wasting Boyce. He spent a while searching the internet for records for Edward Boyce, making notes and recording an address in Tooting Bec which was situated in the right borough and would bear further investigation.

* * *

Ronnie Farley had coffee waiting, and freshly baked fruitcake. The sun was slanting through the kitchen window and one of the cats was asleep on a chair, its paws stretched over the edge. Swift watched Ronnie cut through the still warm cake. It released scents of nutmeg and cinnamon, reminding him of his mother's barmbrack. He felt a wistfulness for things lost and irretrievable.

'This kitchen smells wonderful; like childhood,' he said.

'I have to do something while I'm here, other than cleaning and polishing or I'd go potty,' she said. 'This is my ma's recipe, never fails. And I know you single men; you don't look after yourselves with your takeaway food and ready meals.'

He was about to contest the cliché but decided to eat the cake instead. It occurred to him that she probably pictured him living in a small flat, his socks drying on a radiator, fridge filled with meals for one.

They sat at the table and she poured coffee. Her hands were strong and long fingered with ridged veins on the backs.

'Rupert was here again the other day, checking over the place,' she said. 'He had a good old rummage and informed me he'll keep me on for another month, then review the situation. Told me I mustn't smoke on the premises, not even in the garden.'

'That's a bit mean.'

'Aye, well; he who pays the piper . . . he's full of his own importance, that one.'

There was a tabloid newspaper lying on the table. She turned it round so that Swift could see the headline concerning a retired politician who was being questioned by the police about historic allegations of paedophilia.

'Have you ever dealt with anything like this?'

'Yes, at one time although not that specific area of enquiry.'

'Hardly a day seems to go by now without something like this in the news. What do you reckon; is he guilty?'

'Possibly. I think there have been many unreported cases of abuse, or reported and not believed. Now that victims are being listened to, I'm sure many more will come forward.'

Ronnie tapped the paper, tracing her finger around the politician's face. 'I don't understand why these men behave like that. Some of them have children of their own.'

'It is hard to believe; that's why so many of them have got away with it.'

Ronnie sighed and busied herself pouring more coffee. 'So, what are you looking for here this time?'

He swallowed his cake, savouring the last mouthful. 'My compliments to you and your mother, that was delicious. I'd like to have another look through the house.'

'In case you've missed a clue?'

'Something like that.'

'Well, when you go, take some of this cake with you or it will go to waste.'

He could smell a faint alcohol trace from her again and wondered if Rupert had detected it. Her voice sounded dry and tired and her eyes were pinkish. He thought about her life, coming to another woman's house, baking biscuits and cakes that nobody wanted to eat.

'Have you family, Ronnie?'

'A few cousins in Aberdeen. On my tod otherwise.' She picked up a weighty bunch of keys from the table and put them in her bag. 'Mustn't forget those; no point in being a cleaner who can't get in to clean!'

He started at the top of the house, looking through cupboards and drawers in Carmen's bedroom, finding only carefully hung and folded clothes; the wardrobe held Jaeger suits, shoes ranked in colour gradations and dozens of dresses in individual cellophane covers. The other two bedrooms were sterile and unused with a few books and empty drawers and wardrobes except for spare bedding. The beds were bare, with patchwork coverlets to protect them from dust. The small box room held a sewing machine and a basket with balls of wool in assorted colours. There was an armchair by the window, a cloth bag with wooden handles beside it. A radio stood alongside on top of a slim chest of drawers. From the window, you could see into several back gardens, all beautifully maintained and awash with May colours. Swift pictured Carmen sitting in her armchair and knitting, listening to the radio. He looked through the chest of drawers and saw batches of knitting and sewing patterns, a box of buttons, and an embroidered case holding threads and needles.

He toured back through the downstairs rooms but could find nothing of interest among the magazines and figurines. He opened a walnut cabinet in the dining room that was closely packed with bottles of all shapes and sizes; sherry, gin, vermouths, brandy and whisky, various liqueurs. He noticed that a bottle of Southern Comfort at the front had a misaligned top and guessed that this was Ronnie's current tipple. This Aladdin's cave of assorted alcohol would be a major temptation to a drinker.

He stood, looking at a particularly unattractive and no doubt valuable china shepherdess perched on top of the cabinet, her bonnet tied demurely. He thought of Carmen's private space and how his aunt used to tuck important keepsakes into the lid of her writing box. Ronnie had Johnny Cash playing in the kitchen, bemoaning his fate for killing a man. He went back upstairs and into the box room. He lifted the case of the sewing machine, examined the smooth interior and the base, finding nothing. He sat in Carmen's chair and picked up her cloth bag. Inside was a piece of knitting in progress, in blue and yellow stripes. The pattern enclosing it, published by a cat charity, indicated that it was going to be a toy mouse. He thought that claws would make a quick killing of a woollen mouse but perhaps that was the point.

There were several pairs of needles in the bag and two balls of the wool in use. Swift took everything out and laid the contents on the carpet. A side pocket on the outside of the bag held scissors and a retractable tape measure. Swift unzipped an inside pocket and took out some folded papers. There was a pattern for a dog's body warmer, another for a cat's snuggle and one for hats for donkeys. Swift was fascinated by this whole world of animal fashion he had been ignorant of. He riffled through the papers. Inside the cat's snuggle pattern was a folded letter headed the Pryce Hospice, with an address in Shepherd's Bush. Swift smoothed it out and read the well-formed, sloping handwriting:

My name is William Pennington, date of birth 4.9.1942. I am writing this to state that I am the biological father of Rupert Langborne. My son does not know this and neither did his father, Neville Langborne. I had a relationship with Penny, Neville Langborne's first wife, before they met. We had known each other since school days; I suppose you could say we had been classroom sweethearts. I went away to try my luck in Australia when I left school but I was homesick and I returned to London in 1966 and trained as a librarian.

I met Penny again by chance. She had been married for about a year and was not happy in her marriage. I will make no excuses for what followed. I had an affair with Penny and she became pregnant. She was convinced that the child was mine; I believe women have a way of working these things out. Rupert certainly looked very like me as a child and even more so as he grew up. Neville Langborne had no reason to suspect that Rupert was not his son. Penny broke off our relationship while she was pregnant but she sent me photos of Rupert over the years. I subsequently married but had no children. When Penny was dying of cancer, she contacted me. It seemed important to her that there should be proof, if it was needed at any time, that I am Rupert's father. We did a DNA test; Penny used some of Rupert's hair. This test proved positive. Penny did not wish to tell Rupert about this before she died but she gave me the written DNA outcome, entrusting it to me to use if I ever felt I wanted to tell my son that I am his father.

This has been a heavy burden to me. When I met Mrs Langborne here at the hospice and realised that she is Neville Langborne's widow and Rupert's stepmother, I finally shared that burden. I have cancer and not long to live and I suppose a reckoning is due. Mrs Langborne has been kind and understanding. It is her strong belief that Rupert should be told of his parentage and she has offered to discuss this with him initially, and find out if he wishes to meet me.

I have written this down so that Mrs Langborne can keep it safely and show it to Rupert, to my son. I will understand if he does not want to meet me but at least he will be able to read the truth from my own hand.

The letter was signed and the date added underneath, December 2, 2014. Swift read it through again. What had Carmen been doing at the hospice? She must have been a visitor of some kind but no one had mentioned she had any interest in ailing humanity as well as animals. He had no idea how this could have contributed to her disappearance. If she had told Rupert and he had been angered at receiving the information and at her interference, things might have turned ugly. Would this affect his prospects of inheriting? To go from being the son of a Lord Justice to that of a librarian would be a decline in social status that Rupert was unlikely to welcome or want made public. At last here was a possible motive for wishing Carmen ill. Swift felt a surge of energy, He heard Ronnie's footsteps on the stairs and quickly tucked the letter in his pocket and replaced the contents of the knitting bag.

'Ah, here you are,' she said, appearing in the doorway with a mop and bucket. 'She likes this little den, does Mrs L, spends evenings up here knitting away. Find anything?'

'Nothing. Still, worth having another look. Were there any other charities that you haven't mentioned before that Mrs Langborne was involved in?'

Ronnie shook her head. 'No, I don't think so. I didn't know about everything she did, mind, she could be close with her information, as I've said. I've left you a wee bit of cake on the kitchen table, wrapped in foil.'

Swift fetched the cake on his way out. Ronnie's long-handled bag was open on the table, on top of her cream mac. He saw a whisky bottle inside, beside the huge bunch of keys she carried.

* * *

He decided to go straight to the hospice and was there within an hour. It was in the kind of building he had expected Lilac Grange to be; a sturdy, tall Victorian property, set within large gardens. Inside it was light and airy, painted in pastels and white. At the reception desk, Swift explained who he was and asked to speak to whoever was in charge. The grey-haired woman behind the desk, who wore a badge telling him she was Lettys, spoke on the phone, then smiled at him.

'Mike, our manager, has asked me to take you to the little café we have. He'll meet you in there. Would you like to just sign the visitors' book and follow me? We do ask all our visitors to keep their voices low in the public areas.'

She called to another woman in an office to take over the desk and walked before him, taking him through double doors to a small lounge area bordered on one side by a garden with a veranda. Mozart was playing quietly; there was a small counter where hot drinks and snacks were available and grouped armchairs surrounded by bookcases and plants. Swift could appreciate the effort that had been made to make it homely and welcoming. Lettys left him and he examined the books which were a wide-ranging collection; various classics including George Elliot and Wilkie Collins, spy stories, historical romances, blockbusters involving international financiers and a sprinkling of chick lit. There was a sad lack of pulp fiction. A notice said, *you are welcome to borrow a book but please return it or replace with an alternative.* He wondered what he would want as reading material if he knew he had a limited amount of time left; he visualised a small stack which would include Graham Greene, Beryl Bainbridge, Barbara Vine, Seamus Heaney, some Dan Turner — Hollywood Detective, and Shakespeare's sonnets.

He bought a coffee and stepped through the open patio doors on to the veranda as he sipped it. The garden was lush and riotous with blossom. In the centre was a pond with a water feature. He closed his eyes for a moment, listening to the soothing splashes. A woman with a mobile drip in her arm was sitting on a gardening stool, deadheading flowers.

'Mr Swift? I'm Mike Farrell. How can I help you?' A tall, thin man, with a boyish smile and eager manner appeared behind him.

They sat, Mike Farrell with a bottle of water and Swift explained about Carmen's disappearance and his role.

'Today I was at her home again and found out that she used to come here. No one seems to have known about it. Was she a volunteer here?'

'No, although she visited several times. Mrs Langborne was a regular contributor to collections for us through her church; her husband received some support from us during his final illness. We had a little social gathering last October for people who assist us in any way; cheese and wine, that kind of thing. Mrs Langborne chatted with some of the residents. She became friendly with one in particular and visited him a few times.'

'Would that have been William Pennington?'

'That's right.' Farrell had a habit of nodding eagerly when he spoke, as if to confirm his words.

'So you didn't notice that she had stopped coming here?'

Farrell shook his head. 'She wasn't a regular visitor, you understand, so she wasn't expected. And of course our residents have their privacy about visitors.'

'Would you be able to check when she last came, in the visitors' book?'

'Yes, I can do that.'

Swift finished his coffee, which was surprisingly good for an institution. 'I saw a letter this morning, concerning Mr Pennington. I need to try and find out if it has anything to do with Mrs Langborne's disappearance. I would like to speak to him.' Swift was hoping not to hear of his demise.

Farrell cracked his fingers. 'He's not here at present, he's at home. Mr Pennington comes in for a week or two at intervals for support and pain control.'

'I do need to contact him. Would you be able to phone him and ask if I can visit him?'

'Well . . . it's a bit unusual. It's not as if you're the police.'

'No, and I understand about data protection and privacy. However, there is a woman who has vanished and who might be in great trouble or danger. If you could phone him and say that I'm here and that I have seen a letter he wrote, he might agree to allow me to visit.'

Farrell scratched the side of his neck. 'What if he says no?'

'Then I'll respect that he has said that through you. There are other ways of tracing people, it wouldn't be too difficult for me and I have a job to do.'

'He's a very sick man.'

'I understand that. I think he might be happy to talk to me.'

Farrell asked him to wait. Swift checked his phone and saw that he had a missed call from Nora Morrow. He listened to the message she had left, saying that they had released Lomar for now but would want to question him again; *he says he was at home on the thirty-first with a bad cold but no one to corroborate. We rang ahead to tell Mrs Lomar he was on his way home. Social services don't know them but he's got two previous — for robbery involving knives and a common assault. I've asked a community support officer to call there later. How's the sweet Thames?*

He knew that Nora was going through the motions with Lomar. He thought of Charisse gloomily as he looked up Rupert's address in Berkshire and found it listed under his wife; it was a place called Holly End, a few miles from Cookham.

Mike Farrell returned with a sheet of paper.

'I spoke to Mr Pennington and he's happy for you to call him. This is his number and address. Mrs Langborne last visited here on January the eighth.'

'Many thanks.' He stood and nodded to Farrell. 'This is a pleasant arrangement you have here, people must appreciate it.'

Farrell looked delighted. 'Well, that's kind of you. We do our best and we have loyal helpers.'

On the way back out, Swift saw a donations box. He found a tenner and stuffed it in, glad that others were generous and robust enough to run such a sanctuary and inspired by the trace of guilt always experienced by the healthy in the presence of the dying.

* * *

It was mid-afternoon and his stomach had long forgotten Ronnie Farley's fruitcake. He called at a mini supermarket for a ham sandwich and bottle of water and phoned William Pennington. He answered immediately, speaking hoarsely, with pauses for breath. Swift kept it short, surrounded by the roar of traffic and asked if he could visit within the hour. Pennington agreed and gave him a code for the front door. Swift caught a bus towards Acton and sat on the top deck eating his sandwich and checking directions to Pennington's address. At one stop the bus filled up with boys streaming wildly out of school, hysterical with freedom, bickering their way up the stairs, slapping and taunting each other and generally saturating the air with testosterone. Swift plugged in his earphones and listened to Elvis Costello.

Pennington's flat was in the basement of a four-storey house in a narrow terraced street. Swift negotiated his way past a cluster of bins and down steep concrete steps. He rang the bell, then entered the security code and stepped inside. He found himself in a gloomy hallway filled with shoes, coats and walking sticks and followed the croaky voice that called to him to come through, stumbling over a shopping trolley and righting it against the wall. William Pennington was sitting in a recliner chair in a dark navy tracksuit, his feet bare. Under him was a fleecy white blanket. The phone, a radio, a covered jug of water and a walking frame were beside him and the TV remote was on an adjustable tray poised over his lap. He was extremely thin, his yellowish skin was fine and translucent, his look detached; Swift knew that expression; he had seen it in his mother. Pennington's light was dying.

'Thank you for agreeing to see me,' he said. 'I'll try to be brief.'

'I don't have many visitors. Do sit down. Do you want to open the blinds a little more? I like this twilight world but the nurse tells me off about it.'

'No, this is fine.' He moved a stack of newspapers from a chair and sat. The room smelled fusty, like a burrow. It was small and lined with crammed bookshelves which combined with the clutter and dimness made it oppressive. An empty foil meal container was on the floor, congealed with gravy, bits of unrecognisable meat glued to it. Despite the warmth of the day there was a gas fire on low.

'Let's deal with the elephant in the room first.' Pennington gave him a tired, sweet smile. 'I have lung cancer and a matter of weeks to live. Just to save any embarrassment.'

'Thank you. But I'm not embarrassed. I've come here because Carmen Langborne went missing at the end of January and her stepdaughter has asked me to find her. I found a letter you wrote about your son, Rupert, when I was looking around her home.'

Pennington raised a beaker of water to his lips with a shaky hand and took several small sips. It was hard to see his emaciated features clearly in the gloom but his heavy-lidded eyes and high domed forehead reminded Swift of Rupert Langborne.

'I wondered why Carmen hadn't been back in touch,' Pennington said finally. 'I don't have much energy left for fretting; I thought perhaps she had had second thoughts about involving herself in my affairs. That I could understand.'

'You didn't try to contact her?'

'I have no contact details for her. I saw her only at the hospice.'

'You met her last October, the day she attended the social function?'

'That's correct. I heard her name and recalled that Neville Langborne had remarried. We got talking. She was an interesting woman; no false sympathy, no fussing, very direct. I liked that.'

He paused and held a hand over his chest. Swift waited. The gas fire was sucking the oxygen from the room.

'She came back to see me, and on that visit I told her about Rupert. I needed to tell someone and as his stepmother, it seemed somehow as if she had been sent. I'm not a religious man but I do believe that certain things are meant. Do you think that?'

'I believe in coincidence,' Swift told him.

'Ah, a rationalist. Carmen asked me to write down what I had told her. She said that she would have to consider it carefully, but she thought that Rupert should be told. She had very clear ideas about right and wrong; her view was that Rupert was entitled to know, even if he didn't want to meet me.' He swallowed, his voice roughening.

'Do you want to meet him?'

'To be honest, I'm not sure. I think it would have to be his decision anyway. Could you pour some more water for me? I tend to spill it.'

Swift rose and poured water from the jug, placing the blue plastic beaker back on the tray.

'Thank you. You know you're on the way out when you can't be trusted with a glass and the carers insist on nursery ware. When I was a child, I had a similar drinking vessel with Peter Rabbit on it.' Pennington laughed, then coughed.

'You have no family?'

'No; my wife died some time ago. I have kind ladies and nurses who come in every day and give me orders. What do you think has happened to Carmen? I didn't know her for long but I enjoyed her company and find that I miss her. I've never been a sociable man, you see.'

Swift wondered if Carmen had been his only visitor. 'No trace of her has been found. The police have had no success to date. Did she ever indicate to you that she was going away anywhere or had a new relationship?'

'No. We never talked for long; I get tired easily and Rupert was our only real subject of conversation. I enjoyed hearing about him from her; how his life is now, et cetera.'

Pennington closed his eyes. Swift looked at him, then away; it seemed cruel that Carmen had appeared in his life and offered him company and a chance to be heard, then left him without warning. His hopes for a meeting with his son must have been raised. His solitary suffering and lack of self-pity moved Swift intensely. He stood to look at a photograph on one of the bookshelves; Pennington as a young man with his bride. There was no doubt that he was Rupert's father; the build was slighter, but facially there was a clear resemblance.

He looked around and saw that Pennington was watching him. 'Rupert looks like you.'

'You've met him?'

'Yes, just recently. We had a lunch and discussed his stepmother.'

'You see that shelf, by the window? There's an album at one end. Take a look.'

Swift found a small photograph album propped against a row of books. It contained a couple of pages of photos of Rupert Langborne as a child; some in school uniform, some on beaches, one in a garden. He was smiling in all of them but it was a heart-rending record. Swift replaced it and sat again, moving the chair further back from the fire.

'You must have wanted at times to meet your son, must have been tempted to take a look at least?'

Pennington made a helpless gesture. 'Penny was very firm that I mustn't do anything to rock the boat; too much to lose. Then there was my wife to think of. It seemed best not to interfere.'

There was a placidity about him suggesting that here was a man who had always been instructed by women.

'Do you know if Carmen had told Rupert about you?'

'I've no idea; the last time I saw her I was having a bad day after treatment and she wasn't allowed to stay for long. I don't recall much about that visit; morphine is a blessing but you do tend to check out of reality for a while.'

'What will you do now, about telling him?'

Pennington clasped his hands together on the tray. 'I haven't any fight in me. I've left it too long now. I have written a letter enclosed with my will and the DNA result to be passed to Rupert after my death. My solicitor will see to it.' His voice was reduced to a whisper. 'I think it best that he knows and his mother wanted it.'

'Did Mrs Langborne know about that letter?'

'I don't think so; I don't believe I discussed that.'

Swift stood. 'I'll go now; I've taken enough of your time. Can I do anything for you before I go?'

Pennington held both his hands out and took Swift's. His grip was surprisingly strong.

'This is what you can do; wish for me what I wish for myself; that I will go to sleep tonight and not wake. Will you do that?'

* * *

Poppy Forsyth was drinking vodka and lime; she had come to London with her husband, a paediatrician, she told Swift. They divorced and she stayed on, having become an anglophile. She was wearing jeans and a bright yellow jumper featuring diagonal zips and bits of green leather. On her right wrist she wore a bracelet that jangled musically as she moved; he found it alluring. Her hair swayed about her shoulders and now and again she ran her fingers through it. Swift was glad of the distraction; he would need to sit and think about what he had learned and decide what to do but not tonight. His brain was tired, too tired to process the information. He'd had three glasses of wine and was feeling pleasantly drunk. He told Poppy about Lilac Grange and the Lomars and mentioned William Pennington without providing any details. He told her of Pennington's final request as he was leaving the flat.

'Well,' she said, raising her glass, 'let's wish it for him then, honey. You know the saying? I don't know where it originates but I like it; *may you live as long as you want to and want to as long as you live.*'

'It sounds Irish,' he said, clinking his glass to hers. 'Do you ever get depressed, being around sick people?'

'Not really; sometimes, when children are ill. But you know, it's just part of the human condition. You have good health, you have bad. You're born, you die. It's all quite simple.'

The way she put it, he found himself in agreement. After another drink she put a hand on his knee.

'Want to come back to mine? It's just a couple of blocks, we can walk.'

Her skin gleamed with health, her vitality was infectious. He couldn't think of any reason to say no.

CHAPTER 9

Swift sat in his office, swivelling in his chair, reading over his notes and thinking. There was no point in focusing on Vincent Lomar for now. He had tried ringing Nora Morrow with no luck so sent her an email, thanking her for the heads up on Lomar. He decided not to mention William Pennington, wanting to chew over the situation.

He yawned and stretched. He had woken that morning in a strange, wide bed, feeling rejuvenated. Poppy was already in the shower so he made tea and toast for them both. They left her flat together and he kissed her cheek on the doorstep.

'It was fun, hon,' she said. 'See you soon?'

'Sounds fine,' he said, flagging a taxi.

He didn't know if he would call or if she would; it had been warm and generous and as she said, fun. He would let it lie, see what happened. He switched off the memory of her musical bracelet and refocused on his notes. He knew now what *WP* meant in Carmen's diary, yet she hadn't visited him that day. For a widow who led a quiet life with her charities and knitting, she had certainly got mixed up in some interesting situations. Surely, he thought, she must have broached the subject of his father with Langborne between December and the end of January? It wasn't an issue to delay over, with Pennington likely to die at any time. Being a woman of strong views, she was unlikely to hesitate for long. And if Langborne knew, did Florence? Approaching him was going to be tricky. Swift wanted to make the most of taking him by surprise. He tidied his desk and made a coffee, then sat and doodled for a few minutes. He made a decision which would involve borrowing Cedric's car.

* * *

Saturday morning found Swift on the road out of London early, driving Cedric's burnt-orange Mini Cooper convertible. Cedric used it infrequently so it was in mint condition and smelled new inside. The sun was warm so he had the hood down, the breeze on his face. The traffic was reasonable on the M4 at seven thirty and he cruised just under the speed limit; at this rate, he reckoned, it would take about an hour to Cookham, where he would have breakfast. His plan was to catch Langborne unawares at his country retreat, a place where he would be away from his formal setting and not expecting to be questioned. He aimed to arrive at Holly End around ten a.m., judging that this would be early enough, before a day's activities.

He parked the car near the station just after eight thirty and walked through the pretty streets. There were few people around, mainly men of Cedric's age out to buy their papers. He found a café open and ordered scrambled eggs and coffee and read a selection of their newspapers while he ate. Afterwards, he followed directions to the Thames and walked for half an hour, taking off his jacket and rolling up his shirtsleeves. It was a picturesque place but gentrified in a way that made Swift edgy; he was a city animal and always found the countryside a little alien and unnerving. There were some rowers out on the water and swans gliding. The wooded hillsides were verdant in the sun. He approached the lock, knowing from his Thames lore that the river changed course suddenly at this point and had been highly dangerous for navigating before the lock was built. He stood and watched the flowing water, the convergence of four streams, then turned and walked back to the car.

Holly End was situated off a lane running between high trees that curved and met overhead, forming a green gothic-shaped canopy above the car. A pair of tall wrought-iron gates stood at the top of the driveway. Swift got out of the car and checked them; they weren't electronically controlled or locked. He drove the car further along the lane, not wanting to advertise his arrival. He parked it on the dry verge and walked back to the gates. They were heavy but opened easily. Just beyond them and side by side were two brick-built cottages, double fronted, with fenced gardens. Both had white wooden front doors and porches. They had curtains and seemed lived in but Swift's arrival brought no sign of interest. He walked up the gravel drive towards a white, imposing house with huge sash windows and manicured green lawns curving about it. He had read that it was eighteenth century, Grade II listed, and set in twelve acres, including woodland. To his left he could see a lake, framed by reeds and willows and beyond it a tennis court. There was clearly money to be made from biscuits; would they have servants?

The front door was oak, with a brass knocker posing as a fox's head. Swift knocked twice and waited. He recognised the petite woman who opened the door from the photo he had borrowed at Carmen's house.

'Mrs Langborne?'

'Yes. Can I help you?'

'My name's Tyrone Swift. I was hoping to see your husband. He knows me; we met recently.' He held out his ID.

She was wearing a short white pleated skirt, a cotton T-shirt and white trainers. It looked as if she was about to head to her tennis court.

'Is my husband expecting you?'

'No; I was in the area and there is something I'd like to check with him.'

'Swift,' she said. 'Oh, are you the gumshoe?' Her voice was soft and her accent held a hint of West Country.

'Well, I'm not American so I'm called a private detective.'

She looked past him. 'Where's your car?'

'I left it on the lane.'

'Oh.' This seemed to baffle her. 'Well, I don't know if Rupert is available. Perhaps you'd better come in and I'll speak to him.'

He stepped into a wide entrance hall with a central fireplace, black-and-white marble floor tiles and a staircase rising from the centre. It was panelled throughout in light oak.

'If you take a seat, I'll speak to my husband,' she said, gesturing at an embroidered chair.

She vanished through a door, her skirt swinging. Swift ignored the seat and examined the portraits hanging on the walls; they were of various gentry in eighteenth century costume and he wondered if they had come as a job lot with the house. He recognised a large oil painting over the fireplace of Lord Justice Langborne, wearing a black silk gown and wig and holding a tome, presumably legal. He looked imposing and authoritative. William Pennington was unlikely to have sat for his portrait. To the left of the fireplace hung a framed photograph, showing Daphne Langborne in a field with a minor royal whose name escaped Swift; behind them were the trappings of a country fair and a banner reading *Council for the Protection of Rural England*.

It was a good five minutes before he heard a heavy tread and Rupert Langborne appeared. He was dressed in mustard-coloured cords and a green checked shirt which emphasised his slight paunch. He looked annoyed.

'What are you doing, calling here uninvited?' he asked. 'It's most irregular.'

'I was driving nearby so I thought I'd take the opportunity. Sorry for the inconvenience, but it is important.'

'I'm extremely busy. You could ring me. In fact, why don't you do that on Monday?' He moved towards the front door.

Swift stayed where he was, by the fireplace. 'I'd rather we talked now. It's quite a delicate matter, not really suitable for the telephone. It would be best to be private.'

Langborne stared at him. 'What do you mean?'

Swift moved towards him. 'It's about William Pennington.'

There was a pause. Langborne looked sideways. 'I don't know what you're talking about.'

Swift left a silence. 'I think you do. I believe your stepmother talked to you about him.'

Langborne put his hands in his pockets and rocked on the balls of his feet. 'I honestly haven't a clue what you mean. I'm afraid you've had a wasted journey.' He opened the front door. His wife was crossing the gravel towards the tennis courts, racket in hand, another woman now by her side in a cream tunic and tennis shoes.

'Nice day for tennis,' Swift observed. 'I have the letter Mr Pennington wrote. If you won't speak to me, I'll have to take it to the police. I think you'd rather discuss it with me.'

Langborne looked up at the ceiling, then closed the door with the kind of exaggerated care that spoke of fury. 'Follow me to the garden room.'

They passed through a door at the rear of the hallway and along a narrower passage, past a dining room and library with a billiard table. The oak panelling was repeated everywhere and light spilled in where the ceilings had been exposed and skylights inserted in the roof. Langborne led the way into a wide conservatory that ran the full length of the back of the house. There were half a dozen cane chairs with plump cushions, a couple of full-length sun beds and a huge, elegant telescope on a glass topped table. A walled garden was now visible and several greenhouses. A middle-aged man with a wheelbarrow full of plants was plodding towards the garden. Hens were wandering around outside the conservatory, pecking and fussing. Langborne had a well-balanced life; Whitehall bureaucrat during the week, country squire at the weekend.

Langborne indicated a chair and sat opposite Swift. He placed his hands on his knees.

'Say what you've come to say.'

Swift reached into his pocket and passed across the copy he had made of Pennington's letter. 'I found this at your stepmother's house. I visited the hospice named at the top of the letter and then William Pennington at his home. He told me that Mrs Langborne had said she would consider speaking to you about it. I believe she did.'

Langborne looked at the letter, then threw it back. 'How did you get this rubbish?'

'It was tucked away in Mrs Langborne's house. I do wonder if you've been looking for it yourself; Mrs Farley told me you've been there a few times, checking the place.'

'You can believe what you like. You can't prove that my stepmother told me.'

Swift folded the letter and put it back in his pocket. He looked for a moment at the hens. 'Mr Langborne, you clearly knew about this letter when I mentioned it. You wouldn't bother speaking to me now if you were unaware of it. Your parentage is immaterial to me. I just want to find out what has happened to Mrs Langborne.'

Langborne had flushed at that 'parentage.' He pursed his mouth. 'This is no business of yours. I'm not interested in the ravings of a sick old man. My stepmother is a meddler and should have known better.'

There was a tension snaking from the man. Swift knew that Langborne would like to hit him. 'You must see that your knowledge of this letter would indicate you could have a motive for harming your stepmother.'

'Don't be utterly ridiculous and don't forget my profession; I've spent years dealing with risk and rumours at the highest level. That kind of drivel is a mere nuisance.'

'Hardly drivel if there's DNA proof. And why would William Pennington make this claim? He has nothing to gain from it.'

Langborne had regained control of himself. He sat upright. 'It's of no interest to me why Mr Pennington would say such things. Illness makes some people act strangely. As for DNA; who's to say it was my hair that was used? This is like some bad TV series and I suspect that's what Mr Pennington has been watching.'

'Have you told Florence about this?'

'No, of course not; why would I want to bother her with such nonsense?'

'I can see it's going to be a difficult conversation. Speaking of which, has Florence told you that she and Paul had asked your stepmother for a substantial loan and were questioned at a police station about her disappearance?'

Langborne settled his hands across his stomach. 'I haven't been told that. When did this occur?'

'So many secrets in your family. You'll have to ask Florence; after all, I'm just her employee at present.' Swift changed tack. 'Where were you on January thirty-first?'

'As I have already told the police, I was working here, at home.'

'That's unusual, isn't it? I thought you were in London during the week.'

'I sometimes work from home when I have a report to write.' He made his voice smooth. 'Now, I have spoken to you; you have come here uninvited, impugned my mother and insulted me and I have given you a hearing. I have nothing else to say. If you persist in hawking this letter about, I will put the matter in the hands of my solicitor.' He stood, indicating the door.

There were times when staying seated gave you the advantage. Swift looked up at him attentively. 'Mr Pennington has an album with half a dozen photos of you as a child; ones your mother sent him. Why would she send photos of you to a stranger? You do look very like him,' he said gently.

Langborne's jaw twitched. 'I want you to leave. I don't wish to see or hear from you again. You can leave by the back door.'

He slid back a wide glass door and stood by it. Swift rose slowly and exited. He turned as he stepped on to the gravel, hens scattering near his feet.

'William Pennington is your father and hasn't long to live. You might want to consider seeing him.'

He walked away. The door slammed, the hens clucking loudly in protest. Swift made his way back to the gates, stopping at the cottages. He knocked on both doors. There were no cars parked and no sign of habitation. He looked through the front windows, then went round the back. Both houses were furnished and spick and span, the gardens tended. He wondered if they were rented out; holiday homes, perhaps?

He opened the car roof and sat for a while, listening to silence broken only by occasional birdsong. He imagined that Langborne might already be on the phone, ringing friends in high places, including the Met. He had known about the letter; the question was, had he decided to do something about the bearer of news he didn't want to hear? Pennington was going to die anyway and Langborne didn't know about the information left with his solicitor so Carmen would have been the only real threat.

He started the engine and drove back to London, intending to make the most of the car for the rest of the day. An idea came to him and when he reached the city he headed for Holland Park and pumped coins into a parking meter. He googled stationers in the area and set off on foot to the one nearest Carmen's home. It was a small, stuffy shop and busy but Swift saw that there was a photocopier in a corner at the end of the counter. He waited until the queue had thinned and approached the young man behind the till.

'Hi; I wondered if you might be able to help me.' He took the photo of Carmen from his wallet. 'This lady lives near here and I wondered if she might have come in to do photocopying.'

Name badges were useful; this was Jeremy, looking at the photo and screwing up his mouth in that way people use to indicate deep thought.

'Don't think so but I'm only here Saturdays. Hang on.' He leaned backwards and shouted through a door. 'Sam, got a minute?'

A mature woman with huge glasses and a ponytail came out, cup in hand.

'Can't I even have a tea break?' she said jokingly, poking Jeremy in the ribs.

'Guy here wants to know if this lady's been in.'

Swift proffered the photo again, pointing to Carmen. 'I wondered if she had any photocopying done.'

Sam looked at the photo, then at Swift. 'You plain-clothes police or something?'

'I'm a private detective.' He showed his ID.

'Ooh, very cloak and dagger,' Sam said.

Several people had come in and were waiting in the small space.

'Well, do you recall her coming in here?'

'Jeremy, see to the customers, please.' Sam motioned to Swift to move to the end of the counter. 'Yes, she was here a couple of times.'

'Did she do her own copying?'

'No. Some people do, but she didn't know how to work the machine. I did some for her once or twice.'

'Do you remember what she was copying?'

'There was some charity stuff. We get lots of customers though, it's hard to remember.'

Swift took the letter from his pocket and held his hand over the body of the text, letting her see the hospice heading. 'Does this ring a bell?'

Sam peered, pushing her glasses down her nose. 'I think so, yes. That purple print and the clasped hands; yes, I'd say so.'

'Do you remember when she came in with it?'

'Now you're asking.' She reached for her cooling drink and sipped. 'Couple of months ago at least. Oh, hang on; just before Christmas. We were collecting for the Sally Army and she put a couple of pounds in.'

'Thanks, that's a big help.'

'Why are you asking, anyway?' Alert eyes focused through the jolly expression.

'Her name is Mrs Carmen Langborne. She's missing and I'm looking for her.'

'Oh, crumbs; that's awful. She was very polite, a real lady.'

'So I believe. Well, many thanks again.'

She reached along the counter and pushed a collecting tin under his nose.

'In return for my help, would you care to make a donation? We have a charity collection every month and this one is for Lifeboats.'

That seemed appropriate for a man who liked to spend time on the river. Swift slipped a couple of pound coins in and exited. Back in the car, he dialled Nora Morrow's number. When she answered he could hear shrieks in the background.

'Is this a bad time?'

'Well, I do have the odd day off, you know. Hang on.' There was a pause and she said, 'that's better. I'm at the lido with my nephews. At least you've saved me from being water-bombed for now.'

Swift brought her up to date on his information and his visit to Langborne. 'So if Carmen had this letter photocopied just before Christmas, that suggests that she told Langborne about it around that time; possibly when he went to see her at New Year.'

'Possibly. I'd guess that Langborne wasn't thrilled to see you.'

'No; denied even knowing about the letter but he clearly did. It gives him a strong motive for shutting her up.'

'Hmm. I still have the problem of no body.'

'He says he was working at home on January thirty-first. Did anyone back that up? His wife?'

'She was away at a conference about the countryside, somewhere near Bath. His diary checked out.'

'So he could have been anywhere. He could have been in London, dealing with his troublesome stepmother. It's only an hour's drive for him.'

She sighed. 'I can't see this having legs. To be honest, I'm pushed on this enquiry as it is, I haven't got the staff. I'll have to run it past my chief.'

'What about Lomar?'

'Nasty piece of work. We're charging him with assaulting a police officer but we have nothing else concrete at the moment. Tell you what; find me a body and I can do business.'

'Maybe you'd find a body if you visited Holly End; there's a lake, several empty cottages, woodland; plenty of choice.'

Nora laughed. 'Yeah, I can see me getting a warrant for that. Leave it with me. I have to get back to being bullied.'

Swift rang off, frustrated. He knew that this case would be low on Nora Morrow's radar; missing people always slid to the bottom of the heap. He drove to Tooting Bec, stopping at a garage for fuel and a couple of bananas and orange juice, which he consumed at the side of the forecourt, among the fumes. He could mainly taste oil. He fed another parking meter in the road where an Edward Boyce was supposed to live and looked for number sixty-one, flat 1A. It was a three-storey house on a corner, beside a bookie's. There was a raggedy garden with some sorry looking bushes and an empty bird feeder. A couple of bikes were padlocked to the railings and a tatty, sun faded poster in a front window admonished him to save whales. A removals van was parked near the house, its back doors open, showing bed frames and a fridge-freezer and the front door was propped wide open. Swift accepted the invitation and walked in to the hallway, finding the door to 1A halfway along. There was a bell and a slot for a name, which had been left empty.

A tall man, around his late twenties and with hard eyes the colour of concrete, answered the bell. He was wrapped in a grubby towel, his hair damp. His bare arms were thick and sinewy. He looked as if he'd had a late night. A stale, cheesy smell wafted out from the flat interior; it reminded Swift of the time he had kept white mice in his bedroom until his mother, unable to stand the foetid reek, had insisted that they be removed.

'Hi, sorry to bother you. I'm looking for a friend of mine, Ed Boyce. Haven't seen him for a while, thought I'd catch up as I was passing, have a few beers.'

'Oh, yeah, Ed.' The man adjusted his towel and shuffled his bare feet. One of his big-toe nails was blackened. 'He's not in right now, mate. Away for the weekend, yeah, that's it.'

'Oh, that's a shame. Still, I suppose I could catch him at Purple Spark Productions or Abode, that club he goes to.'

He nodded. 'Yeah, good thinking. He'll be at work on Monday, defo.'

There was a movement from inside the flat. A shadowy figure emerged, a thin younger man, carrying a mug and shaking his head in an agitated manner. His hair was shaved close to his scalp and there was a crusty sore on his lower lip. Hard eyes batted him away, told him sharply to get inside, he'd be in in a minute and waited until an inner door had closed before turning back.

Swift clicked his fingers. 'You must be the friend Ed mentioned he had staying with him; Terry, is it? Sorry, I'm rubbish at names.'

'Pete, that's me, mate.'

'That's right. Hope Ed has a good weekend. Where's he gone?'

The eyes glinted with annoyance. 'Oh, he didn't say, mate. Probably away with his girlfriend somewhere. Yeah, that's it.'

'Okay. Bye then.'

'See ya.'

Swift waited to one side as two men hefted a sofa down the stairs, marking the wall as they went. He was satisfied he had the right Ed Boyce and reckoned that he could have schooled his illegal tenant better in story-telling. He sat for a while in the car, watching the house. He didn't know why he was watching, other than he'd had a sniff of something more than unwashed bodies from Ed's flat. The removals firm finished their work and locked the doors of their van. The driver consulted a clipboard, then accelerated away. Shortly afterwards, Pete emerged from the house, accompanied by two men who kept their eyes down as they walked. One wore a beanie hat and tatty jeans. The other had a limp, his right foot twisted inward. Both wore flip-flops. Neither looked like the skinny man who had appeared earlier. Pete put two cigarettes in his mouth, lit them and handed them one each. He led them to a dark blue transit van; they climbed into the back while he took the driver's seat. When he had driven off, Swift returned to the flat and rang the bell. There was no reply so he rang again, several sharp bursts. The door opened a couple of inches and the shaven-headed man looked around the rim.

'Hi,' Swift said. 'I called and spoke to Pete a couple of minutes ago.'

The man's head shook, the veins in his scrawny neck standing out. 'Pete's not in.' He spoke in a soft monotone.

'Could I come in and wait for him?'

The man edged the door closed another inch. 'I don't let people in.'

'I'm sure Pete wouldn't mind. What's your name?'

There was a silence while he seemed to process the question. 'Billy.'

'Nice to meet you, Billy. I know Ed, who rents this flat to Pete. It would be fine to let me in. Pete won't mind.'

Billy rubbed a hand over his head and looked upwards. 'Pete says no one comes in.'

'I know, but that would be strangers. I'm a friend.'

There was another long pause until Billy said, 'You're a friend.'

'That's right. I'm a friend.'

Billy turned away and disappeared into the flat as if he had lost interest, leaving the door open. Swift stepped in, closing it behind him. There were two rooms opposite him, both with the curtains half drawn. The malodorous air made him gag. Billy had gone to sit on a mattress on the floor in the left-hand front room. He had picked up a magazine and took no notice as Swift walked into the room, then around the rest of the flat. There were two rooms with five mattresses crammed into the one Billy occupied. The larger, second room had a single bed, a wardrobe and chest of drawers and a plasma TV attached to the wall opposite the bed. There were some envelopes on top of the chest of drawers; Swift looked through them and saw a credit card statement for Peter Carmichael with nearly £2000 owing. Along the hall was a tiny, squalid bathroom and narrow galley kitchen, littered with takeaway cartons, dirty crockery and food wrappers. The rubbish bin had no lid and smelled as if something had crawled into it and died. A circle of fat flies danced above it.

Swift returned to where Billy sat, looking at a magazine filled with glossy photos of motor bikes. The room's woodchip walls were painted a dingy yellow and were bare, with marks and patches where pictures or ornaments had hung previously. The floor had thin, stained brown carpet squares, of the type usually found in offices. The mattresses had no sheets, just sleeping bags and there was barely room to step between them. There was no other furniture or fixtures. Small piles of clothes lay under a radiator by the window. Swift squatted down near Billy; he didn't know what kind of disability the man had but he seemed to respond to brief statements.

'Billy, you work with Pete,' he guessed.

After a silence, filled with the sound of a fly throwing itself against the window, Billy said, 'Yes.'

'Pete doesn't pay you. He lets you and your friends live here.'

Billy continued to stare at the same page. 'Yes.'

'There are five of you.'

'Hmm.'

Swift thought about the van. 'You work at people's houses, doing driveways and gutters, odd jobs.'

Billy started humming. Swift waited, breathing through his mouth. Finally Billy nodded.

'Pick fruit soon,' he said.

'Okay. Pete looks after you. He gives you cigarettes and food.'

Billy brought the magazine close to his face. 'I like chips.' He started to hum again, rocking his torso back and forth.

Swift wondered where Carmichael had garnered his serfs from, suspecting the streets or homeless shelters. He wanted to ask Billy how he had come to the flat but thought he might be getting distressed and he had seen and heard enough. He rose to his feet.

'Bye, Billy, good to meet you.'

Before he left he picked up a newspaper lying on a mattress and killed the bluebottle at the window.

* * *

Swift returned Cedric's car to Milo's garage, where it was parked alongside Milo's ancient Vespa, which he could no longer use but kept for sentimental reasons. Back in his office, he considered phoning Mark Gill or Mary but decided to dial 999; as far as he was concerned, slavery was an emergency. He gave details of what he had seen at the Tooting flat and Carmichael's name and a description. He advised that he had previously worked with the Met and Interpol and dropped in Mary Adair's name for good measure. At that point, he was passed to a more senior colleague who assured him that the information would be acted on within twenty-four hours. He then emailed Rachel Breen, giving her the address of the flat and confirming that Ed had a tenant called Peter Carmichael. He explained why he had called the police, adding that Ed was in for a bit of a shock. Over to her and her solicitor to make the most of it, he told her, attaching his final bill. He thought for a moment about his next call, then rang Florence Davenport. Her greeting was not unfriendly so he gauged that her brother hadn't been in touch since the morning.

'Just thought I'd give you an update,' he said. 'I discovered that your stepmother had annoyed a man called Vincent Lomar; she was instrumental in causing his wife to be sacked from the home she stayed at in Kingston upon Thames last year.'

'What home?' she asked vaguely.

'It's called Lilac Grange. I did mention it to you when I came to see you last time.'

'Oh yeah. Sorry, things were a bit hairy.'

'Yes. The police have questioned Mr Lomar and will question him again.'

'They think he has something to do with Carmen's disappearance?'

'They don't know as yet. He would seem to have a reason and he has a previous police record.'

'Oh well, I suppose it's something.'

'Has your brother been in touch with you recently?'

'No, why?'

'You haven't told him about Paul being questioned?'

'No, I haven't. It's irrelevant and he's a busy man.'

'I saw him today. Something came up in my enquiries that I needed to ask him about.'

Her voice lifted sharply. 'Oh, what's that?'

'I don't think it's my place to tell you, it's a bit delicate. You might want to contact him.'

'What are you on about?'

'As I said, I think it's best you contact him. I have to go now; I'll be in touch if I have any news.'

He ended the call and allowed himself a tiny sneak of satisfaction. That should put the cat among the pigeons. It was almost seven o'clock and a fine evening. He checked the tide and saw that it was low so he decided to head for the river. He ran upstairs and changed, ate an apple and filled his water bottle. At the club, which was still open, he checked his boat. As the light would be failing on his return, he attached two white lights on his stern and bow.

He rowed as far as Barnes, spotting several black swans and a great crested grebe and chicks, then made his return journey as dusk approached. In the dimming light, with no one else on the river, the only sound the lapping of the water, he might have been alone in the world. He thought about Langborne; if he was responsible for Carmen's disappearance, he couldn't have effected it in her house as there was no evidence to suggest she had been harmed there. If he was alone at home on January 31, he could have invited her there. There might have been an argument; certainly it was a place that offered plenty of options for disposing of a body.

He was still mulling over this scenario as he pulled his boat up the ramp. He unlocked the boathouse and stowed the boat, towelling his face and neck. He secured the door, bending to the lock in the semi-darkness and had just sensed that someone was approaching when a heavy blow caught him behind his ear. As he fell to the ground, he smelled fish and heard shouting and the sound of running feet. A hard kick landed in his back and he had a sudden desire to vomit.

CHAPTER 10

Mary and Cedric were sitting on either side of Swift's hospital bed. He was propped high on pillows and drinking water. He had been lucky; he had a bruise on his right temple and a fracture at the base of his skull but no swelling or brain damage. His lower back ached where his assailant had delivered that hard kick. He had to stay in hospital for twenty-four hours.

'How are you feeling?' Mary asked.

'Not too bad, considering. I have what's called a simple linear fracture. They told me I mustn't blow my nose; isn't it odd, the minute you're told you can't do something, you feel the need to do it.'

'I don't like to think what might have happened if we hadn't come on the scene,' Cedric said, patting his hand. He looked pale and upset. 'If only we'd been able to get a good look at the chap who did it, but he sped away as soon as he heard us.'

Cedric and Milo had saved him from further blows, emerging from the side alley that led from the pub. It was their shouts he had heard as he fell.

'Did you get a look at him, Ty?' Mary asked.

He remembered just in time not to shake his head. 'No. It all happened in a split second. He must have been hanging around near the club. I wonder what he hit me with.' He smiled a watery smile at Cedric. 'Makes a change for me to be in here, rather than you or Milo.'

They stayed a little while longer. He was glad when they left; his head was aching and he wanted to think. A nurse brought him some more painkillers and warned him again about not blowing his nose, which reminded him that he wanted to. He lay, eyes closed, replaying the scene. The local police had been to see him but he had told the constable he had no idea who could have attacked him. As soon as he had come round, he had recalled the pungent odour of fish and knew that it had been Lomar. The thought of Charisse and what might rebound on her had stopped him speaking. Lomar was going to be done for assaulting a police constable anyway and Swift doubted he would come back and try to finish what he had started. He groaned; he was already frustrated at this enforced inactivity and oddly, his thigh was aching where he had previously been stabbed, as if coming out in sympathy with his head. When another nurse came back to check his temperature he mentioned this and she told him it was a wound memory, the body recalling previous shocks.

'You lead an interesting life,' she observed; 'stabbings and assaults. A bit like working in A & E on a Saturday night. What do you do?'

'I'm a private detective.'

'Really? My uncle used one of those to check on his wife, and they ran off together.'

'The detective and your uncle?'

'You know what I mean; the detective and the wife.'

'Life's hazardous, isn't it?'

She made a note on his chart. 'Yours seems to be. You get some rest while you can.'

Cedric had brought in his laptop and he spent twenty minutes looking up inheritance law. He then slept for several hours, until around six thirty, when he saw Nora Morrow walking towards him.

'This is an honour,' he said.

She was dressed in a black-and-green Lycra gym kit, her hair held back under a bandeau. She looked disgustingly fit and he was conscious of his own feebleness. She sat and fished a bag of peaches out of her rucksack.

'Here, these look tasty. Don't get excited; I'm here to tell you off, as much as to wish you well.'

'Good cop, bad cop?'

'Ha-ha. Your sense of humour hasn't been traumatised, anyway. How long are you in here for?'

'Another night. Then I'm supposed to rest; I should be a hundred per cent within a couple of days.'

She gestured at the peaches. 'Mind if I have one? It'll keep me going through an hour at the gym.'

'Help yourself. Any news on the case?'

She chewed on a peach, looking at him, crossing her legs. 'No body, if that's what you mean. Lomar did this to you, didn't he?'

Swift raised his shoulders a fraction. It didn't hurt. 'I don't know, I didn't see.'

'Hmm, so I understand. It would add up, don't you think? Seems an odd venue for a random mugging. I could pull him in again.'

'That's up to you. Don't do it on my account.'

'Sir Galahad, eh?' Nora said knowingly. She reached for the box of tissues on his cupboard, wiped her mouth and hands and aimed the peach stone expertly at the bin.

'Have you spoken to Langborne?' Swift asked.

'No. Langborne, however, has been speaking to people, as I've no doubt you expected. Top people. My phone was red hot. I've been instructed to leave him alone and to tell you the same.'

Swift eased himself up a little on the pillows. 'Come on, he has clear reason to be hostile to Carmen, given what she knew, given that letter. I've been checking inheritance law and a question over his paternity could possibly affect his share in the Holland Park house, especially if Florence wanted to cause trouble. Given that there seems to be no love lost between them, she might well do. Did you get the copy of the letter I scanned to you?'

'Yes and all very interesting. But . . . I'm under orders. I've passed yours on. You know, it might have been better if you hadn't gone to see him, and left it to me.'

'But you're so busy and understaffed,' he replied sweetly. 'Maybe Langborne had me beaten up.'

'Not his style. He'd be more subtle. Your boat would mysteriously sink in the middle of the river.'

'Is Charisse Lomar okay?'

'As far as I know. I've got to go now and burn some muscle.'

'Thanks for coming.'

'Yeah. Don't go blundering around any further, Swift; certainly not on Langborne's territory. You could nix any chance of finding Mrs Langborne, if he is involved. I'm not going to forget about him but it has to be a softly-softly approach.'

He didn't buy it and he was annoyed that she was standing over him and he was on his back with a throbbing head, in a ridiculous pair of pyjamas covered in bluebirds that belonged to Cedric. 'But you've got your instructions, *from the top.*'

'Oh, take your medication and meddle with something else,' she snapped, striding away.

In the doorway she almost collided with a small, vigorous figure in a floral print dress, carrying a hessian shopping bag. Swift's heart sank; Joyce was all he needed. The worst thing about being in hospital wasn't the injury that had put you there or the hardness of the mattress or the stultifying atmosphere; it was having to accept visitors, whether you wanted them or not.

'Tyrone, my dear!' she said, bending to kiss his cheek, her necklace catching his ear lobe. 'What on earth has happened? I came as soon as I heard.'

'Joyce,' he said heavily. 'How did you know I was here?'

She pulled up the chair Nora had just vacated, loosening the belt on her dress and starting to take items from her deep bag.

'I rang Cedric to thank him for his birthday card and he told me what happened. He sounded very worried. So naturally, I came straight away. Now, I've brought you some bottled water, fruit juice, apples, tissues, hand sanitiser and books.'

He looked at the stuff she was heaping on to his bed. One of the apples rolled out of its bag on to the floor. He could see three hefty thrillers, a short-story omnibus and a colouring book for adults with a packet of felt tips attached. Joyce tapped it and he knew she was about to explain the obvious.

'These are very popular right now. They're supposed to be soothing and absorbing. There was such a huge choice but I got these mandala patterns.'

'So I see. This is very kind of you but I'm only here until tomorrow, you know.'

She patted his hand and retrieved the apple. 'Well, better to have too much than too little. You can take the books home and have a good read while you recuperate. That's a bad bruise. Are you in much pain?'

'No, just tired now.'

Being Joyce, she was impervious to the hint. 'I always think being in hospital is so isolating. Now, when you're discharged would you like to come and stay with me for a couple of days? I'm sure you shouldn't be on your own and although Cedric is upstairs, he can't really be expected to do too much. It won't take me two shakes to get your room ready.' She beamed at him hopefully.

'That's kind but, really, I'll be fine. I'm not an invalid, just a bit bruised.'

'Now, Tyrone, you should let yourself be looked after sometimes. You're an independent man, I know, but there are times when—'

'Joyce.' He sat up as straight as he could manage. 'No. Thank you but no.'

She sighed. 'Oh well, if you're sure . . . I could pop round and do some shopping for you, make a few meals?'

'Again, that's very kind but I'll be fine.'

She looked away, scanning the other beds, then arranged the apples on top of his table. 'You're a difficult person to help, Tyrone.'

'Am I? Perhaps, but I manage.'

She shook her head, then settled back in the chair and told him how much she had enjoyed her party, running through the gifts she had received, talking about people he didn't know. After ten minutes he told her he needed to go to the bathroom, and then he thought he might get some sleep.

'It's been a long day, I'm exhausted. So good of you to come, though.'

She walked out with him, still talking about someone called Roderick and how his wife was in a coma after falling down some steps on a visit to a stately home.

'Now, you will let me know if you don't feel well once you get home?' she said as he opened the door to the men's toilets.

'I will,' he lied, kissing her proffered cheek, backing away from her. He watched to make sure she was exiting through the swing doors, and then splashed his face with running cold water.

Back in the ward, feeling ill humoured, he switched on his phone. It was the first time he'd checked it since the attack. There was a message from Rachel Breen, thanking him for the information about Ed Boyce; one from Poppy Forsyth, saying it would be good to catch up; and one from Mike Farrell at the hospice. He said he thought that Swift might like to know that Mr Pennington had passed away that afternoon. Swift stared up at the ceiling, glad that the ailing man had got his wish. His phone rang. It was Mary.

'Hi,' she said, 'have you been resting?'

'Not much choice.'

'You sound grumpy.'

'I am. Joyce has just been to see me. She brought me a colouring book. And these pyjamas are ridiculous.'

Mary giggled. 'You should buy some and keep them in case of emergencies. How did Joyce know you're in hospital?'

'Cedric told her.'

'Ah, the grapevine. Listen, I'm about to add to your grumpiness. I need to tell you that I've been on the receiving end of phone calls from Whitehall and Met royalty. You've upset Rupert Langborne, I gather.'

Swift gave her a summary of recent events. 'I've already had a warning from Nora Morrow,' he told her.

'Well, do heed it, Ty. I know, I know; why should some people be able to put pressure on the law et cetera, et cetera. I don't like it much either. But then there's reality and with no body, there's no reason to pursue him.'

'There never will be a body unless someone tries to find it.'

'Well, I've told you what I have to. You're your own man but for goodness sake, get better before you work again. Enjoy your colouring in.'

He accepted some mushroom soup for supper, then ate two peaches to get rid of the gritty taste. An email arrived from Ruth, confirming that she could meet tomorrow. He had lost track of time and forgotten that it was Sunday. He replied, confirming he would see her at one. When the nurse who had taken his temperature came to offer him a sleeping tablet, he told her he would be leaving by ten in the morning at the latest.

She looked astonished. 'That will be up to the registrar,' she said.

'No; I think it's up to me,' he smiled. 'Oh by the way, would you like this for the nurses' station? It might pass the time on night shifts.' He handed her the colouring book.

'Thanks; these are all the rage, but they're not cheap.' She flipped the pages, sending a welcome breeze his way.

'So I believe.'

He turned off his reading light when she'd gone and eased onto his side, looking forward to some restored liberty.

* * *

He took a taxi back to the house the following morning. Other than a slight headache and an intermittent soreness in his back, he felt better, less fragile. Hungry after the nauseating hospital fare, he ate cereal and toast and savoured three cups of strong coffee. Cedric was out so he left a message to say he was back and put the eye-catching pyjamas in the wash.

Ruth was ten minutes late and rushed in apologetically, saying one of her students had needed extra help with an essay. She looked at him anxiously as she took her seat.

'What's happened to you? That's a nasty bruise.'

He explained, deciding to order a fruit juice rather than wine. The packet containing his painkillers advised no alcohol.

She took his hand. 'I hate not knowing what's happened to you in between these meetings. But shouldn't you be at home, resting up?'

He looked down at her fingers, the nails short; he could see she still chewed the skin at the side of her thumb. She wore no adornments, no jewellery. She didn't need to add to her beauty.

'I'm all right,' he said. 'Never mind me; you look a bit watery-eyed.'

'Oh, just been on the run, you know.'

She said she wasn't very hungry and chose a plain omelette, with water to drink. She crumbled some dry bread and nibbled it while they exchanged news. When they were eating, she suddenly put her fork down and said she had to go to the loo, rushing away. Her omelette lay on her plate, barely touched. She was gone for more than five minutes and when she returned her face was waxy. She pushed the plate away.

'Sorry, I can't eat any more.'

'What is it? A gastric bug?'

She sipped water, holding her stomach, as if monitoring its progress. Cradling the glass in both hands, she looked at him.

'I'm pregnant, Ty. I found out a fortnight ago. I've been chucking up every day.'

'Well . . . congratulations. I didn't know you were planning a family; you hadn't mentioned it.'

'We weren't; at least not after Emlyn's diagnosis. But then, it's some hope for the future, a child; a refusal to be beaten. Sorry, I have to be sick again.'

He felt as if Lomar had come back and hit him again. He couldn't face what was left of his pasta. He forced himself to check his thoughts and feelings, realising that he had assumed Ruth wouldn't have children, knowing that he felt it as a blow because it cemented her marriage. And why shouldn't it, he chided himself; a marriage should be as solid as cement anyway. What had he been hoping: that Ruth would leave Emlyn, exhausted by what their life had become and turn up at his door? He told himself he was a fool, that these meetings were a betrayal of Emlyn and himself, and he needed to end them.

Krystyna, the waitress, came up to him, looking anxious. 'Is the lady okay? She doesn't seem well.'

'She has morning sickness,' he told her.

'Oh, that's awful; my sister had it bad. But congratulations to you both!'

She went away, humming and he realised she thought he was the father. He couldn't feel any cheaper.

When Ruth came back she was shivering. At least, she said feebly, there couldn't be anything left to bring up. He said she must get home and called her a taxi. Krystyna held the door open for them, nodding and smiling. At Victoria he saw her, as usual, as far as the ticket barrier.

'Sorry about this, I was looking forward to seeing you.'

'Well, it's momentous news. Look after yourself and the baby; sit near the loo on the train. Make sure you get a taxi at Brighton.'

'Don't kiss me,' she said, 'I must smell of sick.'

He ignored the instruction and pressed his lips to her cheek. When she had gone, he went into a bar and, ignoring his medication, had a large brandy. On the way home, he rang Poppy Forsyth; if he was going to feel self-disgust he might as well add to it, use the Dutch courage from the drink and get it all over with.

'Hi, Poppy, thanks for your message.'

'Hi there, hon, good to hear you, how are you doing?'

'I'm okay. Listen; I don't want to mess you around. I can't meet up again just now.'

There was a silence. 'Oh,' she said flatly. 'Any particular reason?'

'I just have some things going on in my life that I need to sort out, some complications. It's not . . .'

'No. Don't say, "it's not you, it's me," that would be too clichéd. It's fine, see you around maybe.'

You couldn't get the satisfaction of slamming a mobile phone down but he knew Poppy would have if it were possible. He was a little sad and relieved. At home, he felt tiredness creep over him so he stood for a long time under a hot shower and tidied up, putting out the rubbish. He checked in with Cedric, returning the damp pyjamas for his tumble dryer but left quickly, not feeling up to conversation. He made coffee, took another painkiller and was going to sit in the garden but it had started to rain so he slumped in the living room, feeling jaded and jittery. He started to write an email to Ruth, saying that he didn't think they should meet again but stopped after the third sentence and deleted it. He at least owed it to her to say it in person. He switched on the radio and listened to a man singing with a nightingale, the voice lilting to the bird's melody. His thoughts turned to Langborne, his old boy network, his patronising air, his belief that he could make difficulties disappear by ringing the right people. He searched for Langborne's Knightsbridge address on the web, suspecting it wouldn't be in the public domain, using credits to access a site where he could find it.

* * *

Langborne's flat was in a secure mansion block two streets away from Harrods, a four-storey red-brick building. Swift arrived there at six thirty and scrutinised the bells on the handsome double front doors. He rang number forty but there was no reply. He crossed back over the street and waited until he saw a woman laden with shopping bags exit from a taxi and open the door with a key. He quickly came up beside her, holding the door for her, nodding cheerily, one resident to another. She smiled and said something in a language he didn't recognise, then tottered away on high heels through doors on the left of the wide lobby. Swift checked the map of the building, which was placed conveniently by the lift, then rode up to the fourth floor. The corridors were wide and deeply carpeted, walls covered in cream embossed paper, small tables holding vases of flowers at either end. There was a deep hush, no noise allowed to penetrate from the grimy streets. The air was stifling and dense; he had a sense of people waiting behind doors, looking through their spyholes when the world intruded. You could murder someone in one of these cocooned apartments and their screams would be muffled by the thick walls. He rang the bell on Langborne's door because it was there, but he wasn't in. Swift walked up and down the corridor a few times, then sat on the carpet by the door, took an *Evening Standard* from his pocket and read it from cover to cover. When he heard the lift he stood, pretending to use his phone, nodding at the couple who exited, taking their briefcases and weariness home for the night.

At seven fifteen the lift hummed and Langborne stepped out, dressed in a flowing calf-length tweed coat, carrying an umbrella and with a Harrods shopping bag in his hand. He saw Swift as soon as he turned from the lift and came towards him, shaking his head.

'Mr Swift, I didn't expect to see you loitering here.'

'You might be able to give the Met instructions but I'm not so biddable.'

'So I see. Well, excuse me for not asking you in but yet again, you haven't been invited. Looking at that bruise, maybe you've been intruding somewhere else as well. Perhaps you were the kind of child who turned up for birthday parties without an invitation?' He took his key and inserted it in the lock.

Swift leaned against the wall. 'I thought you might like to know that your father died yesterday.'

Langborne left his key dangling and stood, looking at the floor. He sighed like a teacher who is having to repeat instructions to a wayward class. He put the Harrods bag down, then did his routine of swaying on the balls of his feet.

'Please spare yourself the bother, Mr Swift. I'm not going to be drawn on the matter.'

Swift decided to take a punt on guess work. 'I think you saw your stepmother on January thirty-first; possibly in Berkshire. Mrs Farley said she seemed in an upbeat mood around that time. I've clarified that she had your father's letter photocopied just before Christmas and I believe she showed you the letter when she next saw you, on New Year's Day. I expect she agreed to give you time to think about it; even she would realise it was a shock. By the end of January, she had decided, with that rigid moral compass of hers that the truth had to come out. Being righteous makes some people cheerful, doesn't it? And Mrs Langborne was a little bored and lonely quite a lot of the time. Knitting doesn't afford much drama; your suddenly revealed paternity must have spiced her days up no end.'

Langborne's control was admirable but his jaw was working from side to side. He picked up his carrier bag, opened the lock and looked at Swift.

'I am going to make myself supper. If you haven't left this building within five minutes, I'll call the police.' He shook the umbrella as he closed the door, spraying Swift with raindrops.

Swift's head was aching again, albeit mildly. He decided to call it a day, knowing that as long as Langborne presented a blank facade, there was very little chance of unearthing any information. At least he'd had the satisfaction of annoying him. A sudden spasm rippled through his lower back as he walked to the lift and he stood for a minute by the wall, massaging it and stretching.

At home, he microwaved a bowl of his soup, ate a lump of cheese, and brewed coffee. Then he lay on the sofa, watching a documentary about the moon. He dozed off halfway through until he was woken by his phone ringing.

'Is that Mr Swift?'

'Speaking.' His throat was dry and he reached for his cold coffee dregs.

'Oh, hi. You came into our shop a couple of days ago. You were asking about Mrs Langborne and her photocopying.'

'Yes. Is that Sam?'

'That's me. Well, I kept that card you left and I thought I'd let you know that one of my part-time girls said something today that might interest you.'

'Go on.'

'I mentioned to her that we'd had a private detective in about Mrs Langborne and her being missing. Doesn't happen every day! Well, Lauren, that's her name, only works three days a week and around the end of January I had a week off, went to Tenerife. Lauren said that Mrs Langborne had dropped some charity leaflet off for photocopying on January thirtieth and Lauren said she'd pop them round when she'd had a chance to do them. We like to go that extra mile for our customers. The shop was ever so busy so she didn't do them till the next day. She lives near Earl's Court and she's got a little car so she dropped them off at Mrs Langborne's about half four that evening, the thirty-first. She's definite that was the date because it was her brother's birthday and she was going on to dinner with him that evening.'

'Did she ring or knock?'

'Hang about, I'm getting to the really interesting bit; well, I think so anyway. She didn't ring the bell, just pushed the envelope through the letterbox. Her car was parked up the road a bit and when she went to drive off she saw a woman going into Mrs Langborne's.'

'Not Mrs Langborne.'

'No. Now, I knew this might be important so I got her to write down what she could remember.' Sam spoke more slowly, reading. "It was a tall woman in a cream-coloured mac. Her hair was short and dark. I didn't see her face because her back was to me but she had a bag with long straps and she was letting herself in with keys."'

Swift gripped the phone. 'This Lauren, she's quite sure about this, about the date and time?'

'Oh, she's very reliable, Lauren and as I said, it was her brother's birthday. You don't get that kind of thing wrong, do you? Well, women don't anyway. You men are sometimes unreliable from that point of view.'

Swift took Lauren's name and phone number. He thanked Sam for the call and immediately rang Lauren, who cheerfully confirmed what he had been told.

'Me and Sam were ever so upset,' she said. 'We sort of remembered news about someone going missing back then but we didn't put two and two together. I mean, you're not expecting that kind of thing, are you?'

She sounded just like Sam; Swift wondered if it was coincidence or if working together made them pick up each other's speech patterns.

'Will I have to talk to the police?' she went on eagerly.

'I expect so. Leave it with me for now.'

'So do you think she's been murdered, this lady?'

'I don't know. Don't talk to anyone else about this for now. I'll be back in touch with you, or the police will.'

He ended the call and paced around the room. It had been in front of him all the time; those keys of Ronnie's, the bunch he had seen at Carmen's house, sitting by the bag with long straps. He recalled her shaking out her cream-coloured mac, smoothing the creases. What reason would she have to harm Carmen? He thought of her height and vigour; she would have had the strength to overpower the much smaller woman. He made fresh coffee and sat for a long time, allowing his memory to snake back over all the conversations he'd had since that first encounter with Florence Davenport. He thought of Ronnie, sitting in charge of the house, accessing it whenever she wanted, sneaking drinks, baking, lounging in the garden, making herself at home. She had possibly been playing him all along, feeding him misinformation about Carmen's mood, sending him along paths she wanted him to walk. He fetched his notes and read them until he was so exhausted that he dragged himself to bed and crashed out fully clothed on top of the duvet.

CHAPTER 11

Swift rang the bell of Carmen's house, just after ten the following morning. There was no reply so he tried Ronnie's phone; it switched to answerphone and he rang off. He sat on one of the steps in the sun and phoned Florence.

'Florence, hi, I'm at your stepmother's, looking for Mrs Farley, I wanted to speak to her. This is one of her days for working here.'

'Well, you won't find her there; Rupert's sacked her.'

'When did this happen?'

'Couple of days ago. He goes in now and again to check on things and said he found her at the sherry. He reckons she's been stealing; drink and some ornaments. He told her he'd get the police in unless she went straight away. I thought you knew; last time you rang, you told me in that oblique way you have that I ought to speak to him about something.'

Swift touched his bruise, which had decided to throb. 'What about the cats?'

'Rupe organised for one of those animal charities to take them. Listen, I was going to call you today; I don't think there's much point in you carrying on with looking for Carmen. You haven't really come up with anything and the police have told me they can't find any evidence about that guy they questioned. If you send me your bill I'll settle up with you.'

'Has Rupert suggested you end my services?'

'No, although I can't say he's sounded too impressed with you.'

'So, what about your stepmother?'

'I'll just have to leave it to the police. I have to dash and pick Helena up from playgroup. Email me your bill.'

'Hang on; before you go, have you got a home address for Mrs Farley?'

'Ahm, I think so. Why do you need to see her?'

'Just a few loose ends.'

'Well . . . if you want to waste your time. Here it is: 3 Carlisle Court, somewhere around Notting Hill. Bye now.'

Not even an attempt at a thank you, Swift thought. He stood and looked up at the empty, silent house and the two door locks that needed those substantial keys. He googled the address he had been given and saw that it was just off Westway. It was time, he thought, that he had a look at Ronnie's home turf. He bought a coffee and waited for a bus, taking one painkiller. The bus crawled along in heavy traffic up to Ladbroke Grove, dropping him outside the tube station. He breathed in the fumes and stepped into the crush of shoppers and tourists heading to and from Portobello Road. He walked under the flyover and in the direction of Westbourne Park. Despite the crowds, he always thought that London was at its best in late spring with white and pink cherry blossom covering trees and sprinkling the pavements; a photo in the free paper he had read on the bus called it 'nature's own confetti' which was twee but accurate.

Carlisle Court was in a cul-de-sac on the left, a block of maisonettes with balconies and a row of shops beneath; launderette, newsagent, minimart. There was a small fenced children's play area with hedging around it. Ronnie's place was on the first floor and as he would have expected, had gleaming windows, front door and paintwork. He had to ring the bell several times before she answered through an intercom, her voice muffled.

'Ronnie? Hi, it's Tyrone Swift. There's something I need to check with you. Florence Davenport gave me your address.'

'Hang on a wee min, I was having a wash.'

He waited for five minutes, looking down on people going to and from the shops, thinking how much pleasanter this social housing was than that occupied by the Lomars. He turned when he heard the door opening. Ronnie was dressed in a fresh white T-shirt and linen trousers and wearing lipstick, but her eyes were bloodshot, her hair flattened at the sides. A wave of alcohol washed towards him. She looked as if she hadn't slept much.

'I'm sorry to disturb you,' he said. 'I did try to ring.'

'That's okay. Come away in.'

She led the way up a flight of stairs to a small landing with four doors leading off it; the one on the left was open into the living room. Although it was a warm day, the windows were closed and the air reeked of cigarette smoke and alcohol.

'Sit you down' she said, seating herself in an armchair with an oval table beside it. It held an ashtray and burning cigarette which she reached for and put between her lips.

Swift sat in an upright chair. The room was sparsely furnished with three single chairs, a TV and a small melamine dining table in the corner by the balcony window. There was one slim white bookshelf with a clock, a couple of photographs and several copies of *The Lady*. The wall next to him had a vintage railway poster of a stag standing among hills with the legend beneath, SCOTLAND FOR YOUR HOLIDAYS. It seemed he wasn't going to be offered coffee or cake.

'I'm sorry to hear you lost your job at Mrs Langborne's; Florence told me when I phoned her.'

'Aye, well; it was going to end soon enough anyway. I never got on with Rupert; he was just lookin' for an excuse to fire me. It's the pussycats I feel sorry for. I wouldnae be surprised if he had them put down, he's a callous one.'

'If Mrs Langborne comes back home, she'll be extremely upset.'

She gave him a neutral stare and pulled deeply on the stub of her cigarette before she squashed it into the ashtray. 'Aye, she will. That'll be Rupert's problem.' She tipped another cigarette out of a packet and lit up.

'Will you be getting another job to replace Mrs Langborne?'

'We'll see. I've a bit put by and my other clients. I might rest my tired feet a wee while. So, what can I do for yez anyway?'

He wondered if she had already been drinking that morning or if her terseness and slight slurring was a leftover of the night before. There was no sign of a bottle or glass but he suspected she had been tidying up while he was waiting outside.

'You remember January thirty-first?'

'Aye, of course.' Her accent had broadened under the influence of the booze.

'When you let yourself into Mrs Langborne's house late that afternoon, did you see an envelope on the floor?'

She sucked on her cigarette, her hand jerking a little. 'What you on about? I wasn't there that day, remember?'

He shook his head. 'Someone saw you going in there at about four thirty.'

She raised her eyebrows. 'That's not right. What someone?'

'The person who delivered the envelope. They saw you from their car.'

'Nah; that's a load of hooey. I was home here, where I usually am, watching telly.'

Swift picked up a shell from a grouping on the window ledge, stroking its ridged surface. 'Why did Rupert sack you?'

She attempted to smile at him but it was more of a grimace, a tightening of the lips; nothing remained of the old Ronnie with the welcoming manner in her borrowed Holland Park empire. She was good at pulling the wool over people's eyes, he had to hand her that; yet he sensed that fooling him hadn't afforded her a malicious pleasure but had been more of a necessity.

'Och, he went on about some ornaments vanishing. I don't know what he was talking about. He was just looking for an excuse. I got those shells in Bournemouth many a year ago. A lovely afternoon on the beach it was. Happier days. When I was little I used to believe you could hear the sound of the sea from inside a shell; you know, if you held a big one to your ear. It was my da told me that. The fibs children get told! He told me as well, my da, that they made blue cheese by putting maggots in it. I didn't touch it for years.' She smiled to herself, then sighed. 'Ach, you can tell children all kinds of tales and they'll believe you. Did you get told those kinds of porkies, Ty?'

Swift stood and looked out at the balcony with its handsome, flower-filled tubs and carefully placed stone frogs and birds. Keeping her external world in order must help her control an inner chaos. He sat again and gave her a smile back.

'I think only the usual stories about witches and leprechauns and fairies. I knew they were make-believe.'

She nodded. 'I must have been more gullible. Maybe it's in the genes; aye, maybe that's it.'

'I think you've lost me Ronnie; you've drifted away somewhere. Speaking of porkies, I think you've been telling me some. I'm not sure now about Mrs Langborne having a gentleman friend. I'm not at all sure about quite a few of the things you've told me. I don't know why you've been spinning your stories but I'll concede you're good at it. I believe it was you at Mrs Langborne's that evening of the thirty-first. I was hoping you'd tell me why you were there.'

'Would you like a wee drink? A whisky? I've a Highland malt, good and smoky.'

'It's a bit early for me.'

'I'll have one, then. Yes, I think I'll have a little drinky.' She rose and opened a cupboard, taking out a bottle and glass and bringing them to the small table. She poured a good measure, slopping it a little and raised it, saying 'slainte!' Swallowing a gulp, she breathed heavily through her nose and pointed a finger at him. 'Did you know, Ty, there are songs about Tyrone, the place in Ireland? My granma used to sing them. She came over from Omagh to pick spuds, met my granda and stayed in Aberdeen. Her favourite was called "The Emigrant's Farewell."' She held the glass to the light and looked at it, then sang in a tuneful, vibrant voice:

Fare thee well my native green clad hills
Fare thee well my shamrock plains
Ye verdant banks of sweet Lough Neagh
With your silvery winding streams
Though far from home in green Tyrone
From where you and I did stray
I adore you Killycolpy
Where I spent my youthful days.

She caught some ash in her hand and deposited it in the ashtray, then poured herself another half tumbler of whisky.

'You've a good voice,' he said.

'Thank you, kind sir. You're all right, y'know Ty, a braw min. Nicer than that bastard Rupert. My granma would have said he'd take the pin out of an orphan's bib. Mean, y'know.'

'You know something about Mrs Langborne, don't you, Ronnie? Maybe you know what's happened to her.'

She blinked, patted her chest and said in that careful way that drinkers have of choosing their words, 'Now, Ty dear, I could tell you that I went to the house that evening cos I'd forgot something and I saw Mrs L lying dead on the floor with a knife stuck through her and the murderer running away out the back. But I didn't!' She laughed. 'Did I get your hopes up?'

'No, Ronnie, you didn't.' Swift went to the photos and pointed at one of her with a young boy, a teenager. Ronnie had her arm hooked through his and was looking at him, smiling. 'This is a lovely photo. Who are you with?'

'That's ma son.'

'What's his name?'

'Liam.'

'Oh, I thought you said you don't have any family here in London.'

She rubbed her forehead with the back of her hand. 'He's dead and gone many a year, my wee Liam.'

'I'm sorry.'

'Aye, I believe you are. Some folk have kind hearts, many more haven't.' She drank again and sank into a reverie, her chin on her chest.

'Yet you repay my kindness with lies?'

She shook her head, not looking at him. 'Who told you kindness meets with kindness? They were fibbing to you. Another tall tale.'

Swift saw a small pile of loose photos at the back of the shelf. On the top was one of Ronnie, standing in a garden in a summer dress; she was younger but the hair was the same. He glanced to check that she was still lost in thought, then took the photo and slipped it into his pocket.

He touched her arm and sat back down. 'Ronnie, if you talk to me I might be able to help you. I'd like to. I think you will have to talk to the police because a witness says you went into Mrs Langborne's that evening and you'll have to explain why.'

She looked up and past him. It was a look that seemed to be gazing into some other vista, far removed from the place they were in.

'Y'know, my life hasn't amounted to much, when all's said and done. No silvery winding streams for me. More of a stormy ocean and I lost my lifebelt somewhere along the way. Have you ever felt that way, Ty, as if you're just drifting, no direction?'

'I have once when I was in a bad way. A woman left me. I felt like that for a long time.'

She topped up her whisky. 'That's why you're kind-hearted. They say that, don't they? They say people who have suffered are more compassionate. I dunno. I think maybe suffering's made me a mean old biddy.' She hiccupped and patted her chest. 'I'm kinda weary now, Ty, and I'm a wee bit blootered. I think I'm gonna get completely blootered. I don't wanna embarrass myself. Ta for coming.'

'Okay, Ronnie. Can I come back to see you?'

'Oh aye. You're always welcome here, Ty dear. I don't think that you'll enjoy it much though, seeing this old boozer.' She raised her glass to him, slopping some drink on her chest.

He said goodbye, knowing that she was going to make it a day with the whisky, and let himself out. Standing under a cherry tree, he phoned the stationers in Holland Park and checked that Lauren was at work. When he reached the shop, Sam was at the till and smiled at him, indicating that Lauren was at the photocopier. She was stacking sheets of paper and seemed excited when he introduced himself. As well as sounding like Sam, she looked very like her, with a similar hairstyle and merry eyes.

'Have you got the police with you?' she asked.

'Not for now. I was wondering if you would look at a photograph for me, see if you recognise the woman.'

'The one I saw going into Mrs Langborne's?

'That's right. Take a look.'

She held the photo, turning it this way and that. 'I only saw the back of her but the hair's right, the colour and shape and she was tall like this, broad-shouldered. It could be her.'

'Okay, thank you.'

Sam came over, full of beans. 'So, any progress with your investigation, Mr Private Eye?'

'Possibly.'

'Have you been at a wedding?' She brushed his collar and some blossom floated to the floor.

'Nothing so exciting; standing under a tree.'

'Did a villain do that?' She pointed at his bruise.

'Yes; crept up behind me and bashed me.'

'Oooh!' both women said, staring at him.

He couldn't help smiling at the double act. Sam presented another collection tin to him. 'As we've been helpful again . . .'

'What is it this time?' He read the label, with the name of a children's charity and put some coins in. He looked at them both, thinking Tweedledum and Tweedledee. 'Are you related?'

They sniggered and Sam said, 'Same mum, different dads! My dad was better-looking.'

'No, mine was!' Lauren elbowed her half-sister and they sniggered again. Then another customer entered and Sam was immediately all business and formality.

* * *

He was feeling famished; he found an Italian café and ordered a toasted sandwich and coffee. While he was waiting for the food he drank a glass of tap water and searched the name Liam Farley on the web. He found several Liam Farleys on LinkedIn, a number with Twitter and Facebook accounts and an American basketball player, then saw a link to an article in a local paper, the *Westbourne Gazette*. He clicked into the page and started reading the brief report as his food arrived.

A verdict of suicide was recorded at West London Coroner's court yesterday for Liam Farley of Carlisle Court, W10. Mr Farley was found hanging in the bathroom of their home by his mother. Mr Farley had been having treatment for depression. The court expressed condolences to Mr Farley's mother.

He checked the date of the paper; June 1998. The sausage and mushroom toastie was delicious but he added extra mustard for a kick. His jaw had started clicking when he ate and he wondered if it was to do with when he hit the ground. He typed *Farley Langborne* into various search engines but drew a blank. He was annoyed with himself for not having checked Ronnie out more carefully at the beginning. He started on his coffee and rang Nora Morrow who sounded even angrier than when he had last talked to her.

'I hear you've been pestering Langborne again, going to his flat. I don't need this shit, Swift, haven't time for it.'

'I don't work for the Met, or has no one noticed? I don't have to follow orders.'

'You will if he takes an injunction out on you.'

'As if. But listen, just for you, I won't go near him again, for now anyway. His sister has ended my contract.'

'Goody.'

'I've found something new. Someone saw Ronnie Farley, the housekeeper, going into Carmen Langborne's house on the evening of the thirty-first around four thirty.'

'So? Maybe she'd forgotten something.'

'Oh come on; why did she not mention it? Did you run any checks on her or where she was that day?'

'Doing chores for other posh people. And you've no reason to keep on asking questions; you're not being paid to. I have to go and interview a real criminal now. I actually have a body and a sound basis for questioning him. Bye.'

He paid his bill and walked the streets in frustration. When he reached home his mood wasn't improved by the letter waiting in the hall. It was franked *St John Beauchamp and Polegate, Solicitors*. There were four wordy paragraphs, informing him that he was causing distress and nuisance to their client, Mr Rupert Langborne, and that unless he stopped they would have to *consider actions open to them*. He tore it up and threw it in the bin and emailed Florence a final bill, reaching for his phone as it rang.

'Hi, thanks for the information you emailed me.' It was Rachel Breen, sounding chirpy.

'A pleasure. Have you heard anything further?'

'It's amazing; all hell's broken loose. My solicitor contacted me earlier. She'd been in touch with the police. They raided the flat in Tooting early this morning. Carmichael was arrested and they said they'll be talking to Ed.'

'Do you know what happened to the men living there with Carmichael?'

Her voice grew solemn. 'Only that they're being looked after, whatever that means. What an awful thing, keeping people in those conditions; seems medieval. What do you think can be done for them?'

'It will depend on what their personal situations are.' He knew that if they had come from the streets, it was possible that they would end up there again.

'Well, Ed rang me a while ago, sounding stunned and meek. He said he'll let me have my stuff back tomorrow and sort out the money with me. It's a good outcome for me although obviously, I wouldn't have wanted this awful thing to have been at the bottom of it all.'

'No. But on the other hand, it has led to those men being freed from that kind of servitude.'

'That's true. You don't think Ed will get into real trouble, do you? I'm sure he didn't know what his tenant was doing. I mean, he's a bastard, but not bad in that way.'

'I'd imagine a heavy fine and the council might choose to prosecute him. His life will be unpleasant for a while. I wouldn't feel sorry for him; what he was doing was illegal in the first place and he can't have checked his tenant out too carefully.'

'I suppose. . . Well, thanks again. I'll be able to get myself back on track at last.'

He was considering what to eat when Cedric texted to say that he had made chicken-and-mushroom pie and there was a spare one if he wanted it. When he collected it, Cedric invited him to come out for an evening walk with him and Bertie and Swift decided to forget about urban servitude and the irritating conundrum that was Carmen Langborne. He strolled the Thames path with Cedric and the dog, stopping to sit outside a pub for a gin and tonic and a dish of water for Bertie.

'It's good to relax and people watch, one of my favourite occupations,' Cedric said. 'You feeling much better now, dear boy? Any news of your attacker?'

Swift told Cedric that he knew who had hit him and explained his reasons for not telling the police.

'Ah, *maiora bona*, for the greater good,' Cedric said. 'I can see your reasoning. I would probably make the same decision in the circumstances.'

'People live such impossible lives, Cedric. They put up with so much, trying to get through the days.'

'We all have our share of difficulties. You've had a portion of troubles yourself.'

They sat for an hour in the glow of the sun, most of the time in companionable silence, while Bertie snoozed at Cedric's feet. Later, Swift ate the pie Cedric had made and opened a bottle of red wine. He sat out in the garden for a long time, listening to the noises of the night, recalling the tune Ronnie had sung. It occurred to him that Langborne and Ronnie might be mixed up in this together somehow but he couldn't figure out why, and finally ditched the idea. By midnight he was pleasantly intoxicated. He decided that his strength was back and he would spend the next day focusing on Ronnie's activities.

CHAPTER 12

The river was fast flowing with a westerly breeze. Swift pulled in near Putney Bridge, donned an extra body warmer and ate a banana. His energy levels were low but at least his headache had gone and his bruise no longer throbbed. He'd had the dream again last night, the same women in a murky room and Ruth there among them, looking up, pleading for something but he had stared down at her, not knowing what she wanted, feeling panic rising in his chest. He had woken from it and lain awake for hours, rehearsing how he would sit opposite her over lunch in the Evergreen, Krystyna neatening cutlery in the background, and tell her he couldn't see her again. The sun slid in and out of fast-moving clouds, which were thickening, promising rain later. He took up the oars and turned the boat.

After a quick shower he dressed in black jeans and a sweatshirt with a roomy hood that he hadn't worn for months. He looked in the mirror, satisfied that he resembled scores of other men on the London streets. By eight a.m. he had stationed himself at the side of Ronnie Farley's block of flats, hood pulled up. There was a low section of wall dividing the building from the health clinic next door and he propped himself on it. The curtains at the front of her living room were still drawn closed. He watched as children were taken to school and women in slippers popped down to the shop for milk and bread. The air had warmed and was still fresh in this early part of the day, at least until the refuse lorry arrived and the bins were emptied with much clattering, releasing a sweet, pungent smell of decay. At nine the curtains were still drawn and Swift sipped water, hoping that Ronnie wasn't on a bender that was going to last for days. After a while he bought a coffee in the shop and as he crossed back to his position he saw the curtains being pulled back and Ronnie stepping on to the balcony with a watering can in hand.

Swift moved further along the wall, into the shadows. Ronnie was in her cream mac, a cigarette in her free hand. She smoked as she watered each tub and her lips seemed to be moving; perhaps she talked to her plants. When she had finished the watering, she readjusted a couple of tubs and picked up some leaves and a crisp packet, shaking her head in annoyance. She glanced at her watch and stepped back into the living room. Swift took a drink of coffee, guessing that she was about to emerge and head to one of her remaining clients.

She appeared within five minutes, walking with her stately, heavy tread, her bag with its long handles over one shoulder. She had another cigarette on the go and waved to a woman who called a greeting as she took a toddler into the play area. Swift allowed her a few minutes head start, then followed her on the opposite side of the road down to Ladbroke Grove and past the tube station where she turned right into a residential street. Swift crossed over and continued after her, keeping his distance. She walked on for ten minutes; the houses grew grander and larger, with big front gardens. Stopping outside one, she finished her cigarette and dropped the butt in the hedge. Then she stepped up the front path, rang the bell and was admitted after a short pause.

Swift finished his coffee and shrugged his hood back, reckoning that she would be in the house at least an hour and possibly longer. This wasn't an area to be seen loitering, especially in a hoodie. He walked the streets for a while, thinking of Ruth; they had considered buying a tiny flat in Notting Hill when they got engaged and had looked at several in the area but in the end, judged it too expensive. He imagined the life they might now be having and then stopped himself, applying hard pressure with his right thumb to the base of his left. It was a trick a friend had taught him, a way of distracting the mind from unwanted thoughts. He doubled back, bought a newspaper and a bar of chocolate and found a bus stop at a junction from where the house Ronnie was visiting was just in sight.

He was bored and hungry by the time Ronnie appeared, just over two hours later. He hoped that she wasn't heading for another job. He tailed her back to the main road where she went into a supermarket, emerging after five minutes with a carrier bag. She walked to a bus stop, read the digital timetable overhead and lit up a cigarette. Within a minute she had started chatting to a woman who was sitting on the slim, uncomfortable plastic bench by the stop, hugging several shopping bags. Swift crossed the road and walked to the door of the supermarket. Ronnie and the woman were deep in conversation and comparing plastic cards, which Swift assumed were bus passes. Various buses came and went; each time, both women looked up, shook their heads and continued talking. After ten minutes a 452 appeared and Ronnie moved towards the stop, signalling the driver and waving goodbye to her friend. Swift walked forwards; it would be tricky, boarding the same bus without Ronnie seeing him. Luckily, in the time honoured tradition of London Transport, another 452 had appeared on the horizon, making sure the first wasn't a lonely traveller. Swift checked that the destination was the same and boarded the second as Ronnie's moved off.

He positioned himself by the exit doors, negotiating several suitcases and shopping trolleys sticking into the aisle, and bent forwards so that he could watch the bus in front. If his driver decided to idle or got caught at lights, his frustrating morning might bear no fruit. Luckily, the driver seemed keen to keep his colleague company and stayed on his tail down towards Kensington, jumping an amber light in the process. Both buses swept into Kensington High Street and Swift saw Ronnie alighting at the first stop, just before Kensington Palace. He allowed other passengers to get off before him and saw that she had turned in the direction of the tube station.

She took a left turn and headed through a leafy square, past a convent, then turned right into a wide street with tall Georgian houses called Tavistock Avenue. She had lit another cigarette and when she stopped outside one of the houses at the end of a terrace she didn't extinguish it. She fished in her bag and took out a set of keys with which she opened the front door of number forty-one and vanished inside. Swift stood by a tall plane tree and considered; the lit cigarette and the keys indicated that the owner of the house was not at home. He decided to stay put for at least half an hour but had only just finished checking his emails when Ronnie exited the house, no longer holding the carrier bag. Swift followed her again; she retraced her route back to a bus stop and she broke into a lumbering run as a 452 approached, going towards Ladbroke Grove. There was a large group of people waiting to board; Swift tucked himself at the back and got on last, watching as Ronnie went upstairs. She got off at Westway and returned to her flat.

Swift adjourned to a café on the main road and ordered coffee and a bacon panini. He ate without interest, barely noticing the taste of his food, thinking over

Ronnie's movements. Weighing up the morning's activities, he decided to return to Kensington and take a look at the house she had access to. The digital timetable at the bus stop promised a 452 within six minutes but when he glanced up again, this had changed to ten, then fifteen minutes. He was about to seek out a taxi when the digital display shivered and vanished and a 452 appeared. Back on Kensington High Street, Swift walked back to Tavistock Avenue where he rang the bell at number 41 and waited, taking in the three door locks and looking down into the basement which had no entry door and iron railings at the window. There was no obvious burglar alarm. He rang the bell again, glancing around; the street was empty, no sign of neighbours. He walked around the side of the house, into the narrow alley that divided it from the next terrace. There was a brick wall, about six feet high, bordering the garden. Swift looked around again and could see no evidence of activity. He gripped the top of the wall and pulled himself up, easing down by a laurel hedge on the other side.

The garden was low maintenance, mainly gravel with narrow borders and some planters containing shrubs. A yellow rose bush scented the afternoon air and apart from the occasional bird trill, the place was silent. Blinds were down at the windows on the first and second floors. Five steps led down to the rear of the basement; this was often the most vulnerable part of a house and was the reason why Swift had high-quality locks on his office. He descended the steps; the window facing him had obscured glass and iron railings similar to those at the front. Despite that security, he saw that the back door had only a cylinder lock and wondered at the lack of logic in many people's home protection; unless there were also interior bolts, he would gain entry without too much trouble. In his youth, he had been an inveterate loser of keys and had taught himself to pick locks rather than regularly pay locksmith charges. He took his slimline lock-pick set from his pocket and set to work, manoeuvring the tension wrench, then inserting the slimmest pick into the upper part of the keyhole for a few minutes until he felt that all the pins had been set. The lock turned and free of bolts, the door opened.

Swift closed the door softly behind him and saw that he was in a dimly lit corridor with a quarry-tiled floor. He stood, listening, and heard no sound. He opened a pine door on his left and glanced in at a shower room with a toilet. To his right, the door was open onto a laundry room. The washing machine and tumble dryer stood silent; the cream mosaic floor, like that in the shower, was dry. Along the corridor at the front of the house he opened another pine door and saw a bedroom with a single bed, wardrobe and bookcase. The place felt dormant and unused.

The ground floor had two large separate rooms; at the front a sitting room, furnished simply and expensively with leather chairs, deep-pile cream carpet and beige walls, at the back a library with floor-to-ceiling bookshelves on three walls, an oak desk and photographs of old sailing ships on the fourth wall. Keys hung from a rack in the hallway and he examined them, sure that they were for the front door. He carried on down the hall into a rectangular kitchen with a butcher's block workstation in the middle and an alcove at the far end with a door on the right. He could smell cigarette smoke. There was no sign of any recent domestic activity but when he touched the kettle it was warm; Ronnie had made a brew. He stood, looking out of the window on to the garden, considering that Ronnie must be looking after the house for its absent owner, hence her fleeting visit. Perhaps her carrier bag had contained cleaning materials.

He flinched, as suddenly he heard a woman's voice counting in a high, quavering tone. Turning, he looked around but there was no one there. He followed the sound to the alcove and stood, listening as she counted to twenty, paused, and then started again. The door in front of him had a substantial bolt under the handle and it was pushed across. He bent to look at it; it was new and untarnished. The counting stopped, then started again, this time as far as ten, then repeated. Swift breathed in, then slid the bolt across as quietly as he could; it moved smoothly. He opened the door slowly and looked in at a small utility room, lit only by a narrow double-glazed window of opaque glass high on the outer wall. There was a thin, elderly woman in blue silk pyjamas lying on a mattress on the floor with her knees hugged to her chest. He knocked on the door and coughed.

'Mrs Langborne?'

She sat up, alarmed, scrambling to her feet.

'Who are you?'

'My name is Tyrone Swift. Please, don't worry. I'm a private detective. Your family asked me to find you and I followed Mrs Farley here this morning.' He stayed in the doorway. The air in the room was stale and smelled of cleaning fluids.

Carmen Langborne stood, gazing at him. Her dark eyes moistened but she quickly regained control, running her tongue across her lips. The coiffured woman of the photos was looking a little dishevelled and weary, the lines on her face more deeply scored. The roots of her hair had grown out so that she had a cap of salt-and-pepper strands on top of the black, and it now reached almost to her shoulders.

'You are here on your own?' she asked, clearing her throat.

'Yes. I had reason to suspect Mrs Farley so after she had gone home I broke in through the basement door. I heard you doing your exercises; counting. Have you been locked in here since January?'

She turned away, not replying, smoothed her hair and took a dress and jacket from the back of a wooden chair.

'I must go home immediately.'

'Are you all right? Do you need a drink, or maybe a doctor?'

She waved a dismissive hand. 'I want to dress.' She opened a sliding door in the far wall; Swift glimpsed a washbasin before she closed it.

The room she had been confined in had a tiled floor and metal shelves with cleaning materials, light bulbs, packets of toilet tissue and tins of food. A mop, bucket and vacuum cleaner stood in a corner. There was a mattress, duvet and pillow, a tray with a plate and mug beside it and a couple of books. On the seat of the chair was a piece of knitting, the needles stuck in a ball of multicoloured wool. The high window had a lock in the centre. Swift marvelled at Carmen's resilience and self-containment; many people would have been reduced to a wreck after several months in such confinement.

She reappeared quickly, dressed in her creased clothing. She picked up her handbag and walked past him into the kitchen.

'Please call a taxi for me,' she said, crossing to the window and looking out. He could see the rise and fall of her chest as she took deep breaths. She smoothed at her jacket, touching the brooch on a lapel.

He made the call, then drew two glasses of tap water and offered her one. She took it and sipped.

'Would you like to use my phone to ring your family?'

'Thank you. I will do that when I get home.'

'The police will need to be told as well.'

'I will see to all that. First, I wish to go home. Shall we wait outside?'

It was an order which he ignored. 'Why has Mrs Farley kept you here like this? Who does this house belong to?'

She looked inside her bag, closed it again. 'I really do want to go outside. I need fresh air.'

'Mrs Langborne . . .'

She held up a hand. 'I have had quite enough of being here.'

She spoke quietly but he could hear the tension in her voice. He understood her desire to escape the confines of the house.

'Very well. Do you want your knitting and books?'

'No.'

'I would like to come with you in the cab, make sure you're okay.'

'No, thank you. I will be perfectly all right on my own.'

She showed no curiosity as he led her through the house, picking up the keys from the hallway. He opened the locks on the front door and she stepped out into the sunshine, wincing. She glanced back once, then moved onto the pavement; bending, she rubbed a speck from her black court shoe. As the cab approached he stepped beside her.

'Mrs Langborne, you are a courageous woman but you might well feel badly shocked once you arrive home. I would like to accompany you.'

'Absolutely not. Thank you anyway.'

She stepped into the cab without another word. He watched as it drove away, feeling amazed, annoyed and stunned. He rang Florence's number and got her answerphone so left a message, informing her only that Carmen was on her way home. He started to call Nora Morrow but then hesitated and phoned for a cab instead; he wanted a chance to speak to Ronnie before the Met got hold of her. Despite what she had done, he had a soft spot for her and wanted to hear her story.

Ronnie's curtains were closed again, shutting out the late afternoon sun. Swift rang her bell several times with no response. He looked through the letterbox and called her name. There was no sign of her and he could hear no movement. He tried her phone but she didn't pick up and he couldn't hear it ringing from within the flat. He left a message, saying he needed to speak to her urgently.

He caught a bus near the tube station and headed towards Holland Park. Heat had been gathering during the day and the air was humid. Carmen's house was glowing in the sun, much as it had been the first day he had visited and Ronnie welcomed him in. As he approached, Swift saw Florence parking and waited outside the house as she locked her car and hurried towards him.

'Has your stepmother called you?'

'Yes, about half an hour ago. She wouldn't tell me anything on the phone, just that she's fine. I've been trying to get hold of Rupe but he's in a meeting. What's going on? What are you doing here?'

'I think we should go in first.'

Florence opened her mouth then shook her head and pressed the doorbell. After a few moments Carmen Langborne opened it.

'Carmen!' Florence shrieked, swooping forward and kissing her on the cheek. 'Where on earth have you been?'

'Do come in, Florence. Why is this gentleman with you?'

'Oh, his name is Mr Swift; I asked him to look for you. Let's get inside and I'll explain.'

Carmen gave Swift a sidelong glance, then led the way in, leaving him to close the door. They went into the living room, where there was a tray with tea and biscuits and a half-full cup. Florence rattled on about how worried she had been. Swift noted that Carmen looked showered and fresh, her hair now rolled into a pleat. She was wearing a blue jersey dress, navy blue pumps and pearls and her face was carefully made up. Swift gauged that she had been home for just over an hour and had made full use of the time. He could only admire her sangfroid.

'Engaging a private detective must have been expensive,' she said to Florence. Her voice was reedy, her diction slow after months of little conversation.

'Carmen, we were so worried about you! We thought . . . well, we thought the worst.' Florence's eyes brimmed; Swift thought it was probably relief at the restoration of the status quo and family finances. 'Where have you been, why didn't you contact us?'

'Where are my darling cats, who is looking after them? When can I bring them home?'

Florence looked at Swift, who shrugged. Ronnie hadn't told her, then, about Langborne's disposal of them.

Florence twisted her hands together. 'Rupert had them rehomed through some charity. I don't know the details. He had to sack Mrs Farley and then there was no one to come in and look after them.'

Carmen closed her eyes, a spasm of distress crossing her face. 'I will never forgive him,' she said flatly.

'I suppose he didn't know what else to do,' Florence said.

Carmen looked at her. 'He couldn't have taken them in, or even you, perhaps? You could have come here and fed them. You don't mind asking me for money but you wouldn't even do that for me.' She put a hand to her mouth.

Swift thought she had aged ten years in a few moments. The loss of her cats had disturbed her equilibrium more than several months of confinement. She was holding herself carefully, containing her emotions.

'Have you phoned the police?' he asked.

She ignored him. 'Florence, I want you to contact Rupert and find out where my darlings are, then let me know. I don't want Rupert to speak to me. Do you understand?'

Florence nodded.

'You can go away now,' she said, 'both of you. I'm here and well. I have things to do.'

Swift moved his chair forward. 'Mrs Langborne, it isn't as simple as that. The police will be here sometime soon and they will want to know where you have been.'

She looked sideways, apparently studying the garden through the back window. After a few minutes she spoke, still gazing outwards.

'I was very troubled about something, a personal matter. I went to stay in a friend's house in the countryside so that I could think and have peace. My friend is abroad for some time. That is all I am prepared to say.'

'But you must have known we would be looking for you!' Florence protested.

Carmen poured some tea into her cup and snapped a biscuit in two. Swift gazed at her; she had clearly decided that lies and silence would be her best policy, but why?

'Mrs Langborne,' Swift said, repeating her name softly until she looked at him. 'Mrs Farley kidnapped you. The police will question her. I know what happened, I broke into a house and let you out of a utility room just a short while ago and I will be telling the police the details. I'm afraid you are going to have to be truthful. You can't really believe that you can maintain a fiction.'

She put the teacup down and sank back, her face blank.

'Mrs Farley?' Florence asked, her voice cracking. 'What's any of this to do with her? What house did you break into?' She had gone pale and was gaping, looking from Swift to her stepmother.

'Florence, why don't you go and try your brother again?' Swift urged. 'I think it would be good for your stepmother to have some information about the cats.' She was going to need whatever comfort she could get to shore her up.

Florence shook her head, then took her phone from her bag and left the room, glancing back as if to check she wasn't imagining Carmen's return.

Swift spoke slowly. 'You have had a terrible and traumatic experience. I don't understand why you are lying about it and I won't collude in the lie. If it helps to know, William Pennington died this week.'

Carmen laughed and shuddered. 'Mr Pennington! How odd; Rupert will probably want to claim him as a father now, rather than the one he thought he had. Such irony!'

'I'm sorry, I don't understand.'

She shot him a look and spoke glacially. 'Why should you? You don't know me.'

'No, but I know about William Pennington and I met him before his death. You saw Rupert that day you went missing, on the thirty-first, didn't you? You were giving him a final ultimatum about acknowledging his natural father.'

She curled her arms around her skinny chest. 'I took the train to Maidenhead and Rupert met me there. He insisted on discussing the matter somewhere neither of us would be known. We lunched in a not very pleasant restaurant. He was twisting and turning, wanting to buy more time. I pointed out that time was one thing he didn't have. I informed him as I left that I would have to advise Daphne; I thought she might be able to make him see sense. He will regret now that he didn't meet William Pennington.'

'Why did Mrs Farley do this to you? Had you harmed her in some way or was imprisoning you related in some way to her son's suicide?'

'Don't be impertinent,' she said, sitting up straight. 'I don't need your concern or your questions and I resent your intrusion. Please go away now.' She rose and walked to the window, retying the curtain holdback.

'I will go, but the police will make my impertinence seem like the height of good manners.'

Swift walked into the hallway as Florence was ending a phone call.

'I can't reach Rupe, he's not going to be available until later. What's going on in there? Where has Carmen been these past months?' She clutched at his arm.

'It's not for me to tell you.'

'Oh, if it's because I terminated your contract, if you're being petty . . .'

He was hot and tired and had had enough of the Langbornes and their incivility.

'Mrs Davenport, it isn't for me to tell you the details now. Your stepmother was kidnapped by Mrs Farley and is in a bad way, despite appearances. I have no idea why she is spinning a story about staying at a friend's place. It may be partly because of shock. You need to look after her and probably you should call Doctor Forsyth. There are difficult times ahead and the police will not accept her lady-of-the-manor behaviour. You should call the police now, especially as a crime has been committed; I think I'll give you that responsibility. I'll speak to them myself in a while to give them details about how I found her.'

She had been chewing at her lower lip while he was speaking. She reached into her bag and pulled out a bottle of water, gulping it. 'But it's all so bizarre!'

'Yes; but what your stepmother has just said is even more peculiar.' He opened the front door. 'By the way, no need to thank me for finding her, despite the fact you'd ended my contract. It would be acceptable if you add a few more days of payment to the final bill.'

Swift left her to it and stepped out of the house, seating himself for a few moments on the wall. He should be feeling sympathy for the woman who had been imprisoned, but he could only think of the woman who had lied while feeding him her home baking. He tried Ronnie's phone again but got no response. A sense of unease nudged at him. He decided to return home to check if there were any messages.

CHAPTER 13

Cedric had left Swift's post by his front door. He put the
bundle on the kitchen counter and made coffee. While it
brewed, he checked for any messages on his landline but
found none. Although it was now six thirty, he had no
appetite; his brain was too busy trying to puzzle out
Carmen's reasons for lying about her captivity. He sat at
the table and checked his emails, opening one from Mark
Gill:

*Hi mate, heard you had a run in with a hard man so hope
you're okay. I thought of ringing you but reckoned this would be
easier by mail. I was passing through Victoria station the other day
and saw you with Ruth. I know you were gutted when she left, so I
just wanted to say be careful. I didn't know whether or not to tell you
this but you know, you always had my back so I decided to go for it.
See you, Mark.*

Swift sighed. You'd think London would be big
enough not to be spotted but Mark was sound and could
be relied on not to mention his sighting to anyone else. It
had started to rain after the moist heat of the day; a light,

desultory misting. He watched it drift in the trees through the back window, then replied:

Hi Mark. Thanks for the good wishes. I'll take care. Catch up soon.

He turned to the post, opened a couple of bills and flyers, then a brown padded envelope with no stamp or postmark and just his name in blue biro and capitals. Inside was a brass key attached to a fob in the shape of a St Brigid's cross and a note in tiny, carefully formed handwriting:

Dear Tyrone. This is the key to my place. I don't want the ambulance or police to have to break down the door and all the neighbours gawping. As I said, you're a braw min and I'm sorry to do this to you but on the other hand I trust you.
You never looked down on me.
God bless, Ronnie.

He threw his jacket on as he called a cab. It was now almost five hours since he had last seen her and several more since he had tried without success to visit her; she must have travelled to his door to deliver the letter but even so, enough time had elapsed for harm to be done. He phoned for an ambulance, emphasising that he was on his way to Ronnie's with a key and waited outside in the rain for the cab, telling the driver it was an emergency. Traffic was easy until they approached Ladbroke Grove and the usual snarl-up appeared. He told the driver to stop, threw him the fare and ran, weaving through the pedestrians. The rain, now more intent, was slicking his hair and dripping down his collar. There was no sign of an ambulance as he raced up the steps and opened Ronnie's door. He left it open, heading up the stairs. The four doors off the hallway were closed. He took a breath and opened the one on his right, looking into the empty bathroom. He wiped his damp hands on his jeans and opened the door to the living room.

She was lying on the floor by the dining table, on her side, her right arm thrown outwards. Her feet were bare, her eyes open and dull. He stepped closer and saw a deep gaping wound, running from the middle of her forehead to the side of her head. The bleeding had stopped and blood had congealed darkly underneath her cheek. He knew immediately that she was dead. He felt a momentary confusion because this was no suicide, then crouched beside her and checked that there was no pulse. There was a smear of blood on the table edge and a mug of coffee had fallen from the top; the mug had broken into three jagged pieces, the coffee staining the curtains of the balcony door and the lower wall. Something caught his eye below her right knee. Leaning carefully over her, he saw two flattened strands of pale purple heather. He took out his LED pocket torch and shone it on them. Then he phoned 999 again, this time for the police.

He stood, looking down on her, noting with a pang of anguish that she had painted her toenails a frosted pink. He went through to the kitchen where all the surfaces sparkled. By the sink were half a dozen packets and bottles of tranquilisers, enough to ensure several deaths. She had planned to end her own life and being Ronnie, had made thorough preparations, but someone had pre-empted her. There was another St Brigid's cross on the wall by the gleaming cooker, this one woven in a frame.

He went back through to the hallway and found her bedroom. It was small, allowing only a single bed, a melamine wardrobe and chest of drawers. There wasn't a speck of dust. On her bedside table was an envelope saying TYRONE. It was heavy and he could feel the shape of more keys inside. He tucked it in his pocket as he heard an ambulance siren whining, then running footsteps. He told the two paramedics her name, that she had planned to commit suicide but had been killed first and that he had called the police. He left them with the body and went back into her bedroom where he sat on the bed and opened the envelope she had left him, taking out three brass keys. The letter was one page, double-sided.

Ty, I'm writing this early in the morning so I'm sober and only a bit heavy headed. I'm going to my morning job when I've finished this. That might seem odd to some when I'm planning to take a heap of tablets later but I don't like letting people down. Sorry for giving you the run around. I have Mrs L locked in a house near High Street Ken. These are the keys to the front door; 41 Tavistock Avenue. She's in a room off the kitchen. Mr Sydney Bailey owns the place and he's been away since January, due back in June. I've been caretaking for him. His details are in my address book, by the phone.

You're a smart one so I know you'll have discovered by now that my son killed himself. When Liam was in his late teens and on tablets for depression he told me that Neville Langborne sexually abused him for about a year when he was fourteen and took him to houses where other men did too. Liam helped out on Saturdays at a car valeting place in Notting Hill where Langborne used to take his car. Langborne got talking to him and that's how it started. I won't go into details, you'll know the picture. Liam told me that once, Langborne took him back to the house in Holland Park. Carmen came home early, as Liam was leaving. Liam said that Langborne made up some story about losing his wallet at the car place and Liam returning it. Liam reckoned she suspected what was going on.

Liam went to the police but was told there wasn't any evidence – this was around 1986. Toffs get away with murder even now and they certainly did back then. He was a shy boy and didn't have the confidence to press his case. I rang social services but nobody ever came back to me.

Liam was never right afterwards. He said to me once that he always felt as if the sky above him was made of ice. Then he hanged himself. I always felt that I should have done more to help him. When my friend Kate told me who she was working for and that Langborne had died, I decided to try and get a job there. I didn't know what I was going to do. I just wanted to see how Mrs L lived

195

and be in a place where my Liam was harmed and suffered. Maybe I was doing some kind of penance.

I had no plan to harm Mrs L. I stole a few things from her, odd bits of money she left around but mainly drink. She had so much there she never noticed and anyway I was her reliable Farley. I've never taken anything from any of my other clients, I want you to know that. And by the way, Florence removed a couple of expensive bits from her house a week ago; I told Rupert that when he accused me, but of course he wouldn't listen. The more I got to know Mrs L, the more I hated her snobbery and her banging on about what was wrong with the world. She used to talk about her husband sometimes, saying what an honest, straightforward man he'd been, that everyone looked up to him because with the Lord Justice, as many people used to remark, 'what you see is what you get.' I nearly laughed in her face when she said that.

I hope this is making sense. One day in January, I heard her talking to Rupert on the phone and got the gist of her having found out something that she was going to tell Daphne and Florence about if he didn't. I could tell that Rupert was arguing with her but she was being high and mighty. That same morning, she was looking at the newspaper, something about Rolf Harris and those other men who'd been raping and molesting and she said they should all be locked up and the key thrown away.

After that I couldn't stop thinking about what her husband had done and the cushioned life she was living and the way she thought she could preach about what other people should do and have done to them when she maybe knew what her own husband had been doing. I mean, they say that the wives usually know, don't they? I brooded on it and I felt a terrible anger. I had this idea to teach her a lesson. She was so big on her animal charities and all. I spun her a story about this lady I worked for in Kensington. I said she was the widow of an Earl – I knew that would appeal to Mrs L. I told her this Lady Hargreave wanted to start a new animal charity and she was thinking of calling it Haven. She was looking for someone to help her with it but wanted to keep it all top secret until it was properly planned. Anyway, I got Mrs L interested and we agreed that I'd go with her to Kensington at five o'clock on the 31 and

196

introduce her so that she could spend an hour with Lady Hargreave before going to her bridge. She was loving the hush bit, agreed not to breathe a word to anyone.

So as you know, I was round there at half past four that evening. We went down to the main road and hailed a taxi. (Mrs L was going to call one to the house but of course I didn't want that because it would be logged so I told her I needed to get something from the chemist on the way.) I took her to Mr Bailey's and once we were in I led her to a utility room off the kitchen and locked her in. It's easy to manipulate someone when they trust you, as her husband had found. I'd put a bolt on the door so her little prison was all ready for her. It's small but has a wee window so she's had light and there's a washbasin and toilet off it. I'd put a mattress, bedding and food and water in there. I told her what her husband had done to my Liam. She said she knew nothing about it but I could tell she was lying. I said she'd have to stay there until she apologised to me for what her husband had done, told the police and agreed to set up a charity in Liam's name.

I've no idea how long I was going to keep it up. I think I've been half mad for a long time. Mrs L never buckled. I went in every day, took her a few clothes, kept her fed. I took her some wool and knitting needles too and books of crossword puzzles. I could see I was going to get nowhere but in the end I just wanted her to know what it was like to feel alone and helpless and hurt by someone, just like my Liam did.

I was a bit surprised that the police and then you accepted my word about everything; the cats were never left unfed of course but I made a big fuss about that because it added to the confusion and made me sound like reliable, caring Farley.

I've been collecting the pills for a while. When you work for wealthy people, you always find sleeping stuff in their bedrooms and bathrooms. I knew once you came to see me yesterday that it was over. I'm glad it is. I wanted to stop it but I couldn't think of a way. When you turned up, I was hoping that you'd find me out so that it could all end and now it has it's a relief.

I did lead you up the garden path and I told you porkies but I hope you can understand. I think maybe you will.

197

When I knew last night that this all had to end, I rang Rupert and told him about what his father had done to my Liam and other boys. I said it would all come out. It gave me some small satisfaction, doing that; he's been horrible to me and I could hear the panic in his voice. I didn't tell him anything about Mrs L or where she was, I wasn't going to show all my cards.

I don't care what anyone says about me. I've cared about nothing and nobody since Liam died.

Ronnie

When the police arrived, he gave them his details and said they could ring Nora Morrow to check him out. A duty inspector called Waring turned up soon after and Swift gave him both the notes Ronnie had written. He read them standing in her bedroom and was told by a constable that DI Morrow had confirmed who Swift was.

'So who's this Mrs L?' Waring asked.

'Carmen Langborne. She went missing in January. Nora Morrow's in charge of the case. The stepdaughter employed me. I found Mrs Langborne earlier today; she's at home now and I asked her stepdaughter to let the police know. You'd better check that Nora Morrow is up to speed about her. I can make a statement about Ronnie Farley later. Rupert Langborne is mentioned in the long letter; underneath Ronnie's head you'll see some pieces of heather. Langborne wears a buttonhole of thistles and heather. He had a strong motive to silence Ronnie.'

Waring nodded, said he would look into it, and went into the living room to speak to forensics. Swift didn't look through as he left. Some neighbours were clustering outside, asking each other for information. Ronnie might have known that they would end up gawping anyway. Swift sat on the wall he had used that morning and emailed Nora Morrow, telling her what had happened. He sat, looking up at the drawn curtains; she had been dead, then, when he had called there in the late afternoon. He could hear the melody Ronnie had sung to him, see her strained eyes and that final image of her lying with her son's photo just a few feet away.

A police car pulled up and Nora Morrow got out, accompanied by a uniformed woman constable. She looked around, saw Swift, crossed over and stood in front of him, hands in her jacket pockets, her expression hard to read.

'Mrs Langborne is home, then?'

'Yes. Florence is with her. She's explaining away the last months by saying that she was troubled and staying at a friend's house.'

Nora's eyebrows shot up. 'She thinks we're going to buy that story?'

Swift stood. He felt suddenly drained. 'When she came up with her version of events she didn't know about Ronnie's death or her letter or that Ronnie had informed Rupert last night about his father's activities. Her instinct was to protect her reputation and maybe there was some concern too for her stepchildren. She dismissed me; after all, I'm low in the food chain. I'm sure you'll have more success.'

Nora gave him a tiny smile. 'I'll be going round to see her once I check-in here. It wasn't Rupert, then, with a body in the lake or concealed on the estate?'

'No need to be nasty. I did crack the case, after all. And, yes, I believe it was Rupert Langborne.'

'How do you mean?'

'I think he killed Ronnie.' He explained about the heather and Ronnie's disclosure that she had phoned Rupert.

Nora rubbed her nose. 'A bit tenuous. When did you see him wearing this buttonhole?'

'A couple of weeks back; the first time I met him. Like father, like son; the father was ultimately responsible for Liam Farley's death and Langborne has seen off his mother.'

199

Nora flexed her shoulders, flicked her string tie; today it was pale blue with one thin green stripe. 'Okay, we'll see. Don't go jumping to conclusions. I'm sorry about Ronnie Farley, despite her criminal activity. DI Waring gave me the gist of her letter; she was a considerate kidnapper, providing materials for pastimes.'

'More sinned against than sinning?'

'Not sure a jury would think that if she was alive to go on trial. Looking on the bright side, Langborne's probably not going to be in a position to complain about you.'

The policewoman was drinking it all in, pretending to examine a rose bush. Nora turned away.

'Well, time's a-wastin'.'

'And you're busy and understaffed.'

She waved a dismissive hand at him and headed for Ronnie's flat. Swift walked away towards the main road, feeling hungry and nauseous at the same time. The rain had stopped, leaving a washed-out, soapy-coloured sky. He stopped to buy a flapjack and coffee and walked to Notting Hill, looking at his phone as he heard a text arriving. It was from Ruth: *I miscarried yesterday. Can I ring you later this evening?*

He stared at the screen for a few moments, then replied: *So sorry to hear that. Of course. I'm working but will text you when I get home.*

He hailed a taxi; he had one more visit to make before he went home. He gave the driver Langborne's address and sat back, drinking his coffee, listening to the hiss of surface water against the wheels. Three distressed women in one day; he suspected that Carmen would prove the most redoubtable.

CHAPTER 14

When Langborne opened the door, Swift pushed against it and stepped in, quickly crossing the room and standing by a marble fireplace. There was an empty Chinese takeaway container on a coffee table, pungent traces of spare ribs still on the air.

'Has murder given you an appetite?' Swift asked.

Langborne stared at him, then closed the door. He sat on the sofa and turned down the radio, muting Handel. He was wearing chinos, a short-sleeved linen shirt and leather slippers.

'Sit down, Mr Swift, and explain yourself. I spoke to Florence a while ago; I understand you found my stepmother and for that I thank you.'

'Very gracious of you.' Swift sat in a chair opposite him.

The light, from two standard lamps, was dim. The place was furnished in heavy oak and mahogany; Swift found it oppressive, like the man. Langborne sounded tired.

'Is Mrs Langborne still refusing to see you?'

'That's correct. She is very upset about the cats and, of course, she's in shock. Florence offered to stay the night but she declined.' He reached for a glass of whisky on the table and sipped. 'I won't ask if you want a drink; I've no wish to detain you.'

Swift gestured at a small suitcase on wheels standing just inside the front door. 'Are you planning to go somewhere?'

'Yes, tomorrow. I have a meeting in Brussels.'

'Is that so? I'm not sure you're going to make it. I found Ronnie Farley's body this afternoon.'

A strange expression crossed Langborne's face; in most circumstances, Swift would have read it as shock. He took another slug of whisky and cradled the glass in his hands.

'I'm sorry to hear that. I hoped to see that dreadful woman on trial for what she put my stepmother through. I understand that she kidnapped Carmen, although I don't have any details yet.

'Ronnie was murdered and I believe the finger points at you, Mr Langborne. Do you want to tell me about it before the police contact you?'

Langborne finished the whisky and placed the glass carefully on the table, straightening the coaster beneath it. The amber glow of the lamp behind the sofa gave his face a jaundiced hue.

'You do like to make allegations about me, don't you? Perhaps I wronged you in another life. I know nothing about a murder. If the police want to speak to me they are welcome. Do you have a weapon with my fingerprints on it?' His voice was steady but his eyes signalled anxiety.

Swift left a silence. A tall grandfather clock by the window counted the slow minutes. There was the softest of thuds as a door closed along the corridor.

'There is clear evidence, including evidence of your motive, and the police have it. The thing is, Mr Langborne, you needn't have gone to the bother. Ronnie Farley had planned to kill herself today, she had the tablets lined up in her kitchen and you interrupted her arrangements. She left me a letter explaining a great deal. I'm sure you've been fitting the pieces of the story together, you're a smart man. Was it a terrible shock when she phoned you last night and told you what your father had done to her son and to other boys?'

Langborne ran his tongue across his lips. 'I was shocked, yes, but only up to a point; you see, Mr Swift, he started with me, when I was six. It was my birthday present.'

Swift nodded. He had never imagined he could feel the slightest glimmer of pity for Langborne, but he did now.

'You seem unsurprised?'

'I'm not surprised. Many abusers start within the home. And Florence? Did he abuse her too or did he just want boys?'

'I don't know. I believe that there's usually a gender preference. Florence has never indicated that she was abused in any way, but then again, I had never mentioned my own experiences to her. We are that kind of family. Although I suppose most families where such things occur maintain their silences.' He sat for a while without speaking, then roused himself. 'I suspected that my father might have abused other boys; I understand that pederasts rarely limit their enjoyment to one experience. When he died, I was relieved but also wary, wondering if the reports of his death would trigger memories and cause people to come forward.'

'You felt safer as the years went by, after his death?'

'Oh no; you never feel safe, Mr Swift, once you have experienced such things. However, that is another matter, and I won't satisfy you with a tale of woe on my own behalf.'

'What Ronnie Farley knew was dynamite, wasn't it? It certainly cast the issue of who your real father was into comparative insignificance.'

Langborne shook his head. 'I didn't see Mrs Farley today or harm her. You'll be disappointed, I know, but I was taking part in a mind-numbing team building exercise all day in Islington; hence the casual mufti.' He gestured at his clothing. 'At least twenty people can vouch for me, from nine thirty until six p.m. when we were blessedly released from the toils of anticipating future challenges and the like.'

He was smiling his practised smile, but there was still a wary apprehension in his eyes and he was edging the coaster backwards and forwards with the sides of his thumbs.

'I suppose you contacted Florence last night, to tell her about Mrs Farley? She would need to know that such information was going to be made public.'

Swift was rewarded by a rapid flicker of Langborne's eyelids.

'I've had a long day, Mr Swift. You can leave now.'

Swift kept his expression neutral as he rose. 'You should call the police and tell them what you have told me, Mr Langborne.' At the door he turned. 'William Pennington didn't strike me as an abuser, if that's any small comfort to you.'

* * *

In the street, Swift stopped outside the railings and moved the jigsaw pieces around in his head, unable to resolve the conundrum of the heather. Langborne seemed to be off the hook but for some reason the knowledge wasn't affording the man the relief it should have done. He looked around and crossed the road, walking to the corner of another tall block of flats and standing under an awning that covered the doors. He had a feeling that Langborne would be on the move soon and had an idea of his destination. It was nearly nine o'clock; he knew that Ruth would be waiting for him to contact her but he tucked that guilt away for now and focused on the door to Langborne's block.

Fifteen minutes later, Langborne emerged, dressed in the same clothes and wearing a blazer. No luggage, which was reassuring. Within moments, a taxi pulled up and he climbed in. Swift followed as it drove off towards the Brompton road. He ran then, looking for a taxi, flagging one after a couple of minutes, by which time Langborne's had disappeared. He went with his gut instinct, giving the driver Florence's address. He asked for the taxi to stop at the end of the street, then walked to Florence's house. The lights were on in the hall and living room and the front window was open. Swift stood by the front door and listened; he could just hear Langborne's voice and the lighter tone of Florence's and gauged that they were in the downstairs room at the back. He looked around; the street was empty, nearby curtains closed with TV screens flickering within.

Swift set to work with his lock pick, taking just two minutes to open the Yale and step softly into the hallway. As he did he heard his name.

'Oh, that bloody Swift!' Florence said. 'What does he know? He's just a troublemaker. He's taken against us and you haven't helped with your attitude.'

'Calm down! What's the matter with you? You're doing that thing of rubbing your eyebrow. I haven't seen you do that since dad died.'

She half laughed, half sobbed. 'More than my eyebrow will be worn away now, there'll be plenty to grieve over; the family name, for starters.'

'Flo, you need to level with me. I believe Swift when he said Farley left a letter with her allegations about dad. Did you go there today to see her? Did something happen? I need to know; *we* need to know what we're going to tell the police.'

'Of course, I bloody didn't go to see her! I had my hands full with Carmen, didn't I? The old bat was raging on about you and those cats. I'd have liked to murder *her* all right! And you'll have to stop calling him *dad*, won't you? Carmen took great pleasure in telling me about your real father. I've suddenly lost half a sibling! There isn't anything else you'd like to reveal to me, is there? Our mother was our mother, was she? We weren't selected from orphanages?'

'Stop being ridiculous and steady yourself. You're a fine one to talk; you never bothered telling me that you'd been taken in for questioning by the police or the little matter of a substantial loan request to Carmen.'

'I suppose Swift told you that.'

'It's a lesson to learn, isn't it? Don't employ a private detective if you want your secrets to stay secret.'

Swift held his breath as he heard the footsteps but Florence paced halfway up the room, her shadow falling on the floorboards, then back to her brother.

'You should have told me about dad's disgusting behaviour before yesterday,' she said sullenly. 'I had a right to know. I couldn't sleep last night, after you phoned, I was so upset. I couldn't stop thinking about what this will do to us. Paul's been away on business so I had no one to talk to. You know what happens with this kind of allegation, all kinds of low life start coming out of the woodwork.' Her voice climbed the scale. 'And now all this today, finding out that Carmen was kidnapped. I can't believe this is happening, it's like being in a nightmare you can't wake up from!'

'Oh now, are you quite sure you never suspected anything about our father?' Langborne spoke softly. 'And would you have believed me? You thought the sun shone from his proverbial. I take it he didn't meddle with you, then.'

'Oh, shut up! No, he didn't. He was the best father to me, until that Spanish cow stole him. God, I need a stiff drink!'

'Give me one while you're at it, will you; whisky if you can still afford it these days.'

There was silence as a cupboard was opened, then the chink of glass and Florence cursing.

'Oh, sit down and let me do it, you're spilling it everywhere,' Rupert ordered.

As he waited Swift's gaze fell on a riding hat and various coats hanging on the hall pegs. On the middle peg was a woman's jacket made of a thin green cotton and on the lapel was a thistle and heather buttonhole, identical to the one he had seen Rupert wearing. He moved closer to it and saw that the base of the heather was frayed.

He left the house, closing the door softly behind him and walked a few paces away. He rang Nora Morrow, willing her to pick up.

'Yes?' she snapped.

'You need to come to Florence Davenport's house right now.'

'Well, I'm trying to raise Rupert at the moment but he doesn't seem to be in. You know, following your heather clue.'

'He's here, at his sister's. He says he has a watertight alibi for today. She has a buttonhole of the same heather, I've just seen it on her jacket and it's clearly torn on one edge. Must be some kind of family thing.'

'What the hell? You've been talking to Langborne? You do know about interfering with police enquiries?'

'We can discuss that later. You need to get round here now. I'll hang on outside the house in case she tries to leave.'

'Give me strength!'

He took that as an affirmative and paced up and down the street. A car turned in from the opposite end and parked in a tight space with a deal of reversing and positioning. Swift saw Paul Davenport get out and trudge along the pavement, carrying a briefcase in one hand and a small canvas bag in the other. He turned away, holding his phone to his ear until Davenport had disappeared into the house. A woman came towards him with a straining dog on a leash and glanced at him. He nodded, saying it was a lovely evening and his cab was taking ages. She nodded back and strode away, trying to keep up with the dog.

It had started to rain again when Nora arrived with two uniformed officers. She slammed the car door and beckoned to him. She looked hot and cross.

'I haven't time for you now. Did you mention the buttonhole to Langborne?'

'Of course not. I was flushing him out; I just said there was evidence. He came straight here after I left him. He rang Florence last night after Ronnie Farley's phone call and told her what Ronnie had alleged. If he hadn't harmed Ronnie that left him to draw an obvious conclusion. The jacket is hanging in the hallway and, no, I didn't touch it.'

The rain was suddenly tipping down. Nora flicked her hair out of her eyes and gestured to the two officers.

'Make yourself scarce now.'

He watched as she rang the doorbell and was admitted, then he hunched his shoulders against the downpour and ran to the shelter of the tube station to wait for a taxi.

* * *

Swift heard Oliver Sheridan's elephant tread on the stairs at just gone eleven as he ate cheese on toast in front of the TV. The forecast was for a heatwave following the rain and he wrote himself a reminder to buy some higher factor sun cream for the river. He had texted Ruth from the taxi and his phone rang as he was washing up and pouring himself a glass of wine.

'Hi, Ruth, how are you?'

'Oh, okay. Heart sick now instead of in the stomach.'
She sounded far away, distracted. 'It all happened very
quickly.'

'Are you in any pain?'

'No, not now.'

'Just in the heart.'

'Yes.'

'Where are you?'

'Walking round the garden. Emlyn's asleep now. He's
taken it worse than me, in a way. He's been crying; saying
he's a useless husband.'

'It's not his fault.'

'No; but he feels — oh, I don't know, contagious, as
if he jinxes people.' There was a silence. 'I hope you don't
mind me ringing you. I needed to talk and Emlyn won't,
he's gone into himself. You're my best friend, Ty; I've
come to understand that.'

He paced up and down the living room. Her words
made him elated and despairing. She shouldn't be speaking
to him in this way. Oliver's raised voice sounded upstairs,
climbing the scale so he went back through to the kitchen.

'It's sad, I know, Ruth, but there must have been
something wrong with the baby presumably.'

'Oh yes, I know. For the best et cetera. To be honest,
I don't know if we'll consider a child again after this.
There's enough heartbreak as it is.'

'You were seeing your pregnancy as something
hopeful when we met.'

'I was. I'm not sure now.'

'That's natural at the moment. You must be depressed
and this isn't a time to make decisions. You'll need a
chance to recover.'

'When did you get so wise? You sound like the nurse
yesterday; she was sensible and kind too.'

'Probably best to accept all the kindness and sensible
advice you can.'

209

'It's a lovely night sky here. I'd best get to bed, try to sleep. Is it okay if I ring you again?'

He assured her that it was, thinking of his previous resolve to end contact. It occurred to him as she rang off that, like Carmen, Ruth had no women friends and that this was unusual. He rubbed his forehead and took a deep draught of his wine, almost spilling it as he heard Cedric shout in pain overhead, a high, agonised cry.

* * *

He grabbed Cedric's key and ran up the stairs two at a time, throwing open the door. In the flat, he saw Cedric sitting, holding his arm and Oliver standing over him.

'What's going on? Cedric?' He crossed to Cedric's chair and saw the bright red mark on his right forearm. He turned to Oliver. 'You just did this, didn't you?'

'Tyrone, it's all right, Oliver was just a little upset,' Cedric said.

Swift saw the fear in his eyes and smelled the aggression from his son, like a feral heat.

'Are you after money again?' he asked Oliver. 'Can't make an honest living?'

'Oh, go away, Mr Plod. You heard my dad. Keep your nose out.'

Oliver was wearing denim dungarees with no shirt beneath. Beads of sweat gleamed in the hollow of his throat. His burly torso, matted chest and hairy arms offended Swift, especially when contrasted with the thin old man in the chair.

'Get out,' he told him.

Oliver smirked. 'You can't tell me to get out. My dad wants me here, don't you, Dad?'

Cedric glanced at Swift, his eyes moist and hopeless. He looked like Charisse. He moved his hand to try and cover the angry weal on his arm and that gesture decided Swift. He hit Oliver sharply on the left shoulder and then on the right, spinning him round, stepped behind him and locked his right arm up his back, thrusting him forward. He propelled him to the door and held him at the top of the stairs, twisting his arm higher as he tried to resist.

'Either you can walk down the stairs or I can throw you down, whichever you prefer,' he said calmly.

'I'll have you for assault,' Oliver shouted, wriggling, then howling as Swift twisted higher. 'Okay, okay, I'll go!'

Swift gave him a shove to help him on his way and he slid on the first few steps before clutching the banister and regaining his foothold. When the front door had slammed, Swift stood for a few moments, breathing deeply. He knew that he had almost broken Oliver's arm and that his anger had only just been controlled. He turned back into the living room and crouched down by Cedric, who was sitting with a hand to his head.

'I'm sorry, Cedric. I couldn't see him harming you and stand by.'

Cedric sighed and rubbed his eyes with the back of his hand. 'Where did you learn to do that?'

'Many years ago, in another life. I haven't had to use it much. Let me get something for your arm.'

He went to Cedric's bathroom and ran a flannel under the cold tap, fetching a couple of ice cubes from the kitchen. He drew a chair up beside the old man and wrapping the ice in the flannel, held it against his arm.

'That will numb it for you.'

'Thank you. Most kind.' Cedric closed his eyes, nodding.

'This isn't right, Cedric. It has to stop. You don't have to let Oliver in, you know.'

Cedric replied, his eyes still shut. 'Please, dear boy, let's not talk about it. Talking doesn't help.'

Swift sat in silence, holding the icy flannel for a few minutes longer. The mark Oliver had made was still livid but slightly less inflamed. He knew that Cedric had to be the one to bar his son; he knew also that this type of violence always increased, especially if the perpetrator knew that their victim wasn't prepared to stand up to them. He worried that one day, Oliver would inflict serious injury. When he returned from wringing the flannel out in the bathroom, he saw that Cedric was dozing. Swift fetched a woven rug from the sofa and draped it over him. He supposed that at least Oliver might stay away for a while, nursing his arm, and brooding.

* * *

Neat, orderly, despairing Ronnie had, of course, left well-ordered arrangements concerning her death; there was a paid-up funeral plan and a will, the kind bought in a stationer, with instructions that she wanted to be cremated. The police had found the contact details for a cousin, Sheelagh Donnelly, in her address book and Swift had a call from her, asking hopefully if he'd like to attend the funeral; *we spoke every couple of months on the phone*, Sheelagh explained, *and Ronnie mentioned you. She'd taken a liking for you and to be honest, she didn't have many friends, there won't be many to see her off.* Sheelagh sounded hesitant and lost. It was her first time in London, she said, and there were so many questions. She didn't know what kind of music Ronnie would want at the service, other than a few hymns; she didn't think the priest would like country and western, it didn't seem respectful. Swift suggested 'The Emigrant's Farewell,' assuring Sheelagh that these days, as far as he was aware, clergy were reasonably open to personal choices at funerals.

The funeral mass was in Our Lady of Fatima church. There was a congregation of just half a dozen: Swift, Sheelagh Donnelly, the priest and an altar boy and two old ladies clad head to toe in black, who Swift guessed were the kind who enjoyed random mourning. It was the first mass Swift had attended since his mother's funeral; on that occasion the church had been packed with relatives from Ireland, colleagues from the college where she taught and local friends. In his numb grief, he had barely noticed the service, unable to grasp that his mother was in a coffin, silent and still.

He stood beside Sheelagh, a tiny, bird-like woman in her seventies with greying hair. Her black jacket had bits of fluff sticking to it and she dusted at it self-consciously. She had broken veins in her cheeks and the high colour of someone who was flustered. She seemed to be overwhelmed with gratitude at his attendance and kept touching his sleeve with little dabs of her fingers, reassuring herself. They sang 'Lead Kindly Light' and 'The Lord is my Shepherd.' Swift had a good tenor voice, trained in the school choir and sang as loudly as he could to make up for the paucity of mourners. The priest mumbled his way through the service, giving a brief all-purpose anodyne homily about Mrs Farley having been a devout parishioner who worked hard, had troubles in her life and had now found peace. Swift thought that a fitting and honest tribute would have been; *she was a bereft mother, a brave woman with a gutsy laugh, a talent for baking and the kindest kidnapper.* At the end of the mass the altar boy disappeared behind a curtain and the church was filled with 'The Emigrant's Farewell,' sung liltingly by a young woman, backed by guitar and violin. Swift was glad that he had been able to introduce some personal element to the anonymous service, recalling the challenging, teasing look Ronnie had given him as she sang to him.

Swift accompanied Sheelagh to the crematorium, where Ronnie was dispatched in the usual utilitarian fashion. When they exited into bright sun, Sheelagh hovered uncertainly, blinking, and he suggested they have a drink and toast Ronnie. He found a small pub and bought a sherry for Sheelagh and a large glass of Shiraz for himself, adding some crisps and peanuts to the order; not exactly baked funeral meats but the nearest he could get.

'Here's to Ronnie,' he said, raising his glass.

Sheelagh nodded and sipped. 'Thank you for singing up in the church, you gave me strength.'

'I liked your cousin, she was a remarkable woman.'

'I still can't believe she kidnapped that Mrs Langborne. Why would she do a thing like that? When we were young any sort of crime, no matter how small was regarded as a terrible sin. Ronnie wasn't a bad person. She liked a drink, more than was good for her, but I never knew her do harm.'

Swift chose his words carefully; it was clear that the police hadn't disclosed the full details of Ronnie's final letter to Sheelagh and he didn't want to undermine their work or have Carmen or Langborne suing him for slander.

'I expect you'll be told in time. I think that she still hadn't recovered from her son's death. She was sad underneath the front she kept up. People behave in strange ways when they're despairing.'

'Aye, I see that. She never said anything when we chatted on the phone; just the usual stuff about her work and the weather. Mind, she was often well on in the drink when we talked; repeating herself, not making much sense. Her husband took off, you know, when Liam was just a wee one. She never heard from him again, never had a penny off him. I didn't know what to say to her when Liam killed himself. What can you say?'

'It's not easy. When did you last see her?'

'It must be ten years or so ago. She came up to Aberdeen for my sixtieth birthday. It wasn't easy, to be honest; she got very drunk and argumentative. One of my sons refused to speak to her again afterwards.'

He opened the nuts and offered some to Sheelagh, then tipped some into his palm. Ronnie was the kind of person who burnt their bridges as they went through life.

'Do you think she was very lonely?' Sheelagh asked. 'She cut herself off after Liam died, I think; just worked and went home, opened a bottle.'

'I do, yes. She liked company but I don't think she came by it easily. She certainly liked chatting to me.'

'I shouldn't eat these nuts, with my dentures.' Sheelagh was relaxing now that her awful task was over. Although she looked nothing like Ronnie, she had a natural warmth that reminded him of her. 'How come you knew Ronnie liked "The Emigrant's Farewell"?'

'She sang a verse to me, told me her grandmother used to sing it.'

Sheelagh reached her tongue to a crumb of nut stuck in a back tooth. 'Aye, she loved a good sing-song, especially after a glass or two; all the old ones. I missed all that after she drifted away from us. Liam's death unravelled the family, in a way. It caused countless little losses.'

They sat for a while longer but Sheelagh refused another drink, saying she was catching the early evening train home. She was staying at Ronnie's and needed to collect her things. Swift saw her to the tube and made sure she knew her stop. At the entrance she slipped a CD from her bag.

'Here, I thought you might like this. It has the track we played at the funeral. Ronnie hadn't much to show for all her years in London, but it's good to know at least she had one friend in you.'

He took the CD, featuring a singer called Orla Malone, a long-haired woman in a flowing red dress holding a guitar, posed on an empty strand. He shook hands with Sheelagh, waved to her and headed for home where he played the CD. He lay on the sofa, listening to the plaintive songs, thinking back to that other funeral held on a similarly sunny day, wishing that he could relive it, participate in the moment instead of being anaesthetised with sorrow. He had been more present for Ronnie than he had for his own mother. With her generous heart, his mother probably wouldn't mind; she had believed that we often received what we needed, even if it came in a guise we couldn't recognise.

CHAPTER 15

Swift had received an envelope with a logo of a hedgehog in the top left hand corner and *Spiny Friends* inscribed below it. Inside was a colourful pamphlet with fascinating facts about hedgehogs, a note informing him that he had won first prize in their raffle and a ticket allowing free entry for up to four people to the sanctuary. He wondered who would like the ticket; it might be Joyce's cup of tea. He made himself French toast, covering it with honey and had a better idea as he poured coffee. He googled *Sally's Bakes* and saw that the shop where Charisse Lomar worked was just a couple of streets away from her home. He had thought of her now and again with a heavy heart; an outing to see hedgehogs wasn't going to solve any of her problems but it might make her forget them for a couple of hours. Posting the ticket could cause difficulties so he would try to hand it to her in person. She could tear it up if she wanted.

Later that morning he stood outside the shop, looking through the window. Charisse was behind the counter in her white overall, slicing bread for a customer. He joined the queue of four and waited his turn. There was no one

behind him when he stepped forward; she hadn't noticed
him until he was in front of her and the smile with which
she was about to greet him vanished.

'Two doughnuts, please,' he said.

'What you doing here?'

'Buying doughnuts; it's a bakery.'

She slung them quickly in a bag and took the five
pound note he was holding out, the ticket attached to it
with a paper clip. She looked at it solemnly.

'What's this?'

'I won it in a raffle. It's for you and the children, if
you want it; a day out.'

She looked at it again, flicked a glance at him, then
tucked it into her pocket and rang through his purchase.

'Thank you,' she said flatly, handing over his change.
'Enjoy your doughnuts.'

He nodded and left as she greeted two young girls
who had arrived to buy their lunch. On the train he ate
one of the doughnuts; it was fresh, light and rich with
raspberry jam, just as a doughnut should be. He resisted
eating the second, saving it for Cedric. He was wiping
sugar from his mouth as his phone rang. He heard a
familiar reedy voice.

'Is that Mr Swift?'

'Yes. Hello, Mrs Langborne. How are you?'

'Very well, thank you. I would like you to do
something for me, but I'm not sure if it is the kind of work
you undertake.'

'If it's anything to do with your family, I can't because
of what has been . . .'

'No, no,' she interrupted. 'I want you to find my cats
for me and return them. I am happy to pay you, as well as
a reasonable amount to whoever has them. I have
established that Rupert had them collected by a rescue
charity, unfortunately one that I have never dealt with. I
phoned the charity; they weren't exactly apologetic but
they said they could understand my distress. My three

darlings have already been rehomed separately. They will be suffering terribly, away from each other and their home with me.'

'Well, I don't know; did this charity tell you where they've gone?'

'Despite their apparent concern for me, they wouldn't give me the details; they said it was best for me not to know and they couldn't possibly contact the new owners and ask for their return. I heard no compassion, Mr Swift; just talk of policies and procedures and confidentiality. When all this is over, I shall contact the charity commission. I understand that people like you have ways of finding things out; I will pay well, over and above your usual fees.'

'What are the details of this charity?'

'Hold on a moment; it is based in Ealing.' She gave him the name and phone number.

'I'll see what I can do,' he said, 'but it may not be possible or I might be able to retrieve just one but not all three.'

'Even one of my darlings back with me would be something.' She took a breath. 'I am desolate.'

'I'll take a look into it and be in touch.'

He produced his ticket for the conductor to inspect and looked out of the smeared window at ramshackle gardens; *people like you.* What a snob the woman was; she spoke of compassion yet seemed to extend none to her fellow humans. Not a word about the traumas her stepchildren had experienced. Still, if he could reclaim the cats for her, it would be a small gesture of repair among all the damage that had been inflicted.

* * *

Nora Morrow rowed fluidly, despite her confession that it had been a while since she was on the water, during a visit back to Dublin. Swift had borrowed a two-person training boat from his club after she rang him, reminding him that he had said they could go on the river.

'I was a bit snappy with you last time we met,' she said. 'Pressure of work and you were being a pain. I could have done you for interfering, you know; that was a big gamble you took, going to visit Langborne.'

'Semi-apology accepted and I'll offer one in return. When I saw the suitcase by his door, I did wonder if he was going to do a Lord Lucan. But come on; you know that a detective sometimes has to take a gamble.'

'Not in the Met,' she said.

'Well, I have a certain leeway that you don't then. We'll just carry on for another half hour or so, as you're out of practice.'

They had pulled in for a breather just beyond Putney and watched a family of swans grooming themselves in the evening light. After a baking day, there was a light pearly mist and a hazy sun. Nora handed him a carton of fruit juice from her rucksack.

'I'll ache tomorrow, although I do manage to get to the gym regularly.'

'You're doing well.'

'I've been meaning to join a rowing club since I came to London but you know how it is — good intentions devoured by the job.'

'I remember only too well. How long have you been here?'

'Just over five years. I used to row regularly in Dublin, out from Islandbridge. Do you know Dublin at all?'

'Only passing through. I visited my mother's family in Clifden a couple of times.'

'Lovely spot. Does your mother still visit?'

'She died when I was in my teens.'

'Oh, sorry. Mine died a while back too. I often think of how she used to annoy me and wish she was still here to do it.'

Swift nodded, smiling. 'Speaking of annoying and dead women, what's the news on Carmen and Florence? I've seen the papers; one of the tabloids has caught a whiff of Neville Langborne's alleged activities so I'd imagine that other victims will soon come forward.'

'I saw that; I'm hoping the information wasn't from us. As you can imagine, hours spent with Carmen and her solicitor. She had to acknowledge in the end that Ronnie Farley kept her locked up but denies that Neville Langborne was a kiddy-fiddler or that he ever brought strange young men back to the house. I guess if she did know, she turned a blind eye because too much was at stake; her social position and all the trappings that went with it.'

'The whole Lady Bountiful world.'

'Exactly. She'll stick to denying it and it will be difficult to prove otherwise unless other witnesses come forward. Regarding Rupert, she says she never knew about any abuse of him and I think that's true; he was an adult by the time she met his father. Rupert Langborne has confirmed that his father abused him but insists he was never aware of any other activities outside of the family. We're liaising with colleagues who have been working on other historic abuse cases just in case we can match information, so you never know, we might get lucky and now that it's out there in the press . . . I searched back but there's no record of Liam Farley's allegation. Different times, different standards.' She sucked up the last of her orange juice noisily. 'You might derive some satisfaction from hearing that Carmen has told Daphne and anyone else who will listen about Rupert's biological father. I expect to read something about *that* in the papers any day, I'm surprised it hasn't been broadcast already. She found out that Rupert had her cats rehomed and such treachery meant that she declared all-out war. She's a hard woman to like.'

'She's asked me to find the cats and try to get them back for her. Says she'll pay well.'

'She knows her own priorities, clearly.'

'Has Rupert's executive poise slipped? It was starting to, last time I saw him.'

'He looked perplexed when I interviewed him but his smooth carapace was still in place. I understand the minister has agreed he should take some leave. I sensed that in a way, he was feeling a kind of release; a burden put down.'

'And Florence?'

'We got the buttonhole and a DNA match. As you said, Rupert had a watertight alibi and he also produced his buttonhole for us. It was undamaged; apparently their deceased mother was half Scottish and they wore them in her memory. Florence took two days to crack but she acknowledged in the end that Rupert had phoned her and told her about Ronnie Farley's allegation. She says she had no knowledge of her father abusing Rupert or any other boys; difficult to know about that and it checks out with what you overheard but she was very close to her father so probably wouldn't want to believe it anyway. I think she was genuinely stunned by the information; she was in quite a state during questioning; we had to get a doctor to see her, especially after I confirmed that Ronnie Farley had been about to commit suicide. She went to see Ronnie early that afternoon; she was going to offer her money to keep quiet although I don't know where she was going to get it, given their financial circumstances; maybe she thought Rupert would cough up. She said Ronnie was drunk, which was borne out by the autopsy. They had a fierce argument. She said Ronnie laughed at her, called her a stuck-up bitch and told her she and her family would be publicly shamed. According to Florence, she felt as if her world was falling apart; first her husband's loss of income and their debts, Carmen's disappearance and now her father's reputation was going to be dragged through the mud. She says she shoved Ronnie because she was in her face, taunting her. Ronnie lost her balance, fell and hit her head on the table edge. Florence thought she was concussed so she panicked and ran; she'd just got to her car when Carmen phoned her. She denies intent to murder, saying she was going to phone the police and explain what had happened but events with Carmen overtook her. Rupert rang her just as she got home that evening, to tell her that you'd been to see him and Ronnie Farley was dead and then, of course, she went into complete panic and denial. We've charged her with manslaughter.'

'Did Ronnie die immediately?'

'Within minutes, due to the head trauma.'

Swift nodded. 'Florence must have been stunned when she found out where her stepmother had been and when I told her that same afternoon that Ronnie was responsible. She looked knocked for six when she turned up at Carmen's house; I reckon I just missed her at Ronnie's. I thought her glazed look was caused by the surprise of seeing Carmen in one piece and hearing the disjointed story.'

'I can't warm to the Langbornes as a family, but I suppose I do feel some pity for them; the Lord Justice certainly left a toxic inheritance.'

Nora reached for his juice carton and threw it with hers into her rucksack, fetching out a couple of plums and passing him one. They ate in a companionable silence. Juice dripped down her chin and she made no attempt to wipe it away. She was smiling into the sun, her eyes half closed, swaying a little from side to side and humming. He liked her forthright enjoyment of life, her lack of self-consciousness and lithe movements. He closed his own eyes.

'Did you go to Ronnie Farley's funeral?' she asked after a while.

'Yes; how did you know?'

'I gave Sheelagh Donnelly your number, I thought you might like to.'

Swift nodded. 'I'm glad I made the effort.' He flipped his plum stone into the water. 'I wonder who will count to six for Helena Davenport now.'

'Pardon?'

He explained about his first meeting with Florence.

'Well, it's her mother who will be on the naughty step for a while. I think Paul Davenport has family; I doubt Rupert or Carmen will be offering to child mind.'

After they had put the boat away, he asked Nora if she would like to have a drink at the Silver Mermaid. She accepted, heading off to freshen up in the cloakrooms. Swift washed his face, noting that his bruise had faded away and ran his fingers through his hair, then packed up his equipment and waited outside the club. The Thames path was busy with people out for a Friday evening stroll. His skin felt burnished by the warmth and breeze. The moon was climbing the sky, pale and full. His phone issued a text alert and he saw it was Ruth: *Can you ring me? On my own at the moment and feeling down.*

He felt a sad confusion. Nora was walking towards him, rucksack over one shoulder, smiling and making a raised-glass movement with her hand. He smiled back but pointed at his phone.

'Sorry, Nora, I need to make a call.'

'Oh, okay. Shall I wait over there?' She gestured to a bench.

'I'm not sure how long I'll be; it's a friend who needs help . . . it's a bit tricky.' He could hear the evasion in his voice and registered her noting it.

Her face clouded. 'Fine, not to worry. Time I got home anyway. See you around. Hope your friend is okay.'

She walked away, slipping into the parade of walkers, vanishing quickly. Swift moved to the wall and leaned on it, looking down at the river's depths. The water was dark and cloudy now, rippled by the reflection of the path lights. He called Ruth's number and waited for her voice, remembering that once it had been the only one he longed to hear.

THE END

Thank you for reading this book. If you enjoyed it please leave feedback on Amazon, and if there is anything we missed or you have a question about then please get in touch. The author and publishing team appreciate your feedback and time reading this book.

Our email is office@joffebooks.com

www.joffebooks.com

ALSO BY GRETTA MULROONEY

ARABY
MARBLE HEART
OUT OF THE BLUE
LOST CHILD

THE LADY VANISHED
BLOOD SECRETS

Printed in Great Britain
by Amazon